SPEAKING OF MURDER

Speaking

OF MURDER

INTERVIEWS WITH THE
MASTERS OF MYSTERY
AND SUSPENSE

Edited by

**Ed Gorman and
Martin H. Greenberg**

BERKLEY PRIME CRIME, NEW YORK

SPEAKING OF MURDER

A Berkley Prime Crime Book / published by arrangement with
Tekno Books and Ed Gorman

PRINTING HISTORY
Berkley Prime Crime trade paperback edition / July 1998

The Penguin Putnam Inc. World Wide Web site address is
http://www.penguinputnam.com

ISBN: 0-425-16145-5

Berkley Prime Crime Books are published
by The Berkley Publishing Group,
a member of Penguin Putnam Inc.,
200 Madison Avenue, New York, NY 10016.

The name BERKLEY PRIME CRIME and the BERKLEY PRIME CRIME
design are trademarks belonging to Berkley Publishing Corporation.

PRINTED IN THE UNITED STATES OF AMERICA

10 9 8 7 6 5 4 3 2 1

Contents

Introduction

BY ED GORMAN

A few years ago, I had lunch with a Chicago talk show producer. The subject was writers and why she felt they made such terrible talk show guests. "I'm sorry, Ed; most of you people are just pretty dull." At least she had the grace to laugh.

I argued with her, of course, naming several writers who were great stand-up comics, deft verbal storytellers, and very appealing human beings: warm, witty, and wise, women and men alike.

"True," she said. "But almost nothing ever happens to any of you."

I started to argue with her again, but you know something? From her point of view, she was absolutely correct. Most of the time, writers lead pretty quiet lives. There is a movie sale here, a foreign sale there; a painful change of agents, perhaps a new, enthusiastic publisher.

Compared to cross-dressing prostitutes, mothers who sleep with their daughter's boyfriends, and UFO abductees who have mysteriously started to dress like Elvis, I guess most of us writers do lead pretty uneventful lives.

For the TV audience, anyway.

For the book audience—that ever-diminishing group of intelligent women and men who prefer the thrills of print to the thrills of channel-surfing—many writers are interesting precisely *because* they're quiet and introspective.

The book you're holding will introduce you to people who are human beings first and writers second. That's the nice thing about having some length to play with. You get more than just a few quips and quotes; you get a real sense of the writer as a person. Some are nicer than others, some are certainly more playful and public than others; some seem to draw back when the questions turn personal, some clearly enjoy the public spotlight.

When I read through these interviews, I was struck, as I always am, by how decent mystery writers are. Every other genre has numerous ego monsters to contend with; there are but two or three in mystery fiction. And mystery writers, I say, are the most talented of all the genre writers. No other category of fiction rivals our field for the diversity of its themes or the excellence of its craft.

If your favorite author isn't in this collection, he or she may very well be in the volume that will follow this one.

In the meantime, you have these entertaining and enlightening interviews to read. I don't know about you, but the more I know about an author, the richer his or her novels become for me. I hope this book provides you with the same experience.

Here, now, are some of the world's most celebrated mystery authors.

Stephen King

INTERVIEW BY LEE SERVER

*S*tephen King, as they say, needs no introduction. But for the sake of our visitors from another planet (no doubt already clutching a few King titles for the return trip), here are a few salient facts. Born, raised, and resides in Maine, U.S.A. Former schoolteacher and janitor. Author, screenwriter, film producer and director, rhythm guitarist. Storyteller. He has been roughly the most popular writer in the world since the mid-1970s. Novels include Carrie, The Shining, The Stand, The Dead Zone, The Dark Half, Desperation, The Green Mile. *Coming to fame categorized as the master of horror—in a practical sense, a publishing category he created—his work now transcends genre or is a genre unto itself. Every year—often several times a year—readers surrender themselves to the latest figments of his imagination, whatever they may be: fantasies; mysteries; blackly comic suspense stories; stories about alienation and loss of identity; elegiac tales of childhood; Dickensian narratives of brutality, misery, and transcendence. With a library-bursting string of best-selling novels and story collections and a never-ending supply of King adaptations and originals appearing on the big and small screens, his comprehensive influence on the popular culture is perhaps topped only by Disney. And Stephen, unlike Uncle Walt's organization, is a one-man band; only his singular consciousness and tapping fingers are required to entertain an audience in the hundreds of millions. Indeed, King has pretty much resisted the allure of Disney/Spiel-*

berg—like empire-building, of cable networks, theme parks, and microwave popcorns, preferring to stick with a writer's lonely calling and his personal visions of life and death and whatever else is out there waiting to get us.

LS: You've joked about that mundane question from fans and interviewers: Where do you get your ideas? I think you answered that you get them from a store in downtown Bangor or words to that effect. Finding things to write about has never been a problem?

SK: It's just that I never worry about material. You never look for material. It just comes. Everything is material, in a sense.

LS: Can we talk about the creative process involved there, how some ordinary materials turn into Stephen King novels? Taking *Desperation* as an example, what was the starting point, and how did you get from there to a finished book?

SK: Well, with *Desperation*, I was bringing my daughter's car back from across the country, from Reed College out West where she had spent the first couple of years before she transferred back to Maine. She flew back, and I said I would go get the car because I had sort of a notion that I might just get an idea; sometimes that's how it happens. And besides that, it's just a great thing to drive across this country.

I was coming through southeastern Oregon, just crossing over into Nevada, and I went through this little town on a day when it was gloomy and overcast. Not a pleasant day. And I drove down the main street of this town on this overcast day and there's nobody on the streets whatsoever. No one on the sidewalks; it's empty. I don't see a soul. And I say to myself, "Where do you suppose all the people are?" And this voice that likes to answer questions like that says, "They're all dead." And immediately I'm playing this game, you know? It's the "story game." So now I say, "Well . . . who killed them?" And that voice, oh yeah, immediately has the answer. It says, "The sheriff . . . The sheriff went crazy and killed them all. . . ."

And that was the nugget of *Desperation*. And I held it. I held onto it without talking to anybody about it, not even talking to myself much. It was pretty much a sort of self-contained scene. It didn't need anything else. It was just that for three years. And then I did this *Insomniac* tour, crossing the country on my Harley-Davidson.

And I deliberately vectored the trip so that I would go through Nevada and not on the turnpikes. And out there, I found something. I found this open pit mine and then I had it. I said, "Yeah, this is the place."

LS: Is the story complete in your mind before you begin writing, or is it still developing as you start hitting the keyboard?

SK: I start writing it. I get to the day and I say to myself, "I'm going to start this book today, and hopefully everything will turn out okay." I get up in the morning and I'm in the shower, and at that point—which is about fifteen minutes before I start—my head turns around to it. Well, how does this thing start? Who's out there? What's going on? It's a woman. A woman and a guy in this car. But I don't see them yet. At first we hear only voices. Everything is blank. We only hear voices, hear this woman saying, "*Oh Jesus . . . Gross!*" And the guy saying, "*What, Mary? What?*" And that's all the foreplay I need. The rest of it just follows, that's all. It's like knocking over the first down. That's the big effort expended, and after that it all takes care of itself.

LS: You've written admiringly about Jim Thompson's *The Killer Inside Me*. I wondered if the sheriff in *Desperation* was a tip of the hat to Thompson's Lou Ford.

SK: Absolutely. I mean, *The Regulators* was dedicated in part to Jim Thompson.

LS: For a while, *Desperation* seems like it is going to be a—for want of a better word—realistic novel. Did it ever seem that way to you?

SK: Yes. Yes, I mean, I started this, really, with the idea that this guy, this crazy sheriff, killed everybody in town.

LS: When did you find out it would be something else?

SK: When the coyotes show up, when he's talking with Johnny, the writer, on the highway. Before he starts to kick the writer all over the road. These coyotes show up, and he starts to talk to them in this other language. Then I knew there was some kind of extraterrestrial force. And part of me was—you know—part of me was bummed by that because part of me is thinking, *Gee, if this was just a crazy guy, then this would be a quote unquote realisic novel in the sense that, hey, these things happen. People go bonkers. Go look at the evening news.* But that's not the story that I had to tell. And one thing I learned at a very early age was that you've got to go with the story. Alfred Bester used to say, "The book is the Law!" and that's what it's about.

LS: The story is never influenced by any other factors, like the expectations of the readers?

SK: I think that my job as a writer should be—this would be in a perfect world for guys like me—my job would be to come down and look and report what's going on. And never mind the motivation. Never mind the *New York Times* analysis. I just want to know what's going on and report what talk I heard and the rest of it. And whatever happens from there happens, you know. That's good enough for me. But I know from sad experience that not only editors but readers want more than that. Why did he do this? What's going on here?

LS: They want to know what it all means.

SK: The fabled Big Picture. Frankly, I hate the Big Picture. I don't care why people do anything. But part of me knows that at some point, you have to go to the next level, you have to start confronting questions. And I can do it; it's just a pain in the ass to do it. So I go along and I'm reporting what's happening, but I've also got to keep looking around and see what else is going on.

LS: Is a resurrected Richard Bachman a way of escaping some of the obligations of writing a book signed by Stephen King?

SK: Oh yeah, he's freedom. He's the place to go when I don't want to be myself. People say to me, "Do you mind being called a horror writer?" And I always say, "No, I don't." I'm writing what I'm writing, and people can call me whatever they want as long as they don't call me late for dinner. I don't care. But part of me down deep feels an obligation as Stephen King to deliver a novel like *Desperation*, where there's this demonic force who's hiding in a hole in the ground. There are a lot of writers out there who are successful in one area. And they may have other areas. We are all multifaceted people, all of us, and a writer may have a whole other side that just doesn't have a mouth. Conan Doyle used to bitch towards the end of his life that he had not been taken seriously as a writer because of the goddamned Sherlock Holmes stories. I can understand that he would feel that way, and you have a right to be crotchety in your old age, when everything sort of hurts, you have to pee forty-five times a day—and besides, I mean, the man was crazy at the end, talking to spirits and stuff like that. But at least he did have all these other mouths he spoke with. He wrote stories about knighthood in flower and he wrote stories about boxing and supernatural and science fiction stories. So he had a lot of things he was capable of doing besides old Sherlock.

So for me, Bachman offers the possibility of doing things that are different. It was great to be in a situation writing *The Regulators* where I could say to myself, "I don't have to be Stephen King today."

LS: You didn't foresee Bachman's continuing usefulness when you reported his death some years ago?

SK: I killed him out of just . . . irritation and depression. I was saying to myself, "I can't have anything!" Like a housewife with three kids running around, one of them breaks the china. You've got this nice thing going with a pen name and there's always a guy who comes along and spoils it. And you're feeling, "I can't have anything nice in this house! You goddamn kids break everything!"

But when I was writing *The Regulators*, it was hard at the very beginning. It felt like such a risk to take the same basic gimmick again, the same MacGuffin, and try to redo it in a different way. So I said to myself, "What if Bachman . . ." Even if Bachman is dead, you know . . .

LS: You constructed *The Regulators* in part out of some previously written material?

SK: There were a number of different things going on that added up to *The Regulators*. There have been things written about the book saying it came from an unproduced story called "The Shotgunners," and that's really only a quarter true. I also had this screenplay called *Rose Red*, which I had worked on for a long time. Steven Spielberg was going to produce it. And I had this idea about the Winchester mansion in California where some psychic told Winchester's widow that she would not die until the house was completed. So she just kept working on the house and adding to it and adding to it, building all these weird rooms and secret passageways, the whole bit. I had approached Steven with this idea, what if we had a story where we had this house and we had these psychic investigators and I told him this story, and he said, "Great." But it didn't happen.

LS: Why didn't it happen?

SK: I wrote the screenplay and rewrote the screenplay and rewrote it again. And finally, he and I got to the point where we just knew it wasn't going to happen. I think he's the most intelligent guy in films that I ever worked with, and I have nothing but respect for him, but I can't deal with the way he works. I absolutely cannot deal with him. So the screenplay was mine and I looked at it—

LS: But what was the problem?

SK: Getting to the point where we're both happy with what we have. And I think there was also a struggle about whose creative vision was going to prevail. So anyway, I had this script which I liked, and there were elements in "The Shotgunners" . . . and I thought, I can combine both of these. And I got really excited about using some of the TV cartoons, talking about violence on TV and kids and violence. But the most important thing that got *The Regulators* going for me was saying that it was a companion piece to *Desperation*, that I could take all the characters like you could in a repertory company. Like it's an acting company and you've got Gena Rowlands playing Lady Macbeth and Peter Falk playing Macbeth one night and then the next night they can play Willy Loman and his wife. And I liked that idea, that was sort of interesting to me. But it's one thing to say, "Theoretically, this should work," and it's another thing to actually say, "I'm going to risk my reputation doing these two overlapping books at the same time." And what saved that book at the very beginning was this guy Bachman came forward and said, "If you're really having a problem with it, stand aside, and I'll take over." And he starts writing, and starts to make fun of the little kids in the store, the whole thing about Margaret the Maggot. And there was this kind of nasty edge to the humor—it kind of hurts when you laugh. And I just stood back and let it happen.

LS: Somebody said, "Bachman is King without a conscience."

SK: Stephen King is a family guy, a grounded individual whose morals are recognizable as roughly the same as the morals of most of the people who read the books. They are fairly well grounded in terms of sanity and morals. Which is good, because a lot of people read the books. I assume that most of them have their wheels on the road. But Richard Bachman does not have all his wheels on the road. That's just the way it is. Bachman is capable of seeing the humor in what's going on on the streets of Wentworth, Iowa, all these people being killed in these horrible ways. You know, *Regulators* was not as popular as *Desperation*. Did okay, because people knew it was me, but it didn't do as well. And there is an element in Bachman's attitude that is really, genuinely disturbing, and I think that was perceived by people. *Desperation* is a disturbing book in a lot of ways. *Regulators* is more so. And it's funny, and that can disturb people. I think there is some funny stuff in *The Regulators*, particularly in the old vet's house where he has all the old animals that smoke and talk and all this, which I got from "Ripley's Believe It or Not."

LS: Did you begin to feel like another person was actually writing the book?

SK: As Richard Bachman, it's easier for me to kill a little kid than it is as Stephen King. I mean, I really agonized over the death of that little girl the cop pushes downstairs [in *Desperation*] and the way that I was able to deal with it was to keep it all offstage. It's all happened and he gets rid of her body as soon as he possibly can. Bachman has *no* problem with that stuff.

LS: I wonder if there was something similar at work with the first-person narrative voice in *Dolores Claiborne*. It reads like you had become possessed by that character. I picture you writing in some kind of trance state.

SK: I don't use the first person a lot, and one of the reasons why is that I feel like you ought to save it for something special. And with *Dolores Claiborne*, I was going to those voices from my past. I was born and raised in Maine, but I had never used that Yankee voice before in any way. And I was thinking about my mother who talked that way and took care of her grandparents and hung out a lot of sheets, you know, on the line. My grandmother was senile at the time, and she'd be yelling, "*Ruth, remember to use three bibs! Not two, three!*" My mother out there freezing her hands off. Or me, my grandmother yelling the same message: "*Stephen! Remember! Three bibs!*" Crazy as a shithouse rat by the end of her life. And I had those voices in my memory. And you're right, it was like being in a trance writing that book. And you start to remember things, they come back to you, just like a person who's been hypnotized. You know, I don't really believe in the subconscious the way that Freudians believe in the subconscious, but I do believe there's a room in your head like a basement where all the shit falls down and it just stays there, unless there's a flood, okay, but otherwise it stays there. I'll tell you, talk about getting a chill, we got a copy of a movie I'd seen as a kid, *The Snake Pit*, that movie with Olivia DeHavilland. And I was watching it this last summer at the summer house. I hadn't seen it since I was a little kid, probably out of WPIX in New York when they used to show the *Million Dollar Movie*. And I can remember how badly it scared me. And I am sure that a lot of my fears as a kid about going insane started with that particular movie. But now I'm watching this as a grownup, as a forty-eight-year-old man, and they're sending the woman to the lunatic asylum, and it's called Juniper Hill. And I realized that Juniper Hill is the name I've been using for the lunatic asylum where all the people go in *It* and in a lot of the other books. I must have pulled that name out of my subconscious. So everything kind of stays around in there, and as a writer, you try and have access to it.

LS: As I recall, you once said—apropos of "Rage," something you wrote when you were very young and published as by Bachman after you became famous—that Bachman was Stephen King, but Stephen King at age seventeen, a kid with a lot of problems. Looking back, how seriously unglued would you say you were in those days?

SK: I think everybody is like that. It's the grace of God that keeps any of us on the rails at that age. If it's not one thing, it's another. You think your head is going to explode and you're going to wind up in a loony bin wearing a straitjacket. If it's not that, it's getting drunk over the state line in Mississippi and coming home at 110 miles an hour. And you know they call that road that goes between

Mississippi and Alabama "Blood Highway," but the miracle is, most kids make it back okay. And I made it back okay, too. But I had a lot of days when I felt like what I would like to do was just go down to Main Street in my hometown, pull out a gun, and shoot everybody that walked out of their store front. . . . I was probably never close to that, but there's no way to tell. When you're imaginative, you have a tendency to take your thoughts to extremes, particularly at that age, and I had not yet found a clear outlet for my imagination. I was writing, but I hadn't yet achieved the ability to access those elemental forces that drive the creative nature. I'm not saying that what I'm doing now is more creative or better, I'm just saying that now it's easier to use those forces creatively. But whether or not I was ever close to just freaking out completely and doing a Charles Whitman or a Charles Starkweather . . . probably not.

LS: Speaking of Starkweather [a legendary multiple murderer of the 1950s], you kept a scrapbook about his exploits. Did the guy interest you from an embryonic novelist's perspective, as intriguing subject matter, or was it a more personal interest—a fan's scrapbook, in other words?

SK: I had a Charlie Starkweather scrapbook when I was about . . . well, I can tell you, I would have been around ten because it was '57, and I was born in '47. My mother was very upset, because she saw it as a morbid interest. But I'll tell you, that was a very healthy interest. I've had murderous impulses and a wide spectrum of people—not everybody, I won't claim that—but a wide spectrum of people have had murderous impulses, and I think we've all had days where if we didn't think we could do a Charlie Starkweather, we felt like Michael Douglas in *Falling Down* and ready to just sort of lose it. You hear that snap in your head and you go off. And yet I can say to myself on a more rational level, "I'm not really very close to that." So what is the difference . . . you want to find out what is it that separates me from a Charles Whitman and a Charles Starkweather? And my Charles Starkweather scrapbook is not that different from my writing *Apt Pupil*, about Dussander, the guy who killed all these people in the concentration camps. I mean, talk about Whitman, Starkweather, these guys are totally inefficient pikers compared to the Nazis. They lined them up six deep and shot them with one bullet to see if they could maximize their kill ratio. And I want to ask, what are these guys like? They tell me Joseph Mengele had a family, loved his kids, he had little girls. And I'm saying, "Holy shit, that's really fucked up. How could that be?" I want to know what's going on with a guy like that. . . . With horror and suspense writers, I think a lot of the time the most fruitful line for the imagination to take is to ask: "How would people like this act?" Or take some experience you're curious about and explore that.

LS: Like an execution? I believe you said that *The Green Mile* grew out of a fascination with the electric chair.

SK: I've always been interested in the electric chair. I read a book when I was a kid called *20,000 Years in Sing Sing* by Louis Lawes. A lot of stories in there got my imagination working. And you say to yourself, "Do people in cold blood walk somebody down that walk and stick them in a chair and electrocute them like turkeys in a microwave or else put needles in their veins or stick them in a room that fills up with gas? Do we really do this?" And you say, "Yes we do." And then you say, "What would that be like, to be part of that experience, to follow it right to the end of the line?"

LS: Has there ever been something that fired your imagination in that way but you decided not to explore it? Anything you would consider taboo as a subject?

SK: A couple of things. I can't very well tell you what they are. . . . That would be telling.

LS: What about *Pet Sematary*? It's been said that you regretted writing it, that you don't like to talk about it. You didn't allow it to be printed for many years, right?

SK: I never said, "This is too awful to publish." What I said was, "I don't need to publish this. I can put this away. . . . I don't have to deal with this book." And I didn't want to deal with it. . . . The idea for it came when my daughter's cat died. There was an actual pet cemetery behind the house where we lived when I taught creative writing at the University of Maine. And the guy who rented us the house took us up there. It was a beautiful day, and there was a path up into the woods, and sure enough, there were all these little things made out of orange crates and tin cans, the handwritten signs, "Smuckee . . . he was obedient," and this kind of thing. We thought, "Isn't this cute. . . ." Until my daughter's cat was run over in the road. Then we knew why there was a pet cemetery where it was. That road was a killer. There were these trucks from a chemical plant that just ran all night and all day. These great big tanker trucks. And a lot of other traffic. And while we were there, two people were killed on a turn just down the highway from where we lived. They weren't the first ones. People there are anxious to tell you, "Nope, they're not the first to die on this curve."

Then, when my daughter's cat died and we buried the cat, she was devastated, and I was sad for her and trying to comfort her. But later on, it's like I was saying about that voice that kicked in with *Desperation*, that voice comes and says, "What if the cat came back to life because the pet cemetery was a magic place?" And I answer, "Well, it wouldn't stay a pet cemetery if things came back from there." So the voice, which has an answer for everything, says, "Well, it's an annex beyond the regular cemetery where things come back to life." And I thought there was a good idea there, but I didn't have a complete story. And then my youngest son, who's in his twenties now but then he was two and a half and just learning the pleasures of running really fast, ran from where we were having a picnic in this field next to the house near the road. And Tabby screamed at me, "Oh Steve, catch him! He's going to run into the road!" And I ran after him, and I could hear one of those trucks coming, one of those big tanker trucks. And I thought to myself, *I am not going to catch this kid.* But he fell down on the edge of the road, and I grabbed hold of him and yanked him back. The truck went by . . . and I had my book.

So part of it was the idea of writing a book based on the near death experience of one of my kids, and there was also the real nastiness of having to confront the grief process. A parent losing a young child is one of the most wrenching life experiences you can have, according to the psychologists. It can tear up families, smash up marriages. It certainly smashes up the illusion that we have a secure life. Because we don't. And then part of the book was the idea of a kid coming back after he's died and the kid is a monster. And I had to deal with the whole issue of: Would you bring your kid back to life if you could, even if the chances were good it would come back without a soul, without any feeling of love for you?

So I finished the book. It was fairly uncompromising, and I just said to myself, I don't need to publish this; I can put this away. There are other things I can write. I don't want to deal with rewriting it. I don't want to deal with the pain of it anymore. So I put it away.

Later on, there was this legal thing that had to do with Doubleday and money they had sequestered. And somebody came to me and said, "You better fix this. They're holding on to a lot of your money, and if you die, your estate becomes liable for the taxes. You've got to get this money out, pay the taxes on it, if not for you then for your wife and kids." So I approached Doubleday and they said, "We can do this for you if you were to do another contract with us." And I'm thinking to myself, another contract, that means another book. And *Pet Sematary* was the book I had. I could give that to them. And I thought to myself, how fortunate, I have this book. And what a perfect book to give to these people under circumstances of duress. It's the most wretched, awful thing. And they published it. And the wretched, awful thing was a tremendous success and it is still the most successful motion picture that I've ever had.

LS: You thanked a couple of morticians in the book. Did you do a lot of research? Any hands-on experience?

SK: Hands-on experience. No, I never actually got working with any of the bodies. I never participated in the burial ceremonies; I didn't think that was necessary. But I talked with the morticians and read some of their literature. They have their own magazine, *American Mortician*. I didn't have to know the technical aspects. What I needed was to find out what Louis would go through arranging the funeral. And when I go down to talk to this mortician and go through his showroom, I see on top of a column a little MasterCard thing: "We take MasterCard." And I say to myself, "That's what I came here to see." The rest was just some bullshit. But in the book, Louis says something like, "And I paid for my son's funeral with my MasterCard." It's a great little moment.

So, I don't repent the book. There are some great things in that book in terms of the writing that I did about the family. I'm pretty satisfied with it, and a lot of that came out on the rewrite. The editor was Sam Vaughan, who was then in charge at Doubleday. He did a great job as editor.

LS: You've lived in Maine all your life, pretty much. A chicken or the egg question: Do you write about it because it inspires you or because it happens to be where you live?

SK: Maine is a great place for a guy like me. All those old Yankee ghosts and stuff. But it depends on the story. You take them where they come. I just finished a Dark Tower novel, which means that I was in some other fuckin' world entirely, which is like combining a fantasy world with the streets of Laredo, or something. But right now I've been thinking about a story—I would love to do it as an original TV miniseries—and that would be set in Maine. If the idea fits this setting, this is where I put it.

LS: Some of your best books, like *The Shining*, were inspired by your being in unusual surroundings, like that big hotel in Colorado. And you said *Desperation* began with a trip through the West. Do you ever consider what inspiration you might find in more long-term travel or if you went off and moved to Japan or somewhere for a couple of years?

SK: Well, I'm sure that's true. And I'm sure that the Nevada desert had an energizing effect on me because it's so fabulously different from what I see every day. I love all that open space. I think the desert has its own kind of Gothic grimness. You see coyotes, barbed-wire fences, and you say, "Something's going on around here." They're not all Gary Cooper out there. But as far as other countries . . . I went to England with the family when I was a younger man, and I finished a novel set in Maine, *Cujo*. And then I waited for something else to come, and nothing else came. I mean, I wrote one story from that period that was set in a London suburb where we got lost. It was kind of a Lovecraftian thing. But the novel I went there to write never got written. So I never really tried again. I've written some overseas, but never based on those locales. American people are my central point of identification. And that's gone when you get overseas. Even in England, though the language is the same, the outlook and the point of view is very foreign. On some level they're more polite than we are, but on another level they're also very unforgiving. My wife calls it "bloody-mindedness." There's a lot of that, and I don't relate to that very well. I'm just glad they read my books overseas.

LS: Are you still a big reader yourself?

SK: Yeah. I don't trust writers who say, "I don't have time to read." I think to myself, "You better have time to read." I think it's very important to keep on reading, to drink from that pool as well as add to it. You know what I'm saying?

LS: You once spoke about Ray Bradbury and certain changes in his work, that he had written all this brilliant stuff when he was young and had lots of problems, and when he worked through those problems, one way or another, his work was no longer as interesting. How do you avoid the process you felt you observed in Bradbury, maintaining your creative fires in the face of success and various contentments?

SK: Well, I think I was wrong in what I said about Ray Bradbury. I think now, looking at the work he's done in the last seven to ten years, a lot of it has been really brilliant stuff. And it could be that Ray went through a twenty-year writer's block. He wrote a lot of things, a lot of poetry and stuff that frankly wasn't very good. But now he's writing some fiction that's really interesting. So it may be that it was just writer's block, and who understands writer's block? It's a cancer of the creative impulse or of the imagination. In my case, I've just tried to go on telling stories and being as honest as I can about the way people feel and the way people react to things. And you have to stay alive emotionally and intellectually. Keep on reading and going to films and plays. Keep alive to wonder, to language, the life of the mind, the life of the imagination . . .

Mary Higgins Clark

INTERVIEW BY JAN GRAPE

Mary Higgins Clark: talk to any writer in the genre about Mary, and you'll hear stories of her charm, wit, generosity, and loyalty, and you'll suddenly realize she's much more than the elegant, sophisticated, and attractive grand dame of suspense; she's a genuine person.

If you wonder what it's like being an icon, Warren Murphy wrote in an appreciation for Bouchercon 27, "She's just like every other writer, scared to death every time she starts a new book, but unable either to suppress the excitement."

My favorite Mary Higgins Clark story (which I usually tell at the drop of a hat) begins when I first met Mary in 1988 at the International Crime Congress held during Edgars week. Mutual friends, Joan Lowery Nixon and Mary Blount Christian, introduced me to Mary Higgins Clark and we hit it off quite well. The next time I saw her was Bouchercon in San Diego that same year. Phyllis Brown hosted the con and asked me to be on a short story panel with Marty Greenberg and Ed Hoch. I'd only had two mystery short stories published, both in small subscription (read small distribution) magazines, and confess to feeling a bit intimidated.

One of the first people I saw as I was taking the elevator to attend my panel was Mary Higgins Clark. We exchanged hellos and Mary asked how I was. I explained about being somewhat nervous, that this was my first panel and nobody knew who I was, and Mary said, "But darling, as soon as you put your foot in your mouth, everyone will know who you are!"

I started laughing and my queasy stomach calmed, the butterflies flew away, and I went and did my panel. It was only much later that I realized how Mary's quick wit had been a great act of kindness to a new kid on the block and it wasn't until much, much (read years) later that I was able to tell her personally how grateful I was for her consideration and humor that day.

Ms. Clark wrote her first short story, called "The Stowaway," while still a Pan Am flight attendant. Six years and forty rejection slips later, she sold it to a magazine. But she didn't give up. Mary liked reading suspense and decided to see if she could write a suspense book. She's been quoted as saying, "It was like a prospector stumbling on a vein of gold." Her first suspense novel, Where Are the Children? *(Simon & Schuster, 1975), became a best-seller, and her contracts now are legendary. For years, when she was introduced, someone would say her name, then attach the dollar amount of her latest contract to it: "Mary Higgins Clark, With the Twelve Million Dollar Contract." Mary herself joked about it, saying this was now a permanent part of her name. When she received the next large contract, that, too, became the new part of her name. The money is nice, but the storytelling is the real joy.*

Mary Higgins Clark, generous to new writers and encouraging to all writers, with her warmth and humor, is the epitome of a grand lady. The past president of Mystery Writers of America and winner of the French Grand Prix de Littérature Policière doesn't let such honors go to her head. Although she continues to reign as the queen of suspense, there's no time to sit back on her laurels; the next deadline is fast approaching. She's looking for a fascinating story with sharp pacing, intriguing characters, and believable settings. As a devoted mother, grandmother, and now a new bride, she plans to slow down "just a little—to smell the flowers," but that won't stop the flow of words. That won't stop the search for the new or bigger idea that her readers, anyone over the age of twelve, wait for with anticipation.

Mary and I tried to do this interview late last fall and again shortly afterward, but in late November, she had marriage plans, and soon the Christmas holidays were upon us. Eventually, on a cold, rainy, raw January day in both New Jersey and Austin, we had a long telephone conversation, and this is more or less how it went.

JG: Congratulations on your marriage. Tell me about John. And how's married life?

MHC: He's absolutely great. As one of his friends wrote to his daughter [she was a woman who had worked with him for many years at

Merrill-Lynch]: "Tell Mary, now she has everything." Isn't that lovely?

JG: That's great. I'm happy for you. Well, shall we start? I read somewhere you wrote poetry as a child. Did you try to write stories or books at that age?

MHC: Not at age seven, no. But I was also talking stories. Friends would stay over or I'd stay over with them, and I'd say, "Let's tell scary stories . . . let's turn out the light, just have one candle, and tell scary stories." And I was writing plays and skits that I made my brothers perform, and I remember once my little brother asking, "Can't I just once be the star?" And I said, "No." In the garage—we had just a single garage and it was under the house—I got the old velvet draperies and I had a stage and wrote plays for the neighborhood kids and charged them two cents to watch.

JG: Oh, great.

MHC: So I was always talking, writing . . .

JG: And telling stories. Do you think storytelling was the influence of your Irish background?

MHC: Oh, yes, the Irish are storytellers. It's just part of what goes into their makeup. They never say anything simply; they have a lyrical way of speaking and a cadence in their voices, and I'm completely Irish. My mother was born here, but all my grandparents were born in Ireland and my father was, too. So it's that ingrained.

JG: That gift of gab?

MHC: Yes, that gift of gab. When I was growing up, we told stories around the dinner table and you had to tell a good story so everybody would listen. Do you know what they say about the Irishman who has kissed the Blarney Stone? (And I did twice.) *He could sell a dead horse to a mounted policeman.*

JG: Who influenced you as a young writer?

MHC: In suspense? Well, I always, always loved to read. To me, the best gift at Christmas or my birthday was a book. I really was a voracious reader. And what I read for just curl-up pleasure was always suspense. I started with Judy Bolton and Nancy Drew, then went on to Agatha Christie, Josephine Tey, Ngaio Marsh, and Mingon Eberhart—I loved her writing. Charlotte Armstrong—these were the writers I thoroughly enjoyed.

JG: At what point did you decide to be a writer?

MHC: It's decided for you, Jan. I mean the ones who become professional writers. Obviously, you have to have some talent. But besides the talent and the desire, it chooses us; we don't choose it.

JG: Who influences you now? Or who do you read now?

MHC: I'm eclectic. I think Anne Tyler is one of our finest contemporary writers—she's a fabulous writer. I read a broad spectrum of nonfiction as well, and I like to reread the classics. And of course I'm always doing so much reading for what I'm writing. Last year, I read books on burial customs for *Moonlight Becomes You*. I read Greco Roman burial customs: *Bury the Past, Down to Earth, The Etiquette of Funerals* from Emily Post, and Amy Vanderbilt. *The History of Newport*—I had to read all the histories of Newport because of the setting. Right now, I'm reading maps of Minneapolis, and things that pertain to what I'm working on, like the newspapers, because I have scenes where my girl goes to Minneapolis in the federal witness protection plan.

JG: I planned to ask you about research later, but we've slipped into it here. When do you do research? A book or two ahead?

MHC: I do it as I'm writing the book. I know where I'm going, like when I was in Minneapolis for Bouchercon. . . . I had been there many times, so I knew Minneapolis. I had even owned property there. But it's been a while, so I needed to know street names and which way you would drive to go to certain places and what hotel a killer would stay in and where the girl's apartment would be. And all of this is important.

Sometimes you get great information from other writers. I meet with a group (The Adams Round Table founded by Clark and the late Thomas Chastain) every month in the upstairs room of a Manhattan restaurant. We often talk about research, and one night, Whitley Streiber said something that helped me. He said, "When I'm writing a book about a city, I get a subscription to that city's newspaper."

JG: Good tip.

MHC: It's a very good tip. Because you get the prices of houses and groceries and what's going on in that area—the politics, the entertainment.

I like to do my own research because sometimes I find things that I didn't know I was looking for. I like the research.

JG: What sparks a new book? Makes you feel you've just *got* to write this one?

MHC: Well, for example, in *Moonlight Becomes You*, I was interested in the fact there are so many nursing homes you see where people are being overmedicated or being so badly treated, and I thought, *What is the reverse? What about in the upscale ones?* About then there was a big article in the *Times* where people would buy their apartment units, but when they die, the space reverts back to the company. So here's a half million dollar unit that's supposed to revert back after you die, and you're only supposed to live seven years or they're losing money on you. I just thought, *What an interesting concept. Here are people who can well afford to pay for care for themselves, and yet they may very well be in danger.* Often the people who died didn't have any family looking out for them. Look at poor Doris Duke, one of the richest women in the entire world. When she died, she had a doctor overdosing her and a butler methodically stealing from her and a nurse pocketing her antiques. Those were the three people surrounding her.

JG: Poor thing. I think also that book touches a chord in us because we all have a fear of something like that happening. I enjoyed reading all those funeral customs. It was a subject I was not too familiar with.

MHC: It's fun to read a subject you would not necessarily go out looking for.

Now the stories in *My Gal Sunday* (which of course is tongue-in-cheek of that old radio show and always intrigued me) instead of the richest, the most handsome nobleman, suppose you had an ex-president. And suppose he married this young congresswoman . . .

JG: A great concept.

MHC: I think they're marvelous fun.

JG: Oh, I can tell you're still having fun with your writing, and that's great after so many books. And it's wonderful because it gives you a break from the more serious things you've done.

MHC: Yes, and they've done very well. But some people were looking for psychological suspense. I got a letter from someone yesterday who said she read the first story and threw up.

JG: Good grief [laughter].

MHC: Well, she just didn't like that kind of story. I've also gotten some very nice letters. But I laughed out loud over that one and thought, *Oh my gosh, honey, that's a bit drastic.*

JG: Are you planning more Sunday and Henry stories, I hope?

MHC: Oh, yes. I owe Otto Penzler a story, and so I'm going to do a Henry and Sunday story when I finish this book.

JG: It's great that you still enjoy writing.

MHC: I do, but I'm not going to try to do two books in a year again; that's too tight. And because I do want to smell the flowers at some point. And that way I can continue on writing indefinitely.

JG: The great thing about writing is being able to continue—no matter what our age—until we're in our coffin, right?

MHC: Of course. Just put a pad and a couple of pens and a glass of wine in my coffin and I'll be all set [laughter].

JG: Okay, back to our task: Several of your books (especially *Loves Music, Loves to Dance*) gave me the creeps. I wanted to make sure all the doors were locked as I was reading, and I wondered if sometimes you scare yourself when you're writing?

MHC: Oh, yes. And yet I love the idea of somebody freezing a body and then dancing with it; there's something rather sweet about it [laughter].

JG: You're a sick person [more laughs]. So how do you research that?

MHC: I had heard an FBI manager at the International Crime Writers Conference discussing cases. I was the chairman of the conference and kept running back and forth from room to room, trying to see if there were enough chairs set up and if there was water at the speakers' table and if the mikes were working, but when the director began talking, I sat down. He had pictures of these seven young girls—their hands bound and their mouths taped and their young eyes terrified. He said he'd taken the pictures. Seven young girls killed over three years. And the common denominator was they had all answered a newspaper ad. They were answering the ad of a psychopath serial killer. And the thought just walked into my head: *Loves Music, Loves to Dance*.

JG: Cool. The book title just walked in and sat down.

MHC: Right. And now on the one I'm doing, I have a young woman in real estate—upscale real estate—selling condominiums in Manhattan, and she witnesses a murder. She brings a guy in to see a property one morning. Later in the evening, she comes back to see the woman owner, and she lets herself in and calls out to her, "Isabelle?" Suddenly she hears a scream and a shot. But she has the presence of mind to slam the front door, pretending she left, and she jumps in the closet. Now she must get into the witness protection plan because the killer was a mobster.

JG: Sounds good. I'll be looking for that one. You often write about things that are current in our lives, like serial killers, empty-nest syndrome, and burial customs. . . .

MHC: And the multiple personalities; in vitro fertilization was another. I really try to do something different and something more than entertaining.

JG: People today want page-turning intrigue.

MHC: Definitely. For instance, in this book, you see a young woman who has to lie about everything, and she's not a liar. She lies about her name and where she came from and what her background is—everything is a lie. But she has to do it or the killer will find and kill her. And if you meet a young man, you soon feel like such a phony because you can't tell the truth.

JG: And how would you remember all the lies—keep them all straight?

MHC: Not easily, but you know that old saying: "*Some people would lie when the truth would serve them better.*" In this case, she has no choice.

JG: Next question: Who has the nerve to critique you? I mean you're *Mary Higgins Clark.* Only your editor or agent?

MHC: I have a couple of family/friend readers, like my sister-in-law, who I often hand pages to. For the legal stuff, my daughter, Marilyn, is a judge, and my son, Warren, is a lawyer and municipal court judge. I get the legal stuff from them or they tell me it's not legal in New Jersey. If they don't know, they can tell me where to go.

Yesterday, I spent a half hour on the telephone with a retired detective finding out where evidence could disappear in a precinct and what the difference is between a U.S. attorney and the New York PD.

And finally my daughter, Carol, is a wonderful, wonderful critic. She was always good at critiquing me, even when she was typing my manuscripts in college.

She didn't mind telling me I couldn't do something. In fact, she was the one who said you can't kill off Alvirah. But I said, "She's gotta go." And Carol said, "She's too much fun, and people will hate you." And she was right. *The Lottery Winner* was a number-one bestseller.

JG: Thank goodness you listened, right?

MHC: And now Carol says she should get the royalties from it [laughter].

JG: Some nerve, huh? Do I dare ask, have any of your books ever been rejected?

MHC: *Where Are the Children?* was rejected by two publishers. They said people don't like to read about children in jeopardy. You have to remember this was twenty-three years ago, and they thought murdering children was too much of a problem.

JG: Which brings me to when you were raising five children and writing about child killers, did you ever get paranoid about your own children?

MHC: My children were in their teens when I wrote those. But once, when we moved and our youngest was three, our house was near a lake. I had been very worried about moving near water. Water is always a problem when you have children. And my God, the very day we moved in, Patty turns up missing. And all I could say was, "Get to the lake."

And you know where she was? Asleep on the couch. It was turned around facing the wall, and you couldn't see her. She got tired, got her security blanket, curled up, and never heard us screaming for her.

Those emotions and feelings all came into play in my early books. That and a true case of a woman who was accused of the deliberate murder of her two children.

JG: Okay, tell us what your writing day is like.

MHC: I get up early. When I've had to, I've gotten up at four o'clock for this book. But I find when I do that, I don't get enough out of it because then I'm so darn tired by one in the afternoon; so I'm not sure that serves me well. I like to get started by seven, seven-thirty. I work all day when I'm on deadline. Yesterday, I worked nine hours straight. The housekeeper brought me up a sandwich, and I ate at my desk.

JG: I was going to ask if you have an office at home or away.

MHC: I have a lovely, lovely tower office. We added a second floor and a third-floor gallery. I don't work neatly, which is why I wanted a place that I could just walk away from. The office is gorgeous and has huge windows and a skylight so that it's very open and sunny.

JG: What do you think you would be doing today if you weren't writing mysteries?

MHC: I have no idea, no idea at all. Well, I would have been working, because I was widowed, you know. Maybe I'd be retired by now and going on a bus to Atlantic City to gamble. I did some radio script writing when I lived in New York. I probably would have been working in an advertising agency, but here again, it would have been writing.

JG: After all these years, do you enjoy going on book tours and doing TV shows?

MHC: It's fun, in a way. Writing is so solitary. Seeing people who are reading the books and enjoying them is very nice; it gives me a feeling of being connected. That way I can find out what they're thinking, too.

I'm comfortable on television. I used to do public relations, so I know what they want. The book tours get tiring. I've tried to cut them down, and now, of course, as an aging bride, I want to be home. John will come along sometimes, especially when he has friends in the city where I'm signing. But I'm cutting down, too. It's one thing to do something in New York in an evening, and another thing to be gone overnight. But I'm always home on weekends.

JG: You usually don't win a lot of awards. Is that a disappointment?

MHC: No. The awards are given by the judges to the ones whom they think deserve it. In France, I won their top suspense award, the Littérature Policière. I don't think I'm particularly honored as a writer among my peers. They think I'm a nice person, but I know a lot of people who don't think I write a good mystery. That is okay with me, because I write the story I want to write.

JG: And as Judy Jance says about not winning awards, "You write stories that sell."

MHC: Yeah, I sure do, but I write a novel of suspense as opposed to a straight whodunit. I'm not a classic mystery writer, and I'm certainly not a literary writer, so I'm not going to get literary awards. The real thing is: Are you read? Do people enjoy you? Do they buy the next book? I think my real critics are my readers, and thank God they keep coming around. I'll settle for that.

JG: You have to be doing something right. What about this new mystery magazine? How involved are you in it?

MHC: I'm involved in the sense that I read the top ten or twelve stories that go into it—I could never read all five hundred or so that are sent in—and I discuss the final decision with Kathy Sagan, who does the really hard work as the editor.

One reason I became involved is because it's another market for fans. It's going to be sold in the supermarket, and none of the mystery magazines has ever gone directly into the supermarket. If you're getting a more mainstream audience like *Family Circle*, you're getting great distribution.

And there's one or two spots for the new writer. They will give good editorial criticism. I think the more mainstream people who buy it, the more interested they will become in reading mysteries—in reading books. So it's a new market, and it's a mass market with a classy magazine. We will keep trying to broaden the mystery readership.

JG: Sounds good. I'm always excited over anything that expands the genre. Any words of wisdom for writers?

MHC: Write. And I think it's wise to somehow be connected to the community of writing. I tell beginning writers, "Take a course." It's not just having the talent, you have to learn the craft.

JG: Okay, now we'll do the more lighthearted questions: Isn't it a kick to be a question on *Jeopardy*?

MHC: Oh, it's a riot. You know, I was a *Jeopardy* question three different times, and the one I love the best is when they said, "Her name is Carol Higgins Clark, her first book, *Decked*, was published in 1992. Who is her mother?" And there were three blank looks and finally somebody pressed the buzzer and said, "Who is Agatha Christie?" We loved it.

JG: And speaking of Carol, how is it to have a daughter who is now a successful suspense writer?

MHC: It's wonderful; really, I'm so pleased for her. And she's suffering just the way I am, and we're on the phone every day moaning to each other. She's writing *Twanged* right now.

JG: *Twanged?*

MHC: It's a country music—

JG: Obviously. Maybe she needs to call and talk to me to get that twang down in her head just right.

MHC: Oh, that's right. It's about a country music singer being stalked and Regan Reilly is hired to protect her. It's due out in the spring of 1998. She's working her fanny off on that one. She's got her deadline, and of course my deadline is the here and now, and we're both working, trying to get finished.

JG: Who would you like to be stranded with on a desert island?

MHC: My husband.

JG: If you could live anywhere in the world, where would it be?

MHC: Right here. I love to travel, but it's like a yo-yo; I always want to come back.

JG: What music do you like?

MHC: I love classical, but I don't know it like John does. I never really had the time to learn. I like the forties kind of music. The big band sounds—always loved that.

JG: What's your favorite color?

MHC: [A brief pause] I'm looking at red walls right now. It's not that I wear red all the time, but I think it's one of the brightest, most fun colors.

JG: And it looks great with your hair and eyes.

MHC: And I like red because it's cheerful. But I wear black a lot, and the dress I wore for the wedding was green and gold. You know, I guess I like the strong colors.

JG: What does your best pal say about you?

MHC: Probably that I'm easy to be around. And I try to be as good a friend as they are to me, and we have fun.

JG: What is your greatest success?

MHC: My family.

JG: Tell me a secret about Mary Higgins Clark.

MHC: I'm as open as apple pie. I don't have secrets.

JG: Somehow, I knew that already.

MHC: What do you want to know? Ask me, and I'll tell you. Some people will try to sidle up to me and try to ask something and I'll say, "What do you want to know? Don't waste your time trying to worm it out of me, I'll tell you."

JG: I know you get interviewed often and are asked the same old questions. What do you wish someone would ask? Then consider that I asked it, and you can answer.

MHC: I wish someone would ask me about my fan mail. Sometimes I'll get a letter like, "Dear Ms. Clark, I was sick and in the hospital and someone gave me one of your books and for the next four hours I forgot my aches and pains." And I've gotten a letter from someone who said, "My little boy was sick and hospitalized and I'm a single mother and for weeks I was by his bedside and I got through it by reading your books." That's lovely and very flattering.

JG: Makes it all worthwhile then, doesn't it?

MHC: Indeed. And since I don't deal with sex and violence, I'm on the reading list from age twelve and up all over the country, and I get letters from kids saying, "I never liked to read, but I liked your book, and now I think reading is fun." Those are the kind of letters that make you feel great.

Then I always keep one that I really love, love, love. "Dear Mrs. Clark, I am twelve years old, and I've read the first half of *Where Are the Children?* You are a wonderful writer. Someday I hope to read the second half."

JG: Oh, that's priceless.

MHC: Isn't that great?

JG: Listen, Miss Mary, I appreciate your time and—

MHC: I'm sorry we weren't able to do this sooner.

JG: No problem. Take care. And thanks again.

A MARY HIGGINS CLARK CHECKLIST

Where Are the Children?
A Stranger Is Watching
The Cradle Will Fall
A Cry in the Night
Stillwatch
Weep No More My Lady
While My Pretty One Sleeps
The Anastasia Syndrome & Other Stories
Loves Music, Loves to Dance
All Around the Town
I'll Be Seeing You
Remember Me
The Lottery Winner
Let Me Call You Sweetheart
Silent Night
Moonlight Becomes You
My Gal Sunday
Pretend You Don't See Her

Joan Hess

INTERVIEW BY CHARLES L. P. SILET

J oan Hess confesses that she has no formal training in writing beyond
the obligatory English class assignments, but since the age of six, she has
been a voracious reader of mystery fiction, consuming everything from
the Hardy Boys to Agatha Christie. Before she began to write them
herself, she read as many as five to ten crime books a week. However informal
her background, since 1986, Joan Hess has published almost twenty novels,
and there is no indication that she intends to slacken her pace. Currently,
she is the author of two highly successful crime series, one featuring the
amateur detective, Claire Malloy, and the other set in the small town of
Maggody, Arkansas.

She began the Claire Malloy books with Strangled Prose (1986), and
since then has written nine more, including her latest, A Holly Jolly Murder. Claire Malloy is a widowed, single mother, who lives with her teenage
daughter, Caron, in the college town of Farberville, Arkansas, where she
owns a bookstore, the Book Depot, located in an old train station. In spite
of her outwardly quiet life, Claire seems to stumble across more than her
share of dead bodies, which she insists on investigating, much to the concern
of her sometime lover, Lt. Peter Rosen of the local police department. Thus
far in the series, Claire has looked into murders at the Farberville high
school, at one of the college sororities, at a bird sanctuary, and at the local
beauty pageant. Solving homicides, struggling to keep her financially pre-

carious bookstore afloat, and coping with the hormonal swings of her daughter keeps Claire a very busy woman and gives the series a wonderful resonance and depth.

The enormously funny and popular Maggody series began appearing in 1987 with Malice in Maggody. Now, there are seven others, including The Maggody Militia (1997). Maggody, Arkansas (population 755), serves as the location for a hilarious set of small-town mysteries that includes a cast of locals who appear to be a cross between characters from Hee Haw and escapees from a Faulkner novel. The books feature Arly Hanks, who went off to the bright lights of "Noow Yark," and returned to Maggody to recuperate from a disastrous marriage. She became chief of police because nobody else wanted the job. The series plays off of the ongoing life stories of Arly's meddlesome mother, Ruby Bee, who runs Ruby Bee's Bar & Grill, and her friend Estelle Oppers of Estelle's Hair Fantasies, and involves the Reverend Verber, Jim Bob and his sanctimonious wife, Raz Buchanan, his prize sow, Marjorie, and an assortment of other eccentric small-town types. Arly works diligently to keep the peace and to establish sanity in this loony community.

Hess also wrote a third series under the pseudonym of Joan Hadley, which featured retired florist, Theo Bloomer, but it ended after only two books, The Night-Blooming Cereus (1986) and The Deadly Ackee (1988). She occasionally threatens to revive it.

CLPS: You got interested in writing by working on a romance novel with a friend.

JH: Well, I was teaching art at the time, and a friend came to me and said we must make our fortunes writing romance novels. I replied with something along the lines of "Huh?" I had never written anything that wasn't due on Monday, and I'd never read a romance novel. This was the early eighties, and the romance market was very, very hot. I finally persuaded my mother to check some out from the local public library. I read one and a half of them and said, "Okay, I get it." I sat down and wrote the first three chapters of a novel and sent it off to Harlequin. I received a very encouraging rejection letter— "almost but not quite"—and asking if I had anything else they could look at. I concluded that it wasn't that hard. Shortly after that, I was at a party late at night, and a friend who did a cookbook and I decided to collaborate, because what on earth does the American woman want more than romance and cooking? We facetiously called it *Recipes for Romance.* We strung together ten or twelve short stories about sisters and various relatives; each resolved the hero and heroine's various problems and sent them to bed. One of my favorite lines is: "Dawn sautéed two chicken breasts in clarified butter as she gazed lovingly across the candlelit dining table." This is what sold. But it was much, much harder to write romances than I realized, and there is only so much you can fake. I did about eight more romance novels, some of them a hundred thousand words, some unfinished, and they were all politely rejected as having too much plot.

CLPS: Didn't that writing experience get you started on your craft?

JH: Yes, it certainly was a valuable learning experience, both the writing and the frustration as well. In November 1984, I investigated a Ph.D. program at the university and was accepted over the telephone. I talked to the head of the education department, and he said he'd give me special admission in January. All I had to do was arrange for my transcripts to be sent down from New York, sign a few papers, and work out the class schedule. I panicked, called my agent, and said, "Stop me!" She suggested that I write a mystery. At that point, I decided I would give myself the spring semester to try to write a first draft; if it didn't sell, then I would go to school. That's when I wrote *Strangled Prose*, and it was so much more fun than writing romances. Romances were very restrictive. I discovered that in the mystery, you could pretty much do anything you wanted. I had probably read ten thousand mysteries by then. Even when I was writing romances, I was reading them. I would go to the library and start with Catherine Aird and work around to Donald Westlake. Then I would just go back and start again.

CLPS: Where did you come up with the idea for Claire Malloy?

JH: When I decided to write a mystery, my agent strongly suggested that I think in terms of a series. It seemed logical to write about a woman, and I chose a woman in her thirties. Claire has barely aged since 1985; I, on the other hand, have been leaping ahead. She's about to turn forty now. I gave her a bookstore because I couldn't think of anything more fun than running a bookstore, because of course all booksellers do all day is sit around and read books. Right? I gave her a daughter because I have a daughter. I made her a widow, which in retrospect was prophetic. At the time, I was very happily married, but by the time the first book was published, I was very happily divorced.

CLPS: Why did you give Claire a teenage daughter while most female protagonists have remained unencumbered by family?

JH: For novelty. I suppose I've always been partial to the traditional mystery, so it seems normal to have a similar format to work around. I very much respect the authors who have characters with small children. Even with a daughter, Claire can go hither and yon without having to arrange for a baby-sitter.

CLPS: It also helps to create a certain amount of the humor.

JH: If Claire were totally on her own, I would still have to manufacture someone for her to talk with. Caron provides an interesting foil, and on occasion, she helps to complicate the plot.

CLPS: So, otherwise, you would have to do more with someone like Lt. Rosen, for example?

JH: I did not intend for Claire to get involved with him. In fact, I had a great deal of trouble in the second book when it became obvious that they were going to have a relationship. I don't even acknowledge the existence of writer's block, but occasionally, I write myself into a corner. In *Murder at the Mimosa Inn*, Claire and Peter went around the far side of the lake and sat on a log for about a week while I tried to figure out what was going to happen. I finally resolved that, but at this point, I would dearly like to have him hit by a bus. In *Dear Miss Demeanor*, a little strain developed in their relationship. In *Death by the Light of the Moon*, Claire grudgingly calls Peter on the phone. In *Poisoned Pins*, there is more strain. Peter keeps appearing less and less. I have a hard time dealing with their relationship and what is going to happen to it.

CLPS: How did you begin the series set in the little town of Maggody, Arkansas?

JH: After I had written all of those romances, I wrote my first murder mystery, the Claire Malloy book, *Strangled Prose*, which I gave to my agent and immediately began another with the same character, *Mur-*

der at the Mimosa Inn. By the time St. Martin's read *Strangled Prose*, I'd finished *Murder*, and they bought those two in the space of a week. That summer my ex-in-laws called for a command performance in Israel, and while I was there, I began work on the first Theo Bloomer mystery, *The Night-Blooming Cereus*. By November, I had written three books in one year. On a trip to New York, my editor expressed his concern about my writing too many books and recommended a third series. He suggested that I set the books in Arkansas. California, New York, Florida, and the big cities were all taken, but nobody was doing a backwoods mystery series. He wanted a small town quite unlike the university town of the Claire Malloy novels. When I returned from that trip, I got in the car and went out to the boonies to explore the small towns around the county. I'd try to find a police station if they had one. In one town, I had to chase the cop all over the place. I'd go to the bank and they'd say, "Oh no, I think he went down to the hardware store." Someone finally radioed and found him. I would ask the police about the problems, their budget concerns, that sort of thing. I did not have a name for the fictional town at that point. At Christmas that year, a group went to Jamaica and rented a house. One afternoon, we were taking a train to the island interior, and we went by a little shack with a weathered sign that said Maggotty. I thought, *Oh, that's perfect*. I wrote it down, but when I returned home, I changed it to Maggody. No one really noticed the similarities in the spelling. I spend a lot of time seeing what I can get past New York. I have a character called Merle Hardcock in the Maggody books. It never, ever occurred to me that they would let me use Hardcock, but I tried it and it slipped past the copy editor. Now, when they object, I say, "Oh no, he's a regular character in the series."

CLPS: How did you decide to make Maggody such a small town with a population of 755?

JH: The look of the town and its size are based on several towns from around here. I went into places like Ruby Bee's Bar & Grill or little, tiny police stations that consist of one room in the city hall. As I prepared to write it, I found myself going through a fairly bitter divorce. I wrote *Malice in Maggody* in less than six weeks in order to get rid of the terrific anger I felt toward my husband. After my editor read it, he called and described it as "239 pages of unrelenting sarcasm." He wanted me to wait a little bit before I did revisions. The original must have been a doozy. But I mellowed a bit, and I reread it after a reasonable amount of time and toned it down. I backed off of some of the characters, especially the less lovable ones.

CLPS: You write the Maggody stories using multiple points of view. What does that allow you to do?

JH: It gives me a great deal of flexibility. When I get confused about what is going to happen, I switch over to see what somebody else is doing, then pick up again with Arly. I try not to get too frenetic, although at the end I do have to pick up the pace, so the scenes get shorter and shorter.

CLPS: You have a lot of different characters in the Maggody books. What does this variety allow you to do?

JH: You may have noticed that not all of the characters appear in all of the books. Some overlap, but others only appear in one book. It allows me to introduce new people all the time. I suspect that before I put away my quill, I may have touched on all 755 people in town.

CLPS: Before the books begin, Arly went away from Maggody to live in Manhattan. Why was that necessary?

JH: It gives her a different perspective so that she can see, to some extent as the readers do, the small town as an alien culture. If she had never left, she wouldn't be able to provide this point of view, provide insight into the characters of the place, or dissect the dynamics. She needed to be forced to realize that there are other cultures, other ways of life.

CLPS: It also allows you to take the series to New York in *Maggody in Manhattan*.

JH: That was an interesting book because I had to move the inhabitants of Maggody out of town, which I did in two ways. Ruby Bee went with the contest winners to Manhattan, and Dahlia and Kevin are on their honeymoon. I really didn't know that Dahlia and Kevin were even going to get married. It also allowed me to create Marvelous Marvin. I was a little worried writing about a black male bank robber. But there he was.

CLPS: He is so much smarter than Dahlia or Kevin, and he is so polite to his victim and hostages.

JH: He is a thoroughly delightful character. Perhaps he'll wander into town one of these days.

CLPS: In all of your books you deal with a string of social issues. Is the mystery novel a good vehicle for social criticism?

JH: Mysteries are morality plays, where good and evil are played out. And they work as social comment insofar as good and evil have a social connection. For example, I value the small town. In *Madness in Maggody*, I wrote about the Wal-Mart experience of potentially destroying the local economy with one large superstore. I wanted to explore behind-the-scenes manipulations of corporate America. In the book that is coming out in the spring, *Busy Bodies*, another in the Claire Malloy series, I deal with another question of social responsibility. That book arose out of a situation in Little Rock, where a man has put some three or four million lights all over his house at Christmastime. He bought the houses on either side so he could decorate them as well. It is an unbelievable display. His neighbors are not happy because there is a traffic jam every night as soon as it gets dark, and they can't get in or out of their houses. They finally brought a lawsuit last year to get some relief, arguing that if someone had a heart attack, they couldn't get an ambulance. The man who decorates these houses finally agreed to a limited schedule that satisfied nobody. I thought that was an interesting problem. It raises issues like freedom of expression versus the rights of the neighbors who are trying to lead some kind of normal life. That's what *Busy Bodies* is about.

CLPS: Both the Maggody and Claire Malloy series are set in Arkansas. In what ways are you a Southern writer?

JH: I am much more Southern than my accent implies. Originally, I did not intend to put Claire in Arkansas. Although the settings for both series are in the South, I think they are more generally small-town and university town atmospheres than anything specifically Southern.

CLPS: You've been fairly active in a number of mystery organizations. What do they do for you?

JH: I was quite amazed with the closeness of the writing community. There are a lot of women who started writing about the time I did, and they have been especially supportive. In terms of advice and encouragement, they help make up for some of the drawbacks of living in Arkansas where there is no one with whom I can carry on a forty-five-minute conversation about mystery writing—or publishing gossip. We discuss mutual problems in the field. I was very active in the Mystery Writers of America at one point and served on the board of directors. But I got on a do-gooder binge and spent an entire year making waves, and finally I resigned.

CLPS: Do you think women have been at a disadvantage in the mystery genre?

JH: They certainly were at the beginning. Women crime writers were thought of as British ladies, mostly dead. That changed with Marcia Muller, Sara Paretsky, and Sue Grafton, and with the realization by the publishing industry that women buy books. In the eighties, women mystery writers did not receive an appropriate share of the reviews. The reviewers were mostly male and tended, I think, to review the writers they read, who were primarily male as well. It was brought to their attention that women writers were accounting for an increasing percentage of the books each year, and things have now begun to change. Women have not yet reached parity, but the situation has certainly improved. Marilyn Stasio began reviewing a wider variety for the *New York Times*, and that made a difference, too, as has the presence of the organization known as Sisters in Crime. It has been criticized a great deal in the last year. The argument that women are storming around the country dominating the industry and taking money out of the poor male P.I. writer's pockets doesn't hold water. Sisters in Crime sponsors booths at the ALA and other conventions and publishes a bibliography of our members to promote our books. The network has been very successful and brings together women mystery writers from all over the country. If I want to know the zip code of the North Carolina State Prison, I have someone to call. If I want to know which bookstore to stop at in Albuquerque, I can find somebody who knows somebody there. If we are all so incredibly powerful and talented, why aren't we all rich and famous? If I had the choice, I would be. Trust me.

CLPS: How have you been treated by the critics?

JH: Pretty well, for the most part.

CLPS: Do you ever learn anything from a review?

JH: I try *not* to. I recently received a whole packet of them from the last book. They were all good except one from Florida that went on about what a silly novel this was. My first response was to send him a letter bomb; my second was to call him and say, "You moron, you failed to notice this and that." My third was potentially disastrous: "Now watch this, I'm going to write a hard-boiled, blood and gore, violent, vicious book to show you that I can do what any of the boys can do." Then I tossed it.

CLPS: Are you writing anything or have you ever wanted to write anything outside of the mystery genre?

JH: No, not too seriously. Mysteries are what I've always read and loved. My son's English teacher asked me if I would still write books if they were not going to be published. I finally said, "No, I probably wouldn't write books because they are an awful lot of work." But I would write short stories for my own amusement and as a form of catharsis. That's not to say that I only write for money, but it sure helps.

CLPS: You have two successful series running. How do you keep them fresh?

JH: I alternate between the two, so I'm only writing one Maggody a year. By the time I finish whichever series I am writing about, I'm thoroughly sick of it, and I'm looking forward to getting to the other one. I don't believe I could write two in the same series in the same year. Each series requires a different mind set and certainly a different vocabulary. Nobody in Maggody knows any words with more than four letters. Four being our favorite number, actually. The multiple viewpoint in the Maggody books is, quite frankly, easier to write, because when I get confused about what is going to happen, I can go check on somebody else and then come back. It is easier to juggle a couple of subplots that way, because they can be from different people's points of view. With Claire, nothing can happen outside of her perception. She can be told things or she can see things. In the Claire series, everything is strictly from her point of view.

CLPS: Tell me a little bit about *Miracles in Maggody*.

JH: The premise is that a famous televangelist/faith healer has come up with a scheme to purchase a large block of land, a thousand acres, to build a Christian theme park, not unlike Heritage U.S.A. I wanted to call it Six Flags over Jesus, but my editor wouldn't let me. However, I think I did manage to work the line in once. Each evening, he holds a tent revival, supposedly curing people, but he's not curing broken legs or anything that would require immediate proof up on stage. Instead, he is telling people that they are cured of diabetes, for instance. The person involved is convinced that she is cured and therefore can go off the diet and can start eating all the wrong foods once again. Another little old lady has been told that she has been cured of her vision problems, so she begins driving around town without her glasses. This is when Arly gets much more involved. I enjoyed doing the research. I did not go to a healing session; I'm too much of a chicken. However, I did find all kinds of books by disgruntled ex-employees of all the big name televangelists. The tricks of the trade are discussed in these books, and I used a lot of that material to expose these people. I think they are truly dangerous.

CLPS: How much research do you do for a book?

JH: In *Miracles in Maggody*, the research consisted mostly of tracking down those books I just mentioned and renting a few videos, not of actual televangelists, but of fictional accounts to try to get an idea of how they operate, how they're set up. The Steven Martin film was funny, and there was one filmed nearby in Eureka Spring, *Pass the Ammo*, and I knew a few of the extras. It is not, however, a good movie.

CLPS: You often deal with social issues in your novels.

JH: Basically, I think that is what we're all interested in. I'm always on the lookout for a contemporary social issue that needs to be lampooned. It is not difficult. I thought when I decided to do the militia book—and it was fairly obvious why I did—that these people wouldn't read fiction, that they wouldn't read anything. But then I discovered if one types "guns" on the search on the Internet, they're very much out there and communicating with each other. If one bozo does not like my book, it will be discussed nationally. I'm getting ready to take on gambling in the next Maggody book, but it makes me less nervous because they don't carry guns.

CLPS: *The Maggody Militia* is the current Maggody book. Tell me a bit about it.

JH: I was watching unhappy events on TV a couple of years ago, and there was a great deal of discussion about the Michigan militia and the Colorado militia, and my brain just said, "Oh, the Maggody militia." The research was rather disturbing. I went to my first and last gun show. I've never been that close to so many guns, or for that matter, that many men in caps. But even more unsettling was that they looked remarkably normal. I would much prefer that they be covered with tattoos and look peculiar so we could recognize them. I picked up a back issue of some magazine like *American Survivalist*, and a man looked over my shoulder and shared with me that he had met his wife through a classified ad in it. "Must like underground shelters." I don't know. This is where I found out about the blowguns, a focal point in the book. It was a very, very uncomfortable afternoon for me. It was the presence of all the guns and bullets and knives. People were sighting through the rifles, and I thought if one shot is fired, there are four hundred people who are going to grab a gun off the counter. But, of course, it was all perfectly civilized.

CLPS: So anyone could be involved.

JH: Even someone's next-door neighbor. I'm not saying my next-door neighbor would come and shoot me, but if I thought he were in the militia, I would be concerned about the number of weapons in his house and the sort of people who might be visiting at night.

CLPS: Is this more of a Southern thing, or is this really all over the country?

JH: It was very big in Arkansas. We had one of the stand-offs at the compound with The Sword, the Covenant and the Arm of the Lord group. They're mostly in prison now. And there are some connections to McVeigh. A weapon stolen from a dealer not far south of me was found in McVeigh's trailer. There is another compound just across the border in Oklahoma. It is very much a Midwest thing because they are appealing to farmers, and of course farmers are having a difficult time with banks and therefore primed to feel that the government is out to get them. All of the Western states—Utah, Montana, Colorado—are exceedingly fond of these groups. I did think it was nice of everybody to start having trials just when my book came out. Let's keep militias on the front page.

CLPS: How is the militia different in Maggody?

JH: After I had read quite a bit of material and listened to them on the Internet, I found the whole subject frightening, more frightening than most people realize. And I was, indeed, going to present them as a very frightening group. But then I decided to present them as a bunch of clowns and make fun of them, and then go into the Author Protection Program. For instance, my guys arrive for their survival weekend, and within forty-five minutes, somebody is going out for pizza. They're not good shots. They have recruited Kevin Buchanan, if that tells you something about them. Arly gets involved when there is a shooting during the survival weekend, and good old Sheriff Dorfer persuades her to deal with it because it is more on her turf than his. In the meantime, she has been investigating a string of burglaries across the county. The perps are using the same MO, but Arly and the sheriff cannot determine what the link is. But it all gets tied up in the end.

CLPS: Let's talk about your latest Claire Malloy book, *Closely Akin to Murder.*

JH: What inspired it was the Anne Perry story, when she was exposed after all these years. I was thinking about that and the eternal "what if" question popped into my mind. In her case, it seemed fairly straightforward. In another situation, perhaps things are not quite that simple. I tried very hard to avoid parallels. I set it thirty years ago in Acapulco because that's where the Hollywood big shots used to vacation. Plus, then you add the language barrier. It seemed very likely that these girls would end up in prison before they knew exactly what was going on. In this case, one of the girls, who is now thirty years older, is threatened by a blackmailer who is threatening to expose her past crime. She asks Claire to find out who the blackmailer is. Of course, Claire had to go to Acapulco, as did I. That was very entertaining. I worked with a travel agent here because I needed a car and a driver for one day. So, indeed, George came to the hotel, and he presumed that we were going shopping and going to the beaches or maybe the bird sanctuary. I said, "No, George, perhaps you should sit down." I wanted to go to the courthouse and the newspaper office. I wanted to know which hotels were here thirty years ago. In most of these places he had to come inside with me in case I needed a translator. I think he was really glad to say good-bye. The police compound was unnerving. There were an awful lot of people with guns and uniforms but no badges. The prison is exceedingly grim. George showed me a hotel that is now closed that used to be where a lot of the big names came like Johnny Weissmuller and John Wayne. Jack and Jackie Kennedy had dinner there on their honeymoon. I changed the name of the hotel, but I didn't change much else about it, although I had it populated now by hookers and dopers. For the Scottsdale side of the book, I went out there for Left Coast Crime, but months and months later, when it was time to write about it, I couldn't remember things so I called the Poison Pen Bookstore about three times a week to ask questions like, "What kind of trees grow in the Tonto National Forest? What's the name of the biggest cemetery in Scottsdale?" In the book I mentioned the bookstore as a little thank-you.

CLPS: What does it do for you to be able to move the series around?

JH: It certainly helps with the Maggodys, because I'm stuck with a basic premise that strange people come to Maggody and then somebody gets killed. We've brought in the movie people, the UFO people, the militia, because I can't kill off the locals. *Maggody in Manhattan* was a nice break, and this gambling book will take place in Mississippi. I have come up with an idea of how to get some of them over there to the casinos, which are just across the river. Once again, someone had to do the research. But they're very fond of me there; I gave them money. And I went over to Tupelo, where Elvis was born; that's going to be in the book, too. I came back through Oxford and looked at the outside of Faulkner's home, but it was after four o'clock, so I couldn't go in.

CLPS: What are you working on now?

JH: I'm getting ready to start the gambling Maggody. At this moment, it's titled *Misery Loves Maggody*, because, believe it or not, there is no gambling word that begins with *M*. I had the same problem when I did the book on baseball teams; there are no baseball terms that start with *M*. If you come up with a gambling one, I'd certainly be interested. There will be another Claire book out this fall, called *A Holly Jolly Murder*, and it is mostly about Druids. My editor wanted a Christmas book, but I really didn't want to write one, so this is more of a winter solstice book. Claire gets involved with a "grove" of Druids, as they call them. Part of the problem is the Wiccans in the group are just not doing the right thing. They prefer to perform their rituals "sky clad." Isn't that a nice word for buck naked? There is a Christmas subplot because Caron has found a job working at Santa's workshop at the mall, where they take photographs. There is a problem out there, and she's being sued for a million dollars for assault and emotional abuse. Santa Claus even walks into this book. He says, "You can call me Ed."

CLPS: Is there anything in the future you'd like to do?

JH: Make the *New York Times'* best-seller list? May not happen, though, because I am perceived as writing genre fiction. I cannot seem to convince people that the Maggodys are social satire as well. I'm still enjoying writing the two series. My agent and I talked about reviving poor Theo Bloomer, but Theo Bloomer will remain lost in the Bermuda Triangle for now.

Portions of this interview appeared in *The Armchair Detective*, 28:1 (Winter 1995), 8–16.

Ed McBain

INTERVIEW BY CHARLES L. P. SILET

van Hunter aka Ed McBain is one of the most prolific and celebrated writers of contemporary crime fiction. His 87th Precinct novels, now numbering close to fifty, stretch back into the mid-1950s and represent one of the longest running, most sustained, and highly regarded mystery series on record. The Matthew Hope books, a second series now entering its third decade, have extended McBain's talent and range.

Writing under his real name, Evan Hunter has been a critically important, best-selling novelist since his early work, The Blackboard Jungle (1954), received acclaim both as a novel and as a hit movie. Through the years, many of Mr. Hunter's other novels have been made into successful Hollywood films. He has also written for the screen, adapting his own fiction as well as the work of other writers. His most notable film project was as script writer for Alfred Hitchcock's classic film, The Birds (1963).

Mr. McBain's output continues to be prodigious. He currently has a new 87th Precinct novel and another Matthew Hope book ready for publication, and he is working on another Evan Hunter. Ed McBain/Evan Hunter books have sold in the millions worldwide. In the process, he has gathered just about all the awards available to writers of crime fiction, including, most recently, Italy's Raymond Chandler Award. In the following interview he talks about his life, his fiction, and confesses his desire to write the book for a Broadway musical.

CLPS: Before you went into the navy during World War II, you studied art briefly at Cooper Union. Do you think your art experience had an effect on your writing?

EM: Absolutely, no question. It's been particularly helpful when I'm doing a screenplay because there you have to call all the shots. But I think of a page in a book in terms of how it looks to the reader's eye. If you have pages and pages of dialogue, the reader's eye will become fatigued and offended. So I break the page like a design and now I know instinctively when there's too much of any one thing, too much exposition, too much dialogue, and I just switch automatically. I also use art in describing a room or a character. It's a cinematic technique as well as an art technique where you give the material that the reader needs in quick flashes so that it doesn't stop the onward motion of the scene, the momentum of the scene. As in real life, you don't come into a room and suddenly have a camera pan the entire room so that you know everything that's in it. You see little things, a fax machine, a bulletin board, and the scene progresses.

CLPS: You often break your books up with illustrations.

EM: Yeah, I like doing that. First of all, I think the reader likes to see these things. The reader says, "Oh this is what it looks like." In this way, the reader has all the information that the cops have. I did a novel called *The Paper Dragon* about a plagiarism trial, and much of the trial hinges on a notebook that the defendant kept while he was an art student, and I reconstructed that notebook with my own illustrations. I loved doing that.

CLPS: During the war, you joined the navy, and when you were aboard ship, you wrote a lot of short fiction. Was it at that point that you decided that you would like to try writing?

EM: It was really interesting because the navy makes use of whatever talents a guy has. So in boot camp they discovered I had gone to art school along with some other guys who had similar training more or less, so they had us lettering signs for the barracks and little tasks like that. On the ship we painted on the stack the words "The First Shall Be First." We were the First Destroyer Squadron, and we were also the first who went to Japan. We painted it on the stack in Japanese so that they could see it and bite their nails. And I drew pictures of all the officers and men and they sent the sketches home to their girlfriends and mothers and wives, and then there was really nothing else to draw. We were in the middle of the Pacific Ocean. After I'd drawn all the gun mounts and the torpedo tubes and the radar antennas, I borrowed a typewriter from the radio shack and I found a little compartment and locked myself in it and began writing and I found it was much more pleasurable. When you go to art school, they train you to see everything with a frame around it. You're sitting on a subway train and you're looking across at the people, and you frame the part of that scene that you want to do. When I began writing, the frame disappeared, it just expanded, and I discovered I could do anything I wanted to do, there was no frame around it; it was wonderful.

CLPS: After the navy, you went to Hunter College, and then you began writing. Where did you come up with the idea for the first 87th Precinct novel?

EM: I think that was an offspring of *The Blackboard Jungle*, which was published in October 1954; the first of the 87th Precinct novels was in 1956. There are many similarities between *The Blackboard Jungle* and the 87th Precinct. The gathering place for the protagonists in *The Blackboard Jungle* was the school itself and the teachers' lunchroom, and in the 87th Precinct it was a station house and the squad room. And the ethnic breakdown pretty much followed what the ethnic breakdown of New York City was at that time. It's a whole different bag of nuts now, but at the time, that was about the ethnic breakdown in the school system and also in the police department. Whereas *The Blackboard Jungle* didn't venture too far out into the city, this was expanded in the 87th Precinct novels, and the whole city became the playing field. I think that *The Blackboard Jungle* and the first of the 87th Precinct novels were—touch close, and in fact, I think over the years, the crime novels have become even closer to *The Blackboard Jungle* than the early ones. I didn't realize this myself at the time, you know; I just recently saw the connection.

CLPS: You were the first to use the ensemble story. Does it bother you that it's been widely imitated now?

EM: Well, I consider it sort of an homage, except when they steal stupidly. In police work, for example, the twenty-four hours preceding a murder and the twenty-four hours after it are considered the most important. The twenty-four preceding because you want to know everything the victim did in order to get to the criminal, and the twenty-four hours following because the gap is widening between the time of the murder and catching the murderer. But I labeled this the "24/24" and a guy in one of his books went into this whole business about the twenty-four hours preceding and the twenty-four hours after, and he said, "In police jargon, this is known as the 24/24." Well, I *invented* that! It doesn't *exist* in police work! So I found that very funny. I do not find the remarkable similarities between *Hill Street Blues* and the 87th Precinct books quite so funny.

CLPS: There was a television show of the 87th Precinct in the early 1960s.

EM: It was only on for thirteen episodes, I think, and it was okay, but they shot it on a studio street instead of out in the big, bad city, and they got Hollywood hacks on it, you know, writing the screenplays, so it went the way of all bad series. It wasn't *too* bad I guess, but it didn't break any new ground, either.

CLPS: Did they use the ensemble cast?

EM: Not all of them. They used Carella, Kling, Meyer, and Havilland, who was a bad guy in the early books. I killed him off later in the novels, but they used him in the series and changed him to a good guy. They took the bad apple out of the squad room, which was a mistake.

CLPS: The 87th Precinct novels are now on television as made-for-TV movies.

EM: I have had very little to do with those, as well. They're okay, just okay. In my estimation, except for the Kurosawa film, *High and Low*, there has never really been a realistic rendering of the books on the screen. I don't know why they resist translation that way. I really don't understand why because there certainly have been many, many television series premised on the 87th Precinct, with which I had nothing to do, that are successful and that get the same gritty feel that's in the 87th Precinct books. So I don't know what it is in the books themselves or in the people who have tried to adapt them over the years that resists this translation. Even the one I did myself, *Fuzz*, once the director got hold of it, he misinterpreted it entirely so that it became a comedy. I think a lot of people misjudge the humor in the books, misinterpret the mix of humor and serious stuff, or go overboard on the violence. They never quite understand the balance in the books. Kurosawa, of course, really did his own movie. He just used the premise of a mistaken identity kidnapping from *King's Ransom* and went off with his own plot and used it to investigate the lower depths of Yokohama. But it was a good movie, and there haven't been many based on the 87th Precinct.

CLPS: You have wide experience as a screenwriter, and the books strike me as very cinematic. Maybe they are too literary.

EM: I don't know, but they sure do resist translation.

CLPS: I've read someplace where you talk about needing not only some bad guys outside, but also somebody inside the squad room as well.

EM: I've got a couple of lazy cops, a couple of stupid cops, a couple of bad cops, a couple of bigoted cops, you know, the whole bag. It keeps all the balls in the air. Robert Parker said this will never end for McBain because he's got so many computations and permutations that he can use, he's got all these characters he can juggle one way or another.

CLPS: What about the time sequence in the 87th Precinct now? The fact that you have not exactly *stopped* time but slowed down. Parker's Spencer keeps getting older.

EM: That's a mistake, I think.

CLPS: How do you decide when to inch the characters forward a little bit in age, the twins for example?

EM: The twins are "inching toward puberty," I like to say. I don't even *know* how old they are; I'll have to look next time I write a book. Carella and the other guys in the squad room are all thirtysomething, that's all I say now, thirtysomething. In one book I said, while talking about a war one of the characters had been in, "He'd almost forgotten *which* war; an American male of a certain age certainly has been in one war or another." In *Mischief*, the book ends with Kling making a telephone call, and *Mischief* was published in August 1993. The one I'm writing right now *begins* with that same phone call. Kling is still making the same phone call to this woman in a phone booth in the rain. That's the first chapter in the new book, which won't be published till Spring of '95. So that makes continuous action a year and a half apart.

CLPS: Each novel in the 87th Precinct Series seems to set up a different kind of writer's problem and then solve it.

EM: I don't know if I consciously set writer's problems for myself, maybe *challenges*, you know. The way to keep a series fresh—for me, anyway—is to find new things about the characters and to find new ways of approaching them. I certainly should know how to describe a character by now; if I don't, I should really hang up my jock. But the fun is to find new ways of doing it. Now, I must have written the scene ten thousand times, where they break the news to someone whose relative has been killed, correct? But in *Lullaby*, a teenage girl, a baby-sitter, is killed on New Year's Eve. So I did a riff instead on it being New Year's Eve and that forevermore for the parents of this girl, this was no longer going to be New Year's Eve, it was going to be the anniversary of their daughter's death. I did the whole riff *before* they knock on the door. It's three in the morning and the parents open the door and it's the police and they're looking at them and Carella says, "May we come in, please?" and that's the end of the scene. I didn't have to play the scene, you see? I look for different ways of doing things that keep the series alive for me, and I'm hopeful this keeps it alive and fresh for the reader as well. Otherwise, it just gets to be hack work.

CLPS: Where did Matthew Hope come from, and why did you start writing about him?

EM: I had just come through a divorce, and I was thinking of divorce as a kind of killing. There's a lot of fallout where people get hurt, you know—the children get hurt and relatives get hurt other than the principals. I wanted to do a serious novel, an Evan Hunter novel, divorce and remarriage, and the effects of divorce on the lives of people who are not necessarily the principals. I got a contract with Harper and Row to do the novel, and it was to be called *The Scene of the Crime*. A crime takes place, but the metaphor really was the divorce. I was going to tell it in terms of a brutal murder that Matthew Hope is investigating, while he himself is having an affair and contemplating divorce. Well, I wrote the book, and it didn't work. It was neither fish nor fowl, neither a mystery nor a straight novel, it was just some curious hybrid. So Harper and Row turned it down and I gave them back the advance money, and there it was, sitting around, and I thought, *This cannot be allowed to happen with a book I spent months writing.* So I read it over again and I figured if I strengthened the mystery elements in it and put Ed McBain on the cover, it could become a mystery novel. And that's what I did. I changed the title to *Goldilocks*, which I thought sounded more mysterious than *The Scene of the Crime*, which to me was a more serious title. It was published here and then it was published again in England. My British paperback publishers threw a party for me, and they were lamenting the fact that Pan Books, their competitors, had all the 87th Precinct novels, and they said it would be jolly good if you had *another* series *we* could publish. So I said, "Well, why don't we? Why don't I do Matthew Hope as a series, using fairy-tale titles?" It was fairy-tale titles at the time; since, I've expanded into nursery rhymes, and—what do you call the stuff like *This Is the House That Jack Built*? I don't know what you call those. And they said great and they gave me a contract and off we went.

CLPS: Why did you set them in Florida?

EM: I was living in Florida at the time, and I usually would write them while we were there for the winter. But also, there was a nice change of pace—like a pitcher with a fastball and a curveball and a slider—setting the books in a place where one doesn't expect that sort of violence. You'd expect palm trees and sparkling beaches and balmy breezes and not that sort of violence. It's a more upscale setting than in the 87th Precinct books. The characters are more upscale, too.

CLPS: They seem sexier and more graphically violent.

EM: Yeah, they are. When I first began the 87th Precinct books, Herb Alexander, the editor at the time, described the books as having what he called "clinical verity." The sex was more concerned with the presence of sperm in a vaginal vault than a steamy sex scene, which I know how to write pretty well, by the way. There had been some sexy scenes in the 87th Precinct books, not between Carella and his wife but between Cotton and some of his women and Bert Kling and some of his women. I think there's a difference in the women in the Matthew Hope novels—who are getting more interesting for me, anyway. But you know, in the 87th Precinct novels, I can have Kling's girlfriend not wanting to go to bed because she just got her period, and I haven't yet done that, get down to the nitty-gritty, in the Matthew Hope books.

CLPS: How is the series evolving?

EM: Pretty well, I think. One of the best books in the series, perhaps one of the best mysteries I've ever written, and in fact one of the best novels I've written, is a Matthew Hope called *There Was a Little Girl*. It is told in five different time frames, a very good book, I think, stylistically an important book. I think writers can learn a lot from reading *There Was a Little Girl* about flashback and flash-forward, about a lot of things. Matthew has evolved as a character in his own right. He's a good character to work with. And he's evolved his repertory company around him now, so he has private eyes who work with him, he has the police, various girlfriends, a daughter. He's got the whole cast of supporting players in place. Which I need. A lot of writers don't need that. Robert Parker does not need his supporting players. He's got one or two, but that's enough for him.

CLPS: What do the Matthew Hope books allow you to do that the 87th Precinct books don't?

EM: They have a different tone to them, I think; the writing is very different from that in the 87th Precinct. They're more leisurely in the unfolding. There's a faster pace to the 87th Precinct novels because they're set in the big, bad city. And they really allow me to have a lead character who is more sophisticated than the cops of the 87th Precinct. As sensitive and as feeling as they are but more sophisticated. So Matthew can have just come back from a trip to Paris whereas Carella would have come back from a trip to North Carolina. Big difference. I can deal with the same upscale characters in the cases that the 87th are investigating, because the city has very rich people in it. It's just in the difference of the personality of the lead character.

CLPS: Is there a relationship between the Matthew Hope books and the 87th Precinct books?

EM: No, not really. Some of the criminals in the Hope books are pretty tough guys. In *Cinderella*, the two heavies that are tracking the book are as heavy as anybody in the 87th Precinct, that's for sure. Maybe the puzzles in the Matthew Hope books are more formal than in the 87th Precinct. I'm not sure. The 87th Precinct has a lot of things going on. Usually, in the Matthew Hope books, there is just one case.

CLPS: Because of the problems with *Lizzie*, you said that experience put you off other novels for a while and that you wanted to concentrate on the 87th Precinct books and make them the best crime novels going. What have you done differently to change them?

EM: I think I've put more social comment in them and that may be a mistake; frankly, I don't know. Although in the new one I'm exploring—I don't know quite how to put this. In *Mischief*, for example, the Deaf Man's plot is really designed to exploit racist attitudes in the city. That becomes a social problem told in terms of a diabolical scheme of the Deaf Man. In the one I'm writing now, Kling is starting an affair with the black woman from *Mischief*, the deputy chief surgeon, so I get to explore what is to my mind one of America's most serious problems, the conflict between races, in terms of two leading characters starting a romance. That's the title of the book, *Romance*. I think that the early 87th Precinct novels were pretty straight mysteries that didn't deal with any social issues. Beginning with *Ice* maybe, they started to change and started to get a lot darker.

Lullaby, Vespers, and *Kiss* are very dark novels where justice doesn't always triumph. *Mischief* is perhaps the darkest one of them. So, the new one—even though it's dealing with black/white relations as the heart beating under the surface of the novel—is nonetheless a simple novel with a straight mystery story line and a straight romantic story line. I'm not certain that the mystery novel *is* the place to explore social problems; I'm not sure of that anymore. I do know I don't like mysteries that are just shoot 'em up, bang bang.

CLPS: What about the 87th Precinct books and social commentary, or commentary in general in the crime novels?

EM: Yeah, I don't know how many other guys are doing it, but a lot of people have talked about this, a lot of mystery writers have talked about it as *subverting* the genre. I don't think the genre *should* be subverted. I think the genre is wide enough *not* to be subverted if you want to make social comments. But I'm not sure the average mystery reader buys a mystery to get social criticism. I'm always aware of a responsibility to the reader. I know the reader didn't buy my book to learn about the social security system in the United States of America or whatever; he bought it because he wants a *mystery*. So I'm aware of that, and if ever I see myself going too far over in another direction, I say, "Hey, hey, hey, get back to what we're supposed to be doing here. We're supposed to be solving a murder. We can't go too far astray."

CLPS: People seem to be doing all kinds of crazy, interesting things with detective writing.

EM: Yeah, how about *cats* solving mysteries. God, I can't imagine what'll be next, *goldfish?* Hold up a suspect weapon in front of a goldfish, it burps up a couple of bubbles. Good grief.

CLPS: Over the past couple of years, you have been writing a new type of Evan Hunter novel. The first one was *Criminal Conversation.* Tell me a little about it.

EM: It's about a woman who unknowingly begins an affair with a gangster her district attorney husband is investigating. None of them know who the others are. So there's an ongoing investigation and an ongoing affair and a threat of discovery everywhere. Will the DA husband discover his wife is having an affair with the gangster? Will the gangster discover she's the DA's wife? And if he does, what will he do about it? Will *she* discover he's a gangster? And what will she do about it? So it's a very steamy novel. "Criminal conversation" is a tort which is a civil wrong for which damages can be sought and "criminal conversation" is the tort of adultery. The actual definition is the tort of debauching or seducing of a wife, defilement of the marriage bed, a breaking down of the covenant of fidelity. That's the law, and that's where the title comes from. I got it on a plane coming back from a book tour. A woman lawyer was sitting next to me. We had a lively conversation, and she mentioned criminal conversation. She said, "Do you know what it means?" I said, "No." She said, "It's adultery." I like the book. It's a good book with some good social comment in it.

CLPS: The second one was *Privileged Conversation*. Both of these books are different, much sexier for example.

EM: Yes, especially *Privileged Conversation*. There I thought, *Wouldn't it be interesting if a psychiatrist who deals with the obsessions of other people would become obsessed himself with this fantasy figure in a Broadway show?* They're both about adulterous love affairs, and you can't write about adultery and have the characters sitting around drinking tea. They have to be screwing; let's face it.

CLPS: In most of your books, the sex is primarily off camera.

EM: In the 87th Precinct novels, most of the time the sex is off camera. Well, in *Romance* there is a lot of onstage sex, but it is mild stuff. This is genuine stuff. I've written some pretty good sex scenes over my lifetime, you know. It's not Jacqueline Susann sex; it's sex, real sex.

CLPS: You started your career making social comments.

EM: I remember when I was writing *Strangers When We Meet* for the screen, talking to Kirk Douglas, and I said would he mind if the character did something—I forget what it was now—but it was something that was unflattering. He said, "Hell, I made my career playing a bad guy." Well, I made *my* career with social commentary.

CLPS: Is there anything you'd like to do that you haven't done so far?

EM: I'd like to do the book for a musical. I once did that; I was working with Jerry Bock, the guy who did the music for *Fiddler on the Roof* and *She Loves Me*. It was a mystery, in fact, a mystery musical titled *Caper*, which was pretty good. There was a good, complicated plot, and Jerry had written some wonderful songs, but it never got off the ground. A lot of things in theater never get off the ground. I wrote a thriller several years ago that was optioned for a play and again never got off the ground. Arthur Penn was supposed to direct it. But I just got a call from someone the other day who had heard about it and asked me to send it to him, and I did, and he said he'd like to do it. So we'll see.

CLPS: A play?

EM: I love the theater. If I could make a living in the theater, that's where I would write. It's very exciting.

Portions of this interview originally appeared in *The Armchair Detective* 27:4 (Fall 1994), 392–399.

Simon Brett

INTERVIEW BY JERRY SYKES

When he came to create the character of Charles Paris, a middle-aged, unsuccessful actor with a glass of whiskey never far from his lips, Simon Brett was able to draw on an insider's knowledge of the fragile infrastructure of show business and the even more fragile creatures that move through that world.

The theater has always been a great love of Brett's, and it was a love that he indulged to the full during his time at Oxford University, playing a number of roles and later becoming president of the Dramatic Society. As well as acting, he also took time to write and direct his own shows. It was this experience that led him to the BBC where for many years he was a producer for Radio Light Entertainment. He later left to become a Light Entertainment producer at London Weekend Television.

It was these years that were to prove invaluable and inspirational in the creation and continuing success of Charles Paris.

Paris made his first entrance in Cast, in Order of Disappearance in 1975, and from the start it was clear that his main interest was in the bottle and young, impressionable actresses rather than a serious acting career. Indeed, Charles had long since ceased to call it a career and now simply referred to it as work.

Charles does, however, make full use of his theatrical training to effect disguises during his investigations, usually taking the form of reprises from *his slim portfolio of character parts. Over the years, those investigations have taken him to all corners of the world of showbiz: TV, radio, West End theater, regional and touring theater, corporate videos.*

In the mid-eighties Brett introduced a second amateur sleuth in the form of Mrs. Pargeter, whom the author has described as "anti–Miss Marple." Certainly she is a world apart from Agatha Christie's creation, being the widow of a high-class crook—or so we are led to believe—whose influence extends from beyond the grave; whenever Mrs. Pargeter is in need of assistance, she can rest assured that the late Mr. Pargeter is owed so many favors that all she has to do is ask.

Brett has also written three nonseries crime novels, among them A Shock to the System, *which was made into a film starring Michael Caine. But it is with his old friend Charles Paris that Brett is most at ease, and he is far too fond of the man to retire him—because if Brett stopped writing about him, who else would give the old rogue any work?*

JS: Let's go back to the start of your career, which presumably started at Oxford. What were you studying? English and Drama?

SB: I've always been interested in the theater and did a lot of amateur acting both in my teens and at university, but I was reading just English. As for the start of my career, I've written for as long as I can remember. The first thing that I can remember writing was when I was about seven. We had an English master who set us seven-year-old boys the task of writing our own epitaphs, and I remember the one I wrote, which is going to be a difficult death to engineer, but it actually said, *"Here I lie, S. Brett by name; killed by a lion I thought was tame."* So there's always been a motif of death running through my work. I wrote a lot of stuff at university: revues, sketches, that kind of thing.

JS: So you were mainly interested in the theater at this stage?

SB: Yes, I suppose so. But I was also writing short stories and five very properly unpublished novels. One of those was a crime story based on my first job, which was as Father Christmas in a department store, called *Death in Toys*, which nobody wanted to publish.

JS: This was after you left Oxford?

SB: Well, I had this rather ugly period where I was unemployed for a couple of months. Then I went to the local Labour Exchange, as it was then called, and got this job as Father Christmas for seven weeks. Later, I joined the BBC as a radio producer and stayed for ten years. That's where I really got into writing Charles Paris.

In the early seventies, I was delegated to produce the series of Lord Peter Wimsey stories with Ian Carmichael, who had just played the part on television. I worked very closely with Chris Miller, who was adapting the stories, and the experience made me less frightened of crime fiction. Demystified the mystery, if you like. I always thought that the plot was paramount, but in making those adaptations, it became clear that character and dialogue were at least as important. I thought, *I'm not sure that I can do the plot, but I can do character and dialogue.* So that's how I got into it.

JS: Had you read much crime fiction?

SB: Not really. I had gone through the Agatha Christie stage in my teens.

JS: Is that where you got the idea that the plot was paramount?

SB: I guess, though if you look back to that time, there weren't that many people doing the *why*dunit. Crime fiction wasn't going through a good patch in the early seventies. There were people who were exploring it, but it was still quite traditional. So I suppose I read the Agatha Christies, the Margery Allinghams, Raymond Chandler a bit, though I didn't really know much about him . . .

JS: He didn't care much for plots, either.

SB: No. Man with a gun, yes, excellent principle. Anyway, I thought I'd written a one-off crime book about an actor until my editor said, "What's going to be the setting for the next one?" and I said, "The Edinburgh Festival." But after the first one was accepted, I did do a kind of crash course in contemporary crime fiction. I just read lots of stuff because I didn't really know about it. I also didn't know that there was this kind of social life attached to crime fiction, that all crime writers knew each other pretty well. I've made a lot of very good friends, but it never occurred to me when I started that I was getting into a whole new world.

JS: Going back to the BBC, you were responsible for launching one of the most successful radio shows of all time, *The Hitchhiker's Guide to the Galaxy*.

SB: Yes, I produced the first episode. Douglas Adams was one of the generation of Cambridge graduates that I first came across when I went to see their end-of-year show with a view to producing a radio version of it. We later worked together on *Week Ending*, a satirical program about the news. I was the producer, and Douglas was writing little bits for me. But I don't think there's ever been a more inappropriate marriage than his kind of imagination and writing serious comedy about news items. But he persevered, and I kept saying, "You really must come up with something of your own, because I don't think this is ideal casting for you." Eventually, he came into my office one Friday afternoon with three ideas, one of which was *The Hitchhiker's Guide to the Galaxy*.

JS: Did you think it was going to be as successful as it was?

SB: I had no idea it was going to be a massive international success. I knew it was good, but I didn't know how good.

JS: It was around this time that you published the first Charles Paris mystery.

SB: A little earlier, in fact. The first Charles Paris was published in 1975.

JS: Was there anything in particular that inspired you? Any particular person?

SB: I think working on the Lord Peter Wimsey series was the main thing. I have this image of actors that I've used in the Charles Paris books, this image of the glove puppet. I often feel that with a lot of actors they only truly come to life when they are in work—they go into a kind of half-life the rest of the time—but suddenly they have a part and it kind of animates them, it gives them a life that they don't have the rest of the time. It's the glove puppet lying on the shelf and then suddenly it's got a hand in it. I was fascinated by the whole process.

JS: Charles Paris is not a very successful actor, but he is dedicated. Do you think many actors are like that, journeymen?

SB: There are a lot of different styles of actor. There are the stars, who are often self-appointed; they have this vision of themselves as stars. Then there are the ones who recognize it as a job of work and find their level fairly soon; they keep doing the same stuff and manage their careers quite skillfully. And then there are a great many actors who are no less talented than the stars but who haven't got the personality or the hustling mentality to keep them going in work, and although they moan about their profession, they know that it's the only thing they can do. It's the same with their children: They can be nasty to them, but if anyone else is rude about them, They will defend them until their last drop of blood. Charles Paris is in that area; he's not a bad actor. It's interesting to see reviews. Sometimes they say Charles Paris is a very bad actor but better as a detective. I've never said he's a bad actor, but I agree with the reviews that suggest that he's not the greatest. I feel he's a perfectly competent actor and given the right breaks, he could have been a lot better than he is, but there is a kind of defeatism in his personality that keeps him where he is.

JS: And his alcoholism?

SB: I've never quite defined whether or not he is an alcoholic. That's something people have picked up on. He is pretty heavily into the booze. Whether he could stop . . . in fact, that's something I'm thinking of exploring in the next book.

JS: Even when the hand is in the glove puppet, he still drinks heavily.

SB: Yes, but in some of the books, when he is in work he doesn't drink as much. I think he probably is an alcoholic but . . .

JS: He doesn't admit it.

SB: Well, he enjoys it, he feels better with a drink than he does without. Maybe that is a definition of an alcoholic.

JS: Paris comes from a generation of actors that have their roots in rep theater, rather than later generations who have had more opportunities in television. Has this created any problems?

SB: Definitely. When I wrote the first Charles Paris in 1974, I didn't actually think I'd still be writing about him in 1997. In the first book, he was 47, and then he aged a year with every book I wrote for the next ten years. But then I thought, *Just a minute, how many jobs are there available for actors in their seventies?* So I froze him in his late fifties. But yes, has he still got that rep background? I'm sure other authors have this problem. Most of them do it by never stating the age in the first place. I think Hercule Poirot was reckoned to be 134 when he solved his last mystery.

JS: I'm always surprised to find the books classified as cozies. Charles Paris is such a dark character.

SB: Yes, I'm always surprised when I go over to the U.S. and find him on the shelves marked British Cozies. Mrs. Pargeter, the other character I write about, is very definitely cozy, but Charles, I think the character is far from cozy. I think they possibly use the definition to mean cozy in the tradition of Agatha Christie. In other words, it's a whodunit where the murder is not brains over the walls; the murder is more the key that starts the mystery. I guess if that's your definition, then in terms of structure, they're cozies. But, no, not based on the characters.

JS: The books were very successful from the outset, enabling you to become a full-time writer. Did the move away from actors make the books, the research, more difficult?

SB: I should say that I've never just written books. I think I would have difficulty making a living if I had just been writing books. I've always kept going with radio and television and anything else that has paid the bills. It did become a problem about two or three years after I ceased being a television producer when I suddenly thought, *My God, I've used up all my research*, because while I was writing and working at the BBC, every time I answered the phone, it was research, because it was going to be an actor, a director, a producer, an agent. The sort of research I do now is to talk to people involved in whichever aspect of the business I'm interested in. For instance, the next book is going to be about a touring production—probably quite a long tour, probably not coming to the West End, which is a phenomenon of theater that's happened in the last five years—and I'm going to have dinner with a guy who's been a production manager on that kind of tour. That's how I do my research now.

JS: Through the Charles Paris series, you've probably savaged most of the showbiz institutions and types. Do you find it difficult finding people that will talk to you about themselves or about their business?

SB: No, I don't think I've ever met anyone that's been offended by it.

JS: All publicity is good publicity?

SB: I think it's partly that, but I've never actually put a real person in any of the books. People will tell me stories and say, "God, you know that thing you wrote about so-and-so, well here's a story about you-know-who," and they'll name names and tell me more stories because people in the business love telling you dreadful stories about other actors and producers and directors.

JS: It's quite a fragile business.

SB: Yes, it is, and that's what I hope appeals about Charles Paris, this mix of the flamboyant and the vulnerable. It's there in every actor I know, and it's why the stars become such megalomaniacs, and I just find it fascinating.

JS: Do you get your plot ideas from the stories people tell you?

SB: With the Charles Paris books, I always start with the setting, which particular area of show business he is going to be in for this one. And then, out of that setting, you get a lot of the cast: If it's going to be a touring production, then you're going to have a producer, touring manager, a director, a star. There are various givens that you can't get away from, and also within that, there are going to be various conflicts, like between the director and the producer, the star and the director. So in a way, once you've chosen the setting, a lot of plotting follows on from that.

JS: After your tenth Charles Paris novel, you wrote *A Shock to the System*. Did you think that was the end of the Charles Paris books?

SB: Some people have adversarial relationships with their protagonists and they want to get rid of them, but as long as there are backgrounds I want to write about, I'll go on writing about him. It was more that there were other things that I wanted to write about. *A Shock to the System* was just an idea that I had, and it certainly didn't fit into the Charles Paris format, and I couldn't see another way of doing it, except as a one-off, so that's what happened. And then I did another one called *Dead Romantic* for the same reason. The third one-off turned out to be the first Mrs. Pargeter. By the time I'd finished that, I knew this was another series character, although I hadn't started out with that in mind.

JS: Didn't that start off as a TV series?

SB: Well, it did and it didn't. I had the first idea working with Irene Handl, who I thought was just wonderful, so full of energy. I started writing a sitcom with her in mind called *Mr Pargeter's Widow*, but I only wrote one-half of the first episode and never showed it to anyone.

JS: Mr. Pargeter is often alluded to as a major figure in the underworld, a Mr. Big type character. Would you go along with that?

SB: I think that's in the mind of the reader.

JS: Certainly all his contacts seem to be a bit shady.

SB: Often, when I do a talk, someone will ask me, "Why don't you do a book where Charles Paris meets Mrs. Pargeter?" But that is so inconceivable. I think of Charles Paris as a real person; it is not impossible that someone like him could exist. Whereas never in a million years could anyone like Mrs. Pargeter exist. She comes from a world of lovable, Ealing Comedy crooks, all with hearts of gold.

JS: I must admit that when I first read her, I was reminded of the old lady in *The Ladykillers*.

SB: I'd be flattered by that comparison.

JS: The Charles Paris books would appear to be ideal for TV. Presumably, there has been some interest?

SB: The series has been going for so long and there have been so many interests—there is an option out at the moment—but who knows? I think there are two problems: One is that television has a dreadful track record of doing showbiz in that it almost always gets it wrong, which is remarkable given the fact that everyone in television has some kind of connection to it. The other thing is that Charles as a character is very interior, and you probably need someone more proactive for television. Personally, I think there are lots of ways one could write it to make him more proactive, but that would worry people a bit.

JS: Have you written any scripts?

SB: I've written a couple. I tried adapting one of the books at one stage when somebody had an option, and then I wrote an original one to show the kind of liberties I thought could be taken. So maybe one day . . .

JS: Any particular actor in mind?

SB: Oh yes, that's been good fun. I'll get a call from an agent or from an actor, they're almost always entirely unsuitable, but they think the way to prove they're right for the part is to take me out for lunch and drink me under the table. So that's quite pleasant. But it does appeal, and there have been some quite eminent actors that have been interested in the character.

JS: For instance?

SB: In all the Charles Paris books, I've never given a single piece of physical description, except in the first one where I said that he had his own hair. I don't really have a physical image of him myself, but there have been various actors over the years who I thought would be fine. The trouble is that most of them are dead now, like Denholm Elliot. Others: Albert Finney, Michael Gambon, someone who has that crumpled but appealing quality to them. I'll tell you about one of the nicest things that ever happened. Do you know the play *Sleuth*? The device is that it is a stage play for two actors, but there are four actors billed on the program. So you keep expecting somebody else to come on, until the end when you realize there were only ever going to be two. Well, whenever the play is done, they list the two actors' names and then the two fictitious actors' names. Someone sent me a review from somewhere near Boston where they had done a production of *Sleuth*, and one of the fictional actors' names was Charles Paris, which I was very chuffed about. Not only that, the reviewer had actually entered into the spirit of the joke and given a short review of Charles Paris's performance. So who knows, maybe Charles Paris can play Charles Paris.

Elizabeth George

INTERVIEW BY CROW DILLON-PARKIN

E lizabeth George is the author of ten novels featuring Detective Inspector Thomas Lynley and Sergeant Barbara Havers of New Scotland Yard. Lynley happens also to be the Eighth Earl of Asherton, and Havers is a working class ex-grammar school girl with a massive chip on her shoulder.

These books are tightly plotted, evocatively located, and beautifully written; incidental characters are as fully realized as the main protagonists, and no matter how much the plots may twist and intertwine, the thread is never broken.

CDP: The first question I'd like to ask is: Why crime fiction and why England?

EG: When I first began writing, I wasn't sure if I could carry off a novel from its beginning to its end, and crime fiction has a natural structure that pulled me through. It's a linear structure with an established through line, and that appealed to me. Additionally, I taught a class called "The Mystery Story," and the more I taught it, the more I began to think that I could write a mystery myself. So it's those two reasons that got me involved in writing crime fiction.

"Why England" is more difficult to explain. When I first started answering that question, I explained that I had taught English literature, that I traveled to England frequently, that in the sixties, when the British influence was very dominant in American culture, I first went to England and I was profoundly affected by the experience. But now I've realized that for me part of writing involves the psychic connection—the spiritual connection—between the artist and the material, if I'm going to write well. And I have a very strong emotional, psychic connection to England. I can't explain why that's the case, but when I see certain locations in England, I feel immediately touched by them, and it's that feeling of being touched in a deep way that allows me to write about the place.

CDP: So you don't go with a plot, you go for a place?

EG: I go with the plot kernel, but for the plot kernel to germinate into a story, the place is essential.

CDP: Because your sense of place is just stunning.

EG: I keep researching locations until I find a place that's stunning to *me*, because not everything I see works for me. A certain amount of what I do is what we in the United States would call a crap shoot: I decide in advance that I'm going to go to a particular section of the U.K. for one reason or another and I single out a number of different towns, villages, great houses, and places of historical, geographical, natural, or topographical significance. I go to see them and to experience them in the hope that somewhere along the line one will work as a location in a book.

CDP: You write well about the English class system. Is that another attraction?

EG: I find it interesting, because it's not analogous to anything in the United States, so it gives me an avenue to explore topics from an angle that's different from what I'm used to. It makes the writing more difficult, because there are elements of the class system that would mean nothing to an American reader, but everything to an English one: For example, the type of cigarette somebody smokes, the type of car he drives, the type of simple vocabulary he uses, whether a person calls what I'm sitting on a sofa or a couch, or the room we're in a sitting room or a lounge. These are details that would go unnoticed to the American reader but would be most revealing to the English reader. And while they make the book more authentic, they make the writing of the book a complete exercise in what my editor used to call "getting it right."

CDP: Are there things, the relationships between classes, and the relationships between the sexes, that are different in England, that might be more interesting to you?

EG: There's certainly an enormous difference in the way we look at class. Class in the United States is based almost entirely on economics and education, not on how old your blood is. For the most part, people could care less how long your family has been in the country. If you're a success at what you're doing, that's what's admired in the United States. So, this British idea of [adopts horrified English accent] "Oh my God, he's in trade!" doesn't apply in the states. Everybody in the United States has been in trade at one time or another. That's how the country grew.

CDP: How much of their [Havers & Lynley] back story do you have?

EG: A great deal. Some of what I know about the character comes from my first novel that was never published. It has the back story on Lynley and his sister, and the death of her husband, Edward Davenport.

CDP: Do you think it's fair to say that your books are more driven by character than by plot?

EG: Absolutely.

CDP: There's an article in *Writers News* that suggests that your plot style has shifted somewhat, with the last three books, in that the death that needs investigating isn't always the first thing that happens, and that gives you more space for exploring character.

EG: That's always been the important area for me. Sometimes I move the murder up front to get the ball rolling, but the creation and the exploration of character were where my commitment was from the very beginning. I begin with the plot kernel (the killer, the victim, and the motive) then design the setting, and then I create the characters. That's a long process, molding them from the ground up, as if I were some sort of god, creating them, not only physically and mentally but spiritually, psychologically, and historically. By the time I start writing about my characters, I have a voice for them, an agenda, a through line, and a pathology. As a result they can emerge much more realistically than if I were just putting names on the page and saying "Now what?"

CDP: It seemed you suddenly got very topical, dealing with the tabloids and parliamentary sleaze . . .

EG: It was purely by chance that, on the plane coming over to do research for my parliament novel, I opened up the British newspaper, and there was the Tim Yeo scandal. I couldn't believe my eyes! I was coming over here to do research about an MP with a love child, and it was playing out in the newspapers, even as I was doing the research! So it couldn't have been a luckier circumstance for me, because the tabloids did everything that I assumed that they would do.

CDP: Do you think you'd ever write something set in America?

EG: I've written one short story set there. I was pleased to come up with the idea, because I'm not a short story writer, at all. My philosophy has always been, why say it in a thousand words when you can say it in six hundred pages . . . It's hard for me to paint with broad enough brush strokes to be concise. In this instance I had an invitation to write something for an anthology at the precise moment that I had an idea for a short story, so I wrote it. It takes place in Southern California, in Newport Beach, close to where I live. I used a quirky little place on Balboa Peninsula where I have my detective have his office up above a place I used to get my hair cut. I really did have to *look* for quirky places because there's not much quirkiness in that particular part of Southern California. One thing that's helpful for me when I'm writing about England is that I notice the details, because it's a foreign country, but in the United States I don't notice the details because I see them every day, and details are an important part of setting, character, and plot.

CDP: How long do you have to spend somewhere, to get that feel?

EG: It depends on the kind of research I'm doing. For location research, it's about a week . . .

CDP: As little as that?!

EG: . . . to get the feeling for the place, yes, about a week, and then I might go back a second time, to fine tune my knowledge of the setting, and then I might go back a third time after I've got the rough draft done, just to make sure I've got everything correct. The more difficult things for me are the telling details that I can use for my characters, because then I have to be able to include the kind of stores people shop in, the kinds of products that they buy, and what those products imply about them. In America, these are things I would just *know*, because I've lived there all my life. For example, one of my students was writing a story in which she placed a man and his wife at their kitchen table, wearing matching bowling shirts. That was it, [clicks fingers]; everybody in the writing group knew what the entire kitchen looked like. All she had to say was they were wearing those matching bowling shirts, because they say everything about a class and a culture. But that kind of detail is really difficult for me to know about England, so that's when I have to get on the phone and call my friends and say "OK, here's the situation, these are the characters, what would they be eating, what would they be smoking?" My friends in England throw themselves into helping me.

CDP: You also deal a lot with the family, the problems in the family.

EG: My books are essentially *about* the family, and the dysfunctional family. I use the crime novel as a device to explore that. I used to read crime novels where no one was related to anybody, including the victim, and I thought it was strange that someone would die and nobody was ever sad or came forward to claim the body. I didn't want to write that sort of novel. I wanted to explore situations in which the killer and the victim had significant others. If a killing arises from a familial relationship, then obviously you're talking about a troubled family . . .

CDP: . . . murder doesn't happen in a family where everybody's getting on all right . . .

EG: . . . and besides, if everyone's getting along all right and communicating, it'd be a boring book, what I call a white bread story. You don't have any drama, you don't have any tension, you have no conflict so you have no novel.

CDP: Your books are whydunits, not whodunits?

EG: It's definitely more why than who.

CDP: You write to find out things, rather than to say things?

EG: Somewhat, certainly. Part of writing is to make it clear to me, and to the reader, why murder was done. If I'm successful, the reader understands the crime completely. To have a psychological motivation that I'm able to explain adequately in the story is important to me. I want my book to pass the refrigerator test. Alfred Hitchcock used to say that if the people who saw a film of his didn't have any questions about it until they got home and opened the refrigerator, then it was a successful film. But, if people were saying "Hang on . . . " while the credits were rolling, then he had a problem. I think that, with books, you want to do more than that. You want the story to linger and to give the reader something to think about.

CDP: How far in advance do you work?

EG: At the moment I'm just writing the next novel, the one that follows *Deception on his Mind*. I'm about three hundred and fifty pages into that.

CDP: So you work quite fast? Well, it seems fast to me!

EG: I do five pages a day.

CDP: Do you do much in the way of rewriting, or do you write it "in best" first time?

EG: The first draft is the most difficult draft. Subsequent drafts are generally polishing. They generally aren't altering anything big in the story. So I take a lo-o-ot of time over my first draft. I'm pretty meticulous, I don't just slam it down on paper and let my editor figure it out, or slam it down and hope that I can rewrite it later on. I try to get it as well done the first time through as I can, so that my work in the second and third draft is fun, rather than agonizing.

Peter Lovesey

INTERVIEW BY ADRIAN MULLER

P eter Lovesey was writing historical crime fiction long before such writers as Edward Marston, Ellis Peters, and Anne Perry came on the
scene. Lovesey started writing as an outlet for his knowledge of sporting
history, much of which related to Victorian England. His expertise in
this period explains the author's decision to set many of his novels in the
latter half of the nineteenth century. In fact, one of his most popular characters is the sovereign's son Edward, the Prince of Wales—more affection-
ately known as Bertie. Lovesey's other Victorian sleuth is Detective Sergeant
Cribb, who debuted in Lovesey's first mystery novel, Wobble to Death.
More recently, the author has added a contemporary detective to his series
characters and now alternates his Bertie books with those featuring Peter
Diamond, a policeman in Bath's present-day police force.

What follows is an overview of the career of an author who has helped
raise historical crime fiction to its current popularity. This profile is based
on an interview held at Lovesey's country home just outside the city of Bath,
in the summer of 1996.

Peter Lovesey was born in Middlesex, England, in 1936. "The same
year as Robert Barnard and Reginald Hill," he says, adding with a smile,
"a vintage year for mystery writers." Brought up in suburban London
during World War II, he was evacuated to the west country in 1944

after the family home was destroyed by a "flying bomb." These war experiences, and those following in early peacetime, were to influence two of Lovesey's later novels, *Rough Cider* and *On the Edge*.

After completing his education at Hampton Grammar School, Lovesey went to Reading University in 1955. Failing his Latin exams meant that he was not eligible to study English because a qualification in the ancient language was a necessary requirement for the modern one. Being a reasonable artist, he decided to study fine art instead. Part of the latter course included history and English as secondary subjects, and due to submitting "some quite interesting essays," as the author puts it, two of Lovesey's tutors, novelist John Wain and literary critic Frank Kermode, helped him get into English studies after all.

By now he had met Jacqueline (Jax) Lewis, his future wife, and he was eager to change courses for more reasons than one. "The big incentive," he recalls, "was that Art was a four-year course and English three. I wanted to get married to Jax, who was doing a three-year course, so I swapped to English." Lovesey, who recalls his time at Reading with much affection, says, "Whilst I didn't do anything remarkable, I managed to get a degree." The statement is a good example of the author's modesty, because his entry in *The St. James Guide to Crime and Mystery Writers* shows that he graduated with honors.

When Lovesey left university in 1958, a two-year stint in the National Service was still obligatory in Britain, and he joined the Royal Air Force. With an eye on the future, he signed up for three years and completed a training course to become an education officer. The rank offered better wages, allowing him to marry Jax in 1959, and also gave him a head start on a teaching career.

In 1961, he left the armed forces for a fourteen-year career in education. Starting out as a lecturer in English at Thurrock Technical College in Essex, he became head of the general education department at London's Hammersmith College for Further Education (now West London College) until he left to become a full-time writer. Lovesey enjoyed teaching and interacting with students but disliked the inroads made on both of these areas by his administrative duties. "There's so much paperwork, so many committee meetings, to the extent that it distracts from the real business of teaching," he says.

By the time Lovesey ended his educational career in 1975, he had already established himself as an author, with two nonfiction books on sport and six of the eight Detective Sergeant Cribb books.

The Cribb novels came about through the author's self-confessed lack in athletic ability. "The first two books I wrote were about sport and their origin goes right back to my school days," Lovesey remembers. "If you wanted to have any status with people in the school, you had to excel at sport. I was useless," he says, laughing. "I was really, really bad." In an attempt to improve his standing, he may have been one of the world's first joggers. Shuffling around the back streets of the London suburb of Twickenham, he tried to improve his times, but frequently, the author claims, he ran into lampposts and was savaged by dogs. As a consequence, he sought a safer alternative to gamesmanship. "I became one of those kids who didn't participate but who knew and could talk about sport a great deal." He would read all the papers and listen to all the commentaries on boxing, football, and so on. Gradually, he began to dream about a career as a sports journalist. Later, when he was a teacher, he started to submit articles to magazines, initially without much success. It took a little while before he realized there was a little-covered topic he could exploit: track and field history. Explains Lovesey, "I thought that if I dug into the past, I could find information for interesting character pieces about great runners." The research brought him into contact with many names in the world of athletics, some of whom became good friends. People like Norris McWhirter, the founder of *The Guinness Book of Records*, and Harold Abrahams, one of the athletes portrayed in the Oscar-winning film *Chariots of Fire*. After Lovesey had spent some ten years writing about sport, it was suggested that he might have enough material for a book. "I thought about it and realized it would require more work," he says. "So I began to expand some of the articles I had written and put them together into a book called *The Kings of Distance*." Peter Lovesey's first book, focusing on the lives of five long-distance runners, was published in 1968. It started off in the early nineteenth century with the story of Deerfoot, an American Indian, and closed some hundred years later with Emil Zatopek, the Czech athlete who dominated the Olympic Games in 1952. The book received good reviews and was chosen as Sports Book of the Year.

In 1969, *The Kings of Distance* was followed by *The Guide to British Track and Field Literature 1275–1968*, a bibliography on sports writing, written in collaboration with Tom McNab. A definitive reference work on the subject, the guide is still used by collectors.

It was also in 1969 that Jax Lovesey spotted an advertisement in the *Times* that would have a major impact on her husband's life. It was for a competition to write a crime novel and, because the cash prize was about as much as her husband was earning in a year as a teacher, Jax suggested he should enter. After all, he had had two books published already. Lovesey was less confident. "I pointed out that those had been nonfiction books about sport, and I had hardly read any crime fiction." Jax was persistent, however, and he finally agreed to have a go.

For this budding novelist, the obvious idea was to use a background in athletics. He entered his manuscript, called *Wobble to Death* and, looking back, he is convinced that it was the novelty value of the story that won him the first prize.

Lovesey first came across wobbles—Victorian long-distance races lasting six days—when he was researching an article in the newspaper library in Colindale. "They seemed very bizarre and extraordinary, involving all kinds of tricks that trainers and runners would use to try to hamper their opponents," he recalls. "They would put laxatives in the refreshments, crush walnut shells into competitors' shoes . . ." However, it was a performance-enhancing drug that fired Lovesey's imagination. To improve their results, runners would take tiny amounts of strychnine. "It is a stimulant if used in a tiny amount, but take a little more and you're writhing in agony!" notes Lovesey. He immediately realized that the wobble setting was a natural for a traditional whodunit: poison, murder, and suspects in a closed environment. All that remained was to find a detective to solve the crime. The author decided an ordinary policeman would be more interesting than a Sherlock Holmes–type character, and he learned about police methods of the day. Enter Sergeant Cribb and his assistant, Constable Thackeray.

It wasn't until Lord Hardinge, the publisher of *Wobble to Death*, handed Peter Lovesey his check and asked him what he would be writing next that the first-time novelist thought about a sequel. "I remember thinking that I could probably write another crime novel," he says, "but for the life of me, I couldn't imagine what it would be about. I didn't think I could go on mining the Victorian world of athletics for very long." For the sequel, Lovesey stuck with the same detectives and again turned to Victorian newspapers for inspiration. In the 1880s, clandestine fistfights took place in the south of England. To get to the secret location, trains would be organized and people would end up in the middle of nowhere having to walk a short distance to the place where the fight would be held. This background was used in the author's second novel, *The Detective Wore Silk Drawers*.

The books developed into a series, mostly exploring various forms of Victorian entertainment. *Abracadaver* dealt with music-hall acts, and *Mad Hatter's Holiday* is set in Brighton, a popular seaside holiday resort.

The fifth in the Cribb series, *Invitation to a Dynamite Party*, focused on Britain's early problems with Irish nationalists. "In that book I used real events more than I had in any other up to that time," says Lovesey. "I found out about Irishmen who, for many of the same reasons as the Irish Republican Army, were blowing up buildings in London in the early 1880s. Terrifying everybody, they were much more successful than the IRA and actually damaged London Bridge and several of London's main railway stations. They even managed to get a bomb into Scotland Yard and blew up part of the building!" *Invitation to a Dynamite Party* ended with an attempt to kill the Prince of Wales by means of one of the earliest submarines, a vessel built by the Irish.

Swing, Swing Together was inspired by the craze set off by Jerome K. Jerome's *Three Men in a Boat*. The latter is a humorous tale of three friends boating up the river Thames. Jerome's book was a huge bestseller in its time, and as a result, trips on the Thames became enormously popular. Reading of all this activity started Lovesey thinking, *Let's have a situation where people join in the craze. In* Three Men in a Boat*, a corpse floats past the boat. Let's weave a story around that.*

Also popular in Victorian times were spiritualists who contacted the dead, and this subject was the inspiration for *A Case of Spirits*.

The last Cribb novel, *Waxwork*, provided a major boost to Lovesey's writing career. Telling a gripping tale of a Victorian woman awaiting execution for murder, *Waxwork* was well received, won the author his first Crime Writers' Association Dagger, and caught the eye of June Wyndham-Davies, an English television producer, who thought the subject might make an interesting television film. The dramatization of *Waxwork* was broadcast in 1979 and starred Alan Dobie as Sergeant Cribb and William Simons as Constable Thackeray. It proved so popular that Granada, the production company, decided to turn the other seven Cribb novels into a television series. Peter Lovesey was shown the scripts, and when he mentioned that one of them didn't feel quite right, the producers asked him if he would do the adaptation himself. The experience proved useful when Granada approached him with the request for a second series. Did he have any ideas for further stories? "You don't turn down an offer like that," says Lovesey. "I came home triumphantly and told Jax about it. She asked me when the company wanted the stories, reminding me that writing a book took me about a year. They wanted six plots in eight months!"

The opportunity and financial rewards were too good to pass up, and it was Jax who provided a solution to the problematic time factor.

Lovesey explains, "Jax always had some influence on the books. We used to discuss the structure of the story, and I would read the chapters to her as I was going along. So, to help me out with the television series, she said she would write three of the stories if I would write the other three. That's how we did it," he says, concluding, "We had our names jointly on the credits."

The television series, shown in some fifty countries, was highly successful and also helped to further popularize the novels. Yet Lovesey decided against writing more Cribb books. One reason was the definitive portrayal of the detective. "I don't in any way want to give the impression that I wasn't satisfied with Alan Dobie's performance of Cribb," he stresses. "I thought he was brilliant in the part, but television is a very powerful medium. After I saw him play my character, it was very difficult to get his portrayal out of my mind. The result was that I couldn't get back to the original concept that I had for Cribb." Moreover, he had exhausted all his ideas for further stories when writing the television series.

After concluding the Cribb novels, Lovesey wrote three books of contemporary fiction under the pseudonym of Peter Lear. The first, *Goldengirl*, focused on a super female athlete. Everyone from the girl's own father to big businessmen seeks to exploit her, even when the distinct possibility arises that she will break down from all the pressure.

Goldengirl was filmed starring Susan Anton and James Coburn, and problems hampered the film's release. "In the book the athlete was an American competing in the Moscow Olympics," says the author. "It was written about two or three years before the actual event was scheduled to take place. By the time the film was ready for distribution, the Russian invasion of Afghanistan led the Americans to boycott the 1980 Olympics. That made it difficult for the studio to promote the film, and it did not do well at the box office."

Two more novels appeared under the Lear pseudonym. *Spider Girl* is about a woman trying to overcome her fear of spiders—so much so that she becomes obsessed, turning almost spiderlike herself. *The Secret of Spandau* is a fictitious account of an attempt to spring Rudolf Hess from his cell in Berlin's Spandau Prison. There has always been speculation as to the motives of Hitler's deputy parachuting into Scotland in 1941. After the war, Hess was sentenced to lifelong imprisonment in Spandau. More recently, questions have been asked about the identity of the now-deceased prisoner, with some people suggesting that the jailed man may not really have been Hess. Lovesey's theory is that the German prisoner of war knew too much sensitive information about the people who wanted to make peace with Germany. "For me," says Lovesey, "the most intriguing thing was not Hess's true identity but the question of his sanity. It is a fact that there were attempts to brainwash Hess in his first few months in Britain. When obliterating his memory proved unsuccessful, he was imprisoned. The Russians were always blamed for keeping Hess in Spandau but," concludes Lovesey, "I think the British had far more interest in keeping him there."

In 1982, *The False Inspector Dew* was published, winning Peter Lovesey a Gold Dagger. The introduction to the novel suggests it is based on true events and then teasingly leaves the reader to try to define which facts are real and which fiction. Lovesey had been reading E. L. Doctorow's *Ragtime* and was much influenced by the novel. "Doctorow had used real people in his book, and I found that very exciting," he says. "I began to think I might do something similar in a detective novel." Lovesey's plot was inspired by Dr. Crippen, the English doctor who murdered his wife, burying her in their cellar. Crippen then attempted to escape to Canada with his mistress on an ocean liner. Unfortunately for the murderer, he was recognized by the captain, who cabled that Crippen was on board. It was Inspector Dew who was sent ahead in a faster vessel to waylay Crippen in Canada and bring him back to face trial. Lovesey read Inspector Dew's memoirs and became more and more intrigued by the policeman's reaction to the murderer. "Dew seemed to like Crippen, even though his name is now almost synonymous with someone like Jack the Ripper," says Lovesey. "In his autobiography, the inspector called Crippen 'the little fellow' and 'my friend Crippen,' portraying him as a Chaplinesque character. That, to some extent, is why Charlie Chaplin makes a brief appearance in my book." A further area of interest for Lovesey was to see how much Dew identified with Crippen, wondering what motivated the murderer, and suggesting ways in which Crippen might have escaped. In the book, Crippen becomes Walter Baranov, and the reader is left guessing to the closing pages whether the very likable villain manages to elude the police. The clever plot twists and surprising ending earned the author his second dagger.

For his next novel, Lovesey stuck to the winning formula of mixing fact and fiction, setting *Keystone* in 1915 at Hollywood legend Mack Sennett's Keystone Film Studios. The plot has an aspiring English actor joining the Keystone Cops to solve a succession of crimes involving bribery, kidnap, and murder. Naturally, the slapstick comedy of the silent-film era forms an integral part of the book.

Up until *Keystone*, the author had not yet written a novel set in a period of time of which he had some personal experience. All this would change with his following two nonseries books.

In *Rough Cider*, the Second World War forces a young city boy out of his everyday environment. He is evacuated to a safe but alien location in the countryside, only to become a crucial witness in a murder case. Though Lovesey's evacuee experiences in Cornwall did not include murder, he still remembers them as unsettling due to the unfamiliar surroundings and strange local accent. Years later, after coming across a west-country recipe for mutton-fed cider, which involves a joint of meat added to barreled cider for extra potency, an idea for a novel sprang to mind, and *Rough Cider* was born.

On the Edge is about "two women who become bored after the war and decide to murder their husbands," says Lovesey. The novel looks at the dissatisfaction of people who in peacetime were forced back into their old, often less-exciting existence. For Rose and Antonia, the two women in *On the Edge*, the situation causes personal conflicts, leading them to kill their husbands. "As with Walter Baranov in *The False Inspector Dew*, I can identify quite a bit with Rose," says the author, describing her mitigating circumstances. "Books that just paint the murderer as a complete blackguard aren't really that interesting. I try to get away from black and white characterizations in an attempt to understand a little of the motives of people. I think it's always fascinating for a reader to be able to understand what drives a person to murder. It's one of those universal questions you can only answer if you have been confronted by it yourself."

Jax Lovesey was especially helpful with *On the Edge*. "Since it was a book about two women," says Lovesey, "I checked with Jax quite a bit. I had an idea of how women talked, but it was the way women talk to men, not how they talked amongst themselves. So Jax put me right on quite a bit of that."

Having set three subsequent books in the twentieth century, Peter Lovesey decided to return to Victorian times for his next novel. The author explains, "I read about Fred Archer, the top jockey of his day, who at the age of twenty-nine committed suicide. His sister came in as he was holding a gun to his head and she heard him say, 'Are they coming?' before he shot himself. I thought the incident would lend itself to a conspiracy theory: Who were 'they,' and what was it all about? It never became clear at the inquest or in the biographies of Archer." In his search for information on the jockey, Lovesey found that Fred Archer, also known as the Tinman, frequently rode for the Prince of

Wales, who was called Bertie by his family and close friends. "I thought, *Why shouldn't Bertie himself take an interest in the case?* I discovered that he had sent the biggest wreath at the funeral, and the more I thought about it, the more I realized that he was perfect to be the detective. As the Prince of Wales he had lots of time on his hands—his mother, Queen Victoria, gave him no responsibilities—so he spent his time playing cards, charming the ladies, and looking for things to do. Also, he was in a unique position: He could order the police to help him if he wanted or, when necessary, he could keep them at arm's length."

Having found his sleuth, the author went on to consider what form the book might take. During research for *The Secret of Spandau*, he learned that a substantial amount of documents regarding Rudolf Hess had been classified as secret, and their release controlled by a time embargo. What if something similar had occurred to Edward VII's personal papers? "Declassification" is how Lovesey would explain the sudden appearance of *Bertie and the Tinman: The Detective Memoirs of King Edward VII*. The author recalls enjoying writing the novel in the first person, allowing his sleuth to solve the Tinman mystery, almost in spite of his bungling attempts.

When *Bertie and the Tinman* was published, one of the favorable reviews referred to the book as "Dick Francis by gaslight." With the year of Dame Agatha Christie's centenary nearing, Lovesey wondered whether it might not be interesting for him to write the next Bertie novel with a nod to the queen of crime fiction. Taking some of the typical ingredients from a Christie plot—a country house setting, a murder occurring for every day of the week, and rhymes being sent as clues—*Bertie and the Seven Bodies* was written.

A third book, *Bertie and the Crime of Passion*, took the prince to Paris where he investigates a murder with the assistance of the great actress Sarah Bernhardt.

In 1991, over twenty years since *Wobble to Death*, after fourteen historical mysteries and numerous short stories, Peter Lovesey decided the time had come to write a contemporary crime novel. Ironically, the title of the first book in this (unplanned) series featuring Detective Superintendent Peter Diamond was *The Last Detective*. When writing his first modern crime novel, Lovesey had to consider how he would deal with unfamiliar subjects such as up-to-date police procedures and current forensic methods. Previously, these matters had been relatively easy to write about because they were less complicated and fixed in time. A solution was soon found. "The procedures and forensics are acknowl-

edged but," says Lovesey, "I've deliberately made my detective a dino-
saur as far as those issues are concerned."

Having explained Diamond's contempt for the latest methods, the
author also made the detective a loner, "Which, for me," he says, "was
more important. A police procedural should involve a great number of
people, it's teamwork. It can be very difficult to engage a reader's interest
when the credit for solving a crime is diffused through a number of
people, and I prefer to write the kind of story where one person gets
the credit and faces the problems himself."

The Last Detective won the 1991 Anthony Award for best novel. It
also left Peter Lovesey with an unforeseen dilemma: "Diamond has this
great row toward the end of the book and storms out of the police
force," says Lovesey, adding, "Initially I had him continue with the case
after being reprimanded. Then I realized that this character had such
integrity, and that he was so volatile, that he would not stay in the force
but would resign. So that's what happened. However, that left me with
a problem when I started thinking about a sequel."

The dilemma was solved by turning the next Peter Diamond novel,
Diamond Solitaire, into an international thriller. "Peter Diamond has a
job as a security guard in Harrods," explains Lovesey, "but is fired when
a Japanese girl sets off the alarms in his department. Intrigued by the
little girl, Diamond becomes involved with her lot when she is kidnapped, taking him first to New York and ultimately to Tokyo where
the whole case is resolved."

In *The Summons*, the author found an ingenious way to return Peter
Diamond to the police force: One of the former detective superintendent's old cases is drastically reopened, forcing the police to ask for his
help. By the close of the novel, Diamond can return to his old job
stating his own terms. *The Summons* was nominated for an Edgar and
won the CWA Silver Dagger for 1995.

Diamond's next case, *Bloodhounds*, was published in the year following a brief controversy in the Crime Writers' Association regarding
the value of traditional versus hard-boiled crime fiction. *Bloodhounds*
focuses on a group of crime fiction readers who gather once a week to
discuss the merits of their preferred genre. When members of the reading group start being murdered, Diamond is called in to solve a variety
of crimes. With the fictional skirmish following so soon after the less
drastic CWA discord, it might seem that Lovesey had found inspiration
right on his doorstep. "Well," he says with a smile, "it might be unwise
to admit it, but there are real people in *Bloodhounds*." He then swiftly
points out why it would be pointless trying to identify any of his fellow

writers. "My characters are often based on real people. I start by thinking so-and-so is ideal for that particular character. Visualizing my protagonists makes them more real for me. Then, as the story develops, they take on a life of their own and become involved with things their real-life counterparts would never consider doing. Therefore, it would be unfair for me to say that a character is based on a certain individual because they have completely changed."

In 1996, for the second year running, the Silver Dagger was awarded to a Diamond novel.

As mentioned earlier, Peter Lovesey has also written many short stories, and they, too, have won numerous awards. Interested readers can find some of them in *Butchers and the Other Stories of Crime* and *The Crime of Miss Oyster Brown and Other Stories.* Calling the short story form "a delight," Lovesey says, "If I could make a living writing them, I would be very happy to do so. They can be done in a short time, and you can experiment with original, exciting ideas. You can take risks with short stories that you can't with a novel." The ideas for the tales bubble up in Lovesey's mind when he is deeply involved in a novel, and he thinks of writing them as a reward to himself for finishing a book.

When writing a novel, he will have worked out a synopsis beforehand. This can run up to eight or nine pages, describing what will happen from chapter to chapter. "It may alter a little as I go along," he says, "but I have to be satisfied in my own mind that the structure is there before I begin." It takes Lovesey eight or nine months to complete a manuscript and, while some of the research is done before he starts, much is also done during the writing of the book itself.

Comparing notes with other authors on their writing methods, Lovesey was amazed to realize that he is one of a small group of writers who know how their novels will end before they start writing them. "In my experience," he says, "the majority of crime writers appear to prefer not to be too clear about where the book is going. They say they can't see the pleasure in writing if they know what's happening. For me, the pleasure comes from putting down the words and finding the appropriate ways of saying things."

The author calls himself a very slow writer, writing approximately two hundred words a day at the start of a novel, but steadily increasing to six or eight hundred words toward the book's completion. One thing Lovesey rarely does is revision, remarking, "What I write is what will go in the book."

Peter Lovesey is unsure what his next project will be. He has recently completed the fifth Peter Diamond novel, *Upon a Dark Night*, and expects to return to Bertie soon. Looking back to his very first detective, Lovesey can draw certain parallels with his more recent contemporary creation. "I suppose we have all been in jobs where we've had some contempt for our superiors, thinking we could do the job a whole lot better without them interfering! That certainly is true of Diamond and Cribb. Also, to some extent, they're both protective about the information that they have gathered, not wanting to share it too much. That trait of being careful of revealing too much is also a convention of mystery writers: You want to surprise the reader, so perhaps you keep back a little." He concludes with what could be a summary of his literary style. "I try and write a fair book, a 'mystery' in the old-fashioned sense of the word."

BIBLIOGRAPHY

Nonfiction

The Kings of Distance: A Study of Five Great Runners. London, Eyre and Spottiswoode, 1968; as *Five Kings of Distance*. New York, St. Martin's Press, 1981.

The Guide to British Track and Field Literature 1275–1968, with Tom McNab. London, Athletics Arena, 1969.

The Official Centenary History of the Amateur Athletic Association. London, Guinness Superlatives, 1979.

Fiction

Wobble to Death. London, Macmillan, and New York, Dodd Mead, 1970. (Macmillan/Panther First Crime Novel Prize)

The Detective Wore Silk Drawers. London, Macmillan, and New York, Dodd Mead, 1971.

Abracadaver. London, Macmillan, and New York, Dodd Mead, 1972.

Mad Hatter's Holiday: A Novel of Murder in Victorian Brighton. London, Macmillan, and New York, Dodd Mead, 1973.

Invitation to a Dynamite Party. London, Macmillan, 1974; as *The Tick of Death*, New York, Dodd Mead, 1974.

A Case of Spirits. London, Macmillan, and New York, Dodd Mead, 1975. (Prix du Roman D'Aventures)

Swing, Swing Together. London, Macmillan, and New York, Dodd Mead, 1976. (Grand Prix de Littérature Policière)

Waxwork. London, Macmillan, and New York, Pantheon, 1978. (CWA Silver Dagger)

The False Inspector Dew: A Murder Mystery Aboard the S.S.
Mauretania, 1921. London, Macmillan, and New York,
Pantheon, 1982. (CWA Gold Dagger)

Keystone. London, Macmillan, and New York, Pantheon, 1983.

Butchers and Other Stories of Crime. London, Macmillan, 1985;
New York, Mysterious Press, 1987.

Rough Cider. London, Bodley Head, 1986; New York, Mysterious
Press, 1987.

Bertie and the Tinman: From the Detective Memoirs of King Edward
VII. London, Bodley Head, 1987; New York, Mysterious Press,
1988.

On the Edge. London, Century Hutchinson, and New York,
Mysterious Press, 1989.

Bertie and the Seven Bodies. London, Century Hutchinson, and
New York and London, Mysterious Press, 1990.

The Last Detective. London, Scribner, and New York, Doubleday,
1991. (Anthony Award)

Diamond Solitaire. London, Little Brown, and New York,
Mysterious Press, 1992.

Bertie and the Crime of Passion. London, Little Brown, and New
York, Mysterious Press, 1993.

The Crime of Miss Oyster Brown and Other Stories. London, Little
Brown, 1994.

The Summons. London, Little Brown, and New York, Mysterious
Press, 1995. (CWA Silver Dagger)

Bloodhounds. London, Little Brown, and New York, Mysterious
Press, 1996. (CWA Silver Dagger)

Upon a Dark Night. London, Little Brown, 1997 and New York,
Mysterious Press, 1998.

Do Not Exceed the Stated Dose (Short Stories). London, Little
Brown and Norfolk, VA., Crippen and Londru, 1998.

Short Story Awards

The Crime of Miss Oyster Brown (Ellery Queen Reader's Award)
The Secret Lover (CWA Short Story Award)
The Pushover (MWA Golden Mysteries Short Story Award)

As Peter Lear

Goldengirl. London, Cassell, 1977; New York, Doubleday, 1978.
Spider Girl. London, Cassell, and New York, Viking Press, 1980.
The Secret of Spandau. London, Joseph, 1986.

Carolyn G. Hart

INTERVIEW BY CHARLES L. P. SILET

Although she is the author of more than twenty mystery and suspense novels, Carolyn G. Hart is best known for her Death on Demand series, which features crime bookstore owner, Annie Laurance, and her lawyer/private detective husband, Max Darling. Set on a resort island off the coast of South Carolina, these novels offer a delightful mix of old Southern charm, eccentric island characters, and crime fiction esoterica.

The first of the Annie Laurance books, Death on Demand *(1987), introduced Broward's Rock Island and the bookstore and a mystery theme, in this case, a gathering of crime writers who begin to die faster than their fictional creations. The novel was nominated for both the Anthony and the Macavity crime writing awards. In* Design for Murder *(1987), Annie organizes a mystery weekend for the annual house-and-garden tour in Chastain, the coastal town nearest the island, and when unexpected bodies begin to appear, the mystery program develops into a real criminal investigation.* Something Wicked *(1988), an Agatha and Anthony winner, plunges Annie into the maelstrom of local theatricals.* Honeymoon with Murder *(1988), also an Anthony winner, finally gets Max and Annie to the altar but not without the usual murderous complications.*

In the next novel, which won a Macavity and was nominated for both an Anthony and an Agatha, A Little Class on Murder *(1989), Annie tries her hand at teaching the art of the female mystery writer at the local Chas-*

tain community college, and Deadly Valentine *(1990)*, an Agatha and Anthony nominee, finds Annie keeping a wary eye on her new husband, even after the local merry widow turns up dead in her own gazebo. In The Christie Caper *(1991)*, also nominated for an Agatha and Anthony, Carolyn G. Hart not only pays homage to Dame Agatha, the author's own favorite classic mystery writer, but she also involves Annie in a classic case of murder during a centenary Agatha Christie convention. Nominated for an Agatha, Southern Ghost *(1992)* is perhaps the darkest of Hart's crime novels and involves two murders that take place years apart. In her latest, Mint Julip Murder *(1995)* Annie has agreed to serve as the author liaison for the five winners at the Dixie Book Festival but soon becomes embroiled once again in murder, this time as the prime suspect.

Now Ms. Hart has launched a new series with Dead Man's Island, which stars Henrie O, a retired newspaperwoman. These are harder-edged, first-person novels written from a more mature point of view than the Annie Laurance books. The next Henrie O book, Scandal in Fair Haven *(1994)*, finds Henrie O investigating a brutal murder in a small Southern town. The third in the series, Death in Lover's Lane *(1997)*, takes her back to her job teaching journalism at a Southern college where she must solve a series of old murders in order to discover who killed a brilliant and beautiful student reporter.

Carolyn G. Hart has been active in a number of crime writers' organizations. She has served on the board of directors of the Southwest chapter and on the National Board of the Mystery Writers of America, and she has been both vice president and president of the organization of mystery writers and readers, Sisters in Crime.

CLPS: Did you experience any difficulties getting started in the business?

CGH: I was a Southwestern woman writer, and this was during the period when it was difficult for American women to sell mysteries. There were Barbara Mertz, who is Barbara Michaels/Elizabeth Peters, Dorothy Gilman, Charlotte MacLeod, Dorothy Kallen, Jane Langton, Amanda Cross, who managed to sell throughout the 1960s and 1970s; but generally, American women mystery writers were not being published. The reason is because the market was dominated by dead British ladies and American male hard-boiled writers. The perception by many of the critics in the U.S. is that The Mystery is the Dashiell Hammett–Raymond Chandler–Robert B. Parker kind.

These are the critics who in a pejorative sense coined the term "the cozy" to describe the Agatha Christie kind of book, pointing out that Miss Marple in her little village couldn't have gotten involved in all those murders. Well, in point of fact, private detectives do not in reality spend their lives righting society's wrongs, as they do in a Hammett or Chandler novel. They're out chasing married men, and they're trying to find deadbeats who haven't paid bills; they're hunting for fathers who owe child support. In the cozy, you find a much more real world, the world in which most people live, than the world that is portrayed in the hard-boiled private detective books. Now we've got a new breed of editors in New York, and they talk very excitedly about cozies.

CLPS: So, what made the change?

CGH: Three things happened about the same time that made an enormous difference to American women mystery writers. One is that Marcia Muller in 1978 published the first Sharon McCone, the first hard-boiled woman private detective written by a woman. Marcia was not the writer who got the greatest amount of attention, because here came Sue Grafton and Sara Paretsky and the three of them were suddenly writing The American Mystery with the hard-boiled P.I. It was valid because it was the hard-boiled P.I., even though it was written by women and the protagonists were women. But these three were the ones who first opened the window for the rest of us because their books became so popular that the effect in New York was to enhance the perception that women's mysteries were very, very hot. Well, not all women write about hard-boiled female private eyes, but after the success of Muller, Grafton, and Paretsky, the editors were then willing to look at traditional mysteries. The second thing that happened, I think it was about 1985, was that the big publishing houses—Bantam, Ballantine, Pocket Books—decided to publish paperback original mysteries. Prior to that time, most mysteries had been in hardcover first and then reprinted in paperback. So, suddenly you had a combination of an enormous number of slots that had to be filled by editors and this emergence of three women hard-boiled writers, and it opened the doors for all of us. Of course, the other event that I think has made a big difference was Sisters in Crime, which was created basically by Sara Paretsky.

CLPS: How did you finally make a breakthrough in your writing?

CGH: I had been teaching writing in the journalism school at the University of Oklahoma. I was terribly discouraged because I had about seven manuscripts in New York, and nobody was interested in buying them. This was in about 1984 or 1985. I thought, *This is really dumb.* I had about thirteen books published, and nothing very exciting happened with any of them. I thought, *I'm going to write one more book, and then I'm going to quit.* Of course, I'd threatened this a lot, and my family never believed me. I went to a mystery meeting in Houston. I belong to MWA. The Southwest Chapter's headquarters are in Houston, and once a year it hosts a daylong seminar for its members and invites authors to speak and editors to come, and they very kindly invited me to speak. I sort of slunk down there because I felt like this enormous failure. I was very depressed, but the real upshot of that meeting was that I realized how much I love mysteries. Always before, I had tried—and this is a mistake so many writers make—I had tried to figure out what the market was looking for. The agent I had at that point said, "Nobody is buying mysteries. You might as well forget it. There's no way in the world you're going to sell a mystery." I had had five mysteries sell in England and four of them have never sold in the U.S. That agent said, "You know, you've got to write romances. That's all anybody's buying today." I did disguise one mystery as a romance and I sold it to Harlequin as a gothic, but that was not much fun. After this daylong talk about mysteries, I thought, *I am going to write the mystery I have always wanted to write, and if it doesn't go, then I'm just going to quit.* And I wrote *Death on Demand.*

CLPS: At what point did you realize that you had a series?

CGH: Well, actually, that was the basis upon which it was sold. Kate [Miciak] said she wanted three more with the same characters. She's very, very strong on series. She does a few single titles, but most of her authors do series. I was perfectly agreeable. At that point in my career, the idea that anybody would even buy a book was thrilling, and so I thought that sure, of course, I can do a series.

CLPS: It's wonderful the way you build from that first book when we're introduced to Annie and to Max, and then you follow with the courtship book and the book when they get married.

CGH: Well, I have to admit Max gets a little bit of a short shrift in *The Christie Caper* because he's offstage quite a bit. I couldn't handle him and the implications of the story at the same time, so he does not have a very strong role in that novel. In the next, *Southern Ghost*, he has a major role.

CLPS: Where did the idea of the bookshop come from?

CGH: I don't know why I made it a mystery bookstore—I guess just for fun. I decided if I was going to stick with writing, I was going to have a lot of fun with it. I changed my idea about who the heroine was going to be, and I moved the bookstore from California to South Carolina.

CLPS: Why South Carolina? Why an island?

CGH: Because at this mystery meeting I went to in Houston, Ruth Cavin was speaking, and she was then an editor at Walker and as just a sort of throwaway line in her discussion, she mentioned that 50 percent of all manuscripts she received were set in California. I had originally intended to set the bookstore in Carmel. I'm not completely stupid; I didn't want to set a book where 50 percent of all books in the mystery world are set. I only knew one other vacation area, and that was Hilton Head Island, South Carolina, because we have vacationed there since the mid-1970s, and I wanted a resort background.

CLPS: Obviously one of the advantages of setting it on an island is that you have a small, contained community, and especially with a resort community, you have the locals who remain there all year round and the constant stream from outside, but isn't that restricting in any way?

CGH: Well, yes, for example, when I was talking with my editor about *Southern Ghost*, she said, "I want you to do a Southern gothic." I realized that I couldn't possibly do a Southern gothic on Broward's Rock Island because the old Southern families are not still entrenched the way they are on the mainland. If I were going to do a family-type mystery in an old house, which is what Kate was looking for, then I needed the background on the mainland. So that's the only way in which it's restrictive. In other words, the Old South is not really on the resort islands, except just little patches of it. Mostly, everybody's from Ohio.

CLPS: Why did you decide to have your central character, Annie, get married?

CGH: That's a very perceptive question. Because I was making a very deliberate statement. I truly believe that happy marriages are quite possible. I have been married for thirty-five years, and I think marriage is a wonderful institution, but I know that there are a great many women who have had difficult lives: they are estranged from people, they are divorced, they are unhappy. But you *can* have a good marriage, it really can exist, and that was what I wanted to celebrate with Max and Annie.

CLPS: There is a domestic quality not only to Max and Annie but their whole world.

CGH: I try to deal with the same thing that Agatha Christie did in her books: life in a very realistic fashion, with the kind of people that you go to work with, that you go to school with. What Christie did was write parables. The traditional mystery, in my view, is a parable of life; I think it has a reality that the hard-boiled private detective books don't. They, oddly enough, are the more truly romantic books because they are about the white knight on a quest. The private detective is trying to remain incorruptible in a corrupt world, and this is truly a romantic vision. In my view, what I write touches much more directly on reality.

CLPS: How do you go about thinking about the next book?

CGH: It's always hard. If it were easy, I guess everybody would be writing. I'm not really sure exactly what I'm going to do until I really get into it. I do have a theme I'm thinking about when I'm writing a book. In *Deadly Valentine*, for example, I was demonstrating how totally screwed up everyone's life gets if nobody loves them. Of course, in *The Christie Caper*, it had to do with how sensitive authors are to critics. I sometimes don't really know exactly what it is that I'm doing until I have finished the book, and then I can look back and I can see more clearly. *Southern Ghost* is a story of a family where the lack of love has twisted everyone's relationship in this family. I didn't really discover that until I got about halfway through it.

CLPS: Do you find the series limiting?

CGH: Only with Annie's age. Otherwise, it's wonderful because a series gives you a chance to get to know your characters much better than you ever would if you just did one book with them. It's just like knowing people well or knowing them only slightly in life; if you spend more time with someone, you're going to get more from them. No, I really don't feel a series is limiting. But I am excited about doing two series rather than just one.

CLPS: One of the things that's always bothered me is that genre fiction has had to take a backseat to straight fiction or mainline or serious fiction. How do you respond to that?

CGH: I think mainstream is secondary now. Mysteries are going to become more and more popular, generally, with readers across the country because they are becoming aware of the strengths of genre books and they suddenly are available, easily available. I think they will capture the readership that mainstream fiction is losing because so much of mainstream fiction doesn't tell a story, and mysteries tell a story. People are truly hungry for that. I don't make any apology about the kind of books I write because I consider a mystery to be intellectually extremely challenging. A successful mystery is a wonderful achievement. I don't think so-called serious fiction is any more serious than what we write. So I don't feel second rate in any sense.

CLPS: But are mysteries formula fiction?

CGH: I don't think it is a formula. I truly don't think so. Women's lives have changed enormously in the last twenty-five years, or at least women's perceptions of what they can do and what they should do and what they will do has changed, and that is reflected in the books by women writers today. Basically, they are approaching life as independent human beings and they are not going to wait to be rescued in the last chapter by the handsome guy. That is not part of the scenario.

CLPS: What about equality for women writers?

CGH: Inequality is enormous in the mass market. It is still very difficult for women writers to be distributed on the greater mass market; I'm talking about paperbacks. If you go into your local grocery store, you're going to see Clancy and Parker and now occasionally you'll see Grafton or Paretsky. You'll see the romance section, and the horror, but American women mystery writers are still not well distributed in the greater mass market.

CLPS: Do you think that Sisters in Crime has really made a difference?

CGH: Oh, yes. There's no doubt about it. We started off with 5 members in 1987; we now have 2,200 members in the U.S. and eleven foreign countries.

CLPS: Where do you think the group is going to go now? Are you going to publish a magazine?

CGH: No. We will continue to do our *Books in Print*, which has been enormously successful for us, and to sell a map that shows the location of many women sleuths across the country. Our greatest hope is to continue to increase the visibility of women's mysteries. A handful of us visited for the first time the American Library Association meeting in Atlanta in 1991. We thought, *Well, is there really any point in six or seven members of Sisters in Crime going?* We took our map and our *Books in Print* catalog and were swamped every day at our booth by librarians who were enormously excited at the prospect of visiting with women mystery writers. We sold more than a thousand dollars worth of the maps at five dollars a map. We realized that the excitement about the mystery has yet to be truly understood on a national scale. We had the greatest weekend we had ever had. Sisters in Crime attended the 1992 and 1993 ALAs, and they were even more wonderful. ALA is now a yearly event for Sisters in Crime. We had a booth at the ABA in 1992, which was interesting but not as valuable because booksellers received the *Books in Print*. We've been told by many booksellers that they use the *Books in Print* to stock their mystery sections. Sisters in Crime will attend some bookseller events.

CLPS: Tell me a bit about *Southern Ghost*.

CGH: In *Southern Ghost*, I made it up to Max since he didn't get to be quite as much onstage in most of *The Christie Caper*. It's through the Confidential Commissions connection that he becomes involved in an inquiry in Chastain about two deaths that occurred on the same day, father and son, twenty years before. He's hired by a young woman to investigate. One death was ostensibly a heart attack and the other a gun accident. He starts investigating, and the young woman who hired him disappears. So, then, he's in trouble. Chastain police begin looking at him suspiciously. He and Annie take up residence in Chastain and pursue this inquiry, which involves some characters we've met before in Chastain: Miss Dora, the old curmudgeon; and Sybil, the attractive, late-thirties, rich gal. It involves that family. So there's a great deal about the background of the Tarrant family and Tarrant House, which is an old Southern mansion, and they have just a wonderful Southern gothic time of it. It's a little bit different. As a matter of fact, when I was writing it, I was worried because in a sense the tone is very different from *The Christie Caper*, but there's only one book that could ever be *The Christie Caper* because there was only one Agatha Christie. I hope that readers who enjoy it will also enjoy *Southern Ghost*, even though it's a more somber and darker family story. Well, it does have one lighthearted aspect. Laurel is not on the scene, but she is very much in evidence over the telephone, as she often is, and she's finding out all about the ghosts of South Carolina. Interspersed with this rather somber family tragedy, we have Laurel's report on all these marvelous ghosts all over South Carolina. It's very different, and I had fun with it.

CLPS: What about the future? Are Annie and Max going on together?

CGH: They do in *Southern Ghost*; but *Dead Man's Island* will inaugurate a new series. I've done three short stories with a character named Henrietta O'Dwyer Collins. She's a retired newspaperwoman, and she's teaching journalism at a small liberal arts college in Missouri. The neat thing about this college is that almost all the faculty are old professionals. This is my dream about what a really wonderful journalism school would be because you can eliminate the dichotomy between the academic and the professional. I think it would be fun to have all these old professionals who are at the end of their careers but who can still teach. There are so many things that I can do with this, and I like Henrietta. She has a very strong personality. Her nickname is Henrie O, and it was given to her by her late husband, Richard, who said she could pack more surprises into a single day than O. Henry ever did into a short story. So I'm looking forward to it. Then I hope to alternate a Henrie O and an Annie and Max. I thought it was very interesting when I was at a women's mystery seminar in Berkeley a couple of years ago, a young student came up to me and confessed that she was surprised that I was so much older than she had thought I would be. I said, "Well, obviously, I'm not twenty-six years old, as Annie is." And that does narrow the range that I can do, because with Annie, I'm looking at life through a twenty-six-year-old's viewpoint. With Henrie O, who is a much more cynical and jaded character than Annie, it will be refreshing for me to have a different voice.

CLPS: Tell me a little bit more about *Dead Man's Island*.

CGH: It is also set on an island off the coast of South Carolina but a very different kind of island from Broward's Rock. It is one of those little sea islands. They're just about a mile across, belong to individual families, and usually they serve as hunting preserves. This particular island belongs to a media magnate, a multimillionaire, and there's only the one house on it. He is a figure in Henrie O's past, and he calls on her for help and asks her to come to this island for a visit. She arrives and discovers that everyone there is someone who might have been guilty of an attempt on this man's life earlier in the summer, and so he wants her to help him figure out who might have done it, and also there is a hurricane approaching.

CLPS: *Dead Man's Island* was shot as a made-for-TV movie. What was that like, seeing one of your novels turned into film?

CGH: It was amazing, really. I think I enjoyed the most the actor who played the secretary. When I saw him, it was just like the character walked off the page. I thought the casting was very good. However, I would say very honestly that, although Barbara Eden is very charming, she is not my picture of Henrie O, and I really regretted that they gave her a Texas accent. Trust me, honey, that's not a Texas accent. If they had wanted a Texas accent, they should have talked to me. My guess is that they wanted to differentiate it sharply from *Murder, She Wrote* with the New England background. But Henrie O is not from Texas and has no accent; she grew up abroad. The other thing I regretted was that they changed the locale from the East Coast to the West Coast, and in the novel the hurricane has an enormous impact on the book. Of course, they couldn't have a hurricane on the West Coast, so they just had a big storm, and it wasn't quite the same.

CLPS: That's too bad, because your depiction of the hurricane is one of the real achievements of the book.

CGH: I felt that way, too. Nevertheless, it was a very pleasant experience. My husband and I had the opportunity to go out and watch a couple of days of the filming, and Barbara Eden is just as nice as you might think she would be. It was exciting.

CLPS: In general, did the film conform to your view of the story and what you had in mind when you wrote it?

CGH: In the main part, it did. The ending was different, and I thought that was very interesting. Perhaps it's a rather subtle point, but in the novel when Henrie O ultimately realizes what happened, she decides that she cannot prove it, and therefore it would be futile to broadcast it to the world. Of course, part of her motivation is to protect her daughter from realizing her true parentage. The script was written by a man, and I suspect that it didn't even occur to him as important. To me, it was a very important point in revealing Henrie O's personality. Other than that, I think they did a really good job.

CLPS: As you have in the past, in the second Henrie O book, *Scandal in Fairhaven*, you deal with wealth and privilege in a small Southern town. Then you peel back the thin layer of respectability.

CGH: I was trying to show that a woman who meant well, who truly tried hard to do the right thing, could absolutely put herself at risk in failing relationships with people simply because she wasn't very empathetic about how her actions affected others. I think that's a fascinating concept because the whole point in mysteries is how relationships are fractured. Patty Kay, my victim, was really a good person, but she truly had a limited vision of the world around her. I find that an interesting theme to explore.

CLPS: You also explore the history of old families, which the South has in abundance.

CGH: There is nothing closer to anyone than their family. Those relationships have an enormous impact on our present lives and grow out of what happened in the past. What happens in the past is prologue: We can't divorce ourselves from the past. You have to come to terms with who you are and the effect of your family on your life. I think that is one of the reasons I like to write about family relationships.

CLPS: Also, history seems to be especially present in the South.

CGH: In the South, it's not how much money you have or what your job is, it is who your people are. There is also a very definite sense of place. Whether you feel you belong or not is another question, but you definitely are encapsulated. I can't speak for the rest of the world. I don't know if that is true of a New England village or in Seattle, but in the South it is definitely true.

CLPS: Let's talk about your latest book in the Death on Demand series, *Mint Julip Murder*.

CGH: That was sheer fun. The opportunity to be a part of the Southern Book Festival several years ago gave me the idea for that book. What I really did was just to transfer the Southern Book Festival from Nashville to Hilton Head and have a lot of fun dealing with what writers are like and what it's like to go to these kinds of events.

CLPS: You often have multiple possible murderers in your books.

CGH: I create characters who have some kind of relationship where there is the possibility for anger or hate or fear. Basically, when you write a mystery, the second most important decision you make is the identity of the victim, because it is the people who are in the victim's life who are going to figure in that person's death, and that gives you your cast of characters. I create a victim and then I think who did this person know, who did this person work with or was afraid of or hated.

CLPS: Annie is accused of the murder in this book.

CGH: That's a device authors often use because it gives the character a very clear and present reason to wish to solve the crime. In this novel, Annie felt a responsibility to the authors because she was their liaison. She also has a tendency to lose her temper about things, and this always gets her in trouble. A friend of mine once said about the Annie and Max books, "You know, Carolyn, they are really a fantasy." And I said, "Well, yes, in a way they are." We have this very happy young couple, the celebration of mysteries in the bookstore, and a cast of interesting characters. In a way, they are very complex books to write and perhaps in a sense harder to write than the Henrie O books.

CLPS: In *Mint Julip Murder* you continue your satire on Southern life and on Southern writers. What was the attraction?

CGH: Well, I know so many writers. This is the world I live in. It was just lots of fun to have fun with them. I do think writers are interesting people and very emotional and very creative. It is fun to put them in moments of jeopardy. I heard Nancy Pickard speak recently. Nancy is a brilliant writer and a wonderful speaker, and she was talking about two friends of hers who are very adventurous. The point she made was, as a writer she sits in her office and creates adventures and dangers in which she never participates. I think that is true of most of us. I just like to write about writers.

CLPS: Your latest novel, *Death in Lovers' Lane*, is the third Henrie O book. Tell me as much as you can about it.

CGH: It was mentioned in the previous two Henrie O books that she taught journalism at a small college in Missouri, and in this book she is pictured for the first time on that turf. She is teaching in a journalism school, and she has a very beautiful and abrasive student who wants to write an investigative series. She is focusing on three unsolved crimes that have occurred over the past fifteen years in this small college town. Henrie O is very unimpressed when this is broached, because she says, "What you are talking about is just rehashing old facts and there is no point to that; that is not investigative reporting." The student assures her that you can always find out something new and that she will. Then the student's body is found in lovers' lane, which was the site of one of the previous crimes where a student couple was found dead about five years before. So Henrie O, of course, feels a sense of responsibility, because she is concerned whether it was her insistence on really raking out new information or the facts in the student's personal life that led this student to her death. Henrie O has to solve the earlier crimes to solve the present one.

CLPS: You've used a campus as a setting before in one of the Annie Laurance books. What's the attraction of a college campus?

CGH: For one thing, I taught for three years in the journalism school from which I graduated at the University of Oklahoma, so I know that background, I feel very comfortable with it. Personality clashes and violent disagreements are not uncommon on college campuses. I love dealing with a journalism school because to me it is very exciting and interesting background. I felt that it was time that Henrie O was seen doing what she presumably does. I probably will not do it again because I've now done it twice.

CLPS: You end the novel with the line: "Have laptop. Will travel." What is the advantage to keeping Henrie O moving around?

CGH: I didn't really want her to be in one continuing background because it is the hallmark of the Death on Demand books. I wanted to have her free to find adventure wherever she might go. As a matter of fact, the next novel is complete, and it is called *Death in Paradise*, and it occurs on the island of Hawaii.

CLPS: You've won practically every major award given for crime writing. What does winning those awards do for a writer?

CGH: To be specific, I have won three of the four major awards, and I doubt if I will ever win the fourth, the Edgar, because it is always chosen by a committee of five authors, and often the hard-boiled writers are given preference by that committee. The awards I have won are voted by readers. Quite frankly, that means more to me than what five authors think. What matters to me is to be read; that is the whole point of writing. You want to communicate; that is why you write. Winning the awards like the Agatha and the Anthony and the Macavity says to me that I have reached out and communicated with readers. So they mean a great deal to me.

CLPS: What are your plans for the future?

CGH: Well, right now, I am working on *Yankee Doodle Dead*, which is the next Death on Demand book. So guess who gets killed? Then I hope to continue to write about Henrie O. I just love writing mysteries, and as long as Avon wants to publish me, I will write them.

Portions of this interview appeared in *The Armchair Detective*, 24:4 (Fall 1993), 46–49, and *Mystery Forum*, No 4 (1993), 32.

Marcia Muller

INTERVIEW BY JAN GRAPE

Quick now: Who was the first contemporary female to write a female private eye series? P. D. James with her Cordelia Gray novel An Unsuitable Job for a Woman? Or Maxine O'Callaghan with her first Delilah West short story published in 1974 in Ellery Queen? Or Marcia Muller with her first Sharon McCone book, Edwin of the Iron Shoes (1977)? What about Sue Grafton with her Kinsey Millhone or Sara Paretsky's V. I. Warshawski? No. The winner is, of course, Marcia Muller. James only wrote two Cordelia books. Although O'Callaghan's story was published before Muller's Edwin, the first Delilah book, Death Is Forever, didn't see print until 1981, Grafton's "A" Is for Alibi and Paretsky's Indemnity Only both debuted in 1982. Marcia says the idea of writing a strong, independent female protagonist was in the air. She just happened to get her book published first and happened to continue the series.

It never entered Marcia's head nor did she aspire to ever be called "The founding Mother of the contemporary female hard-boiled private-eye," by Ms. Grafton; a quote both women are haunted by but can never escape. Marcia Muller only wanted to write something a little different and something that might sell. She was trying to make a living writing, after all. And that she has done and quite well.

But Marcia Muller paid her dues; she wrote two books a year for a time, one a McCone and the other either a Joanna Stark or Elena Oliverez.

She wrote numerous short stories, she and husband, Bill Pronzini, wrote a suspense/thriller, and together they edited an abundance of anthologies. The Joanna stories were meant to be a trilogy from the beginning. The Elena stories died on their own after three. Marcia had become more energized with her pal, Sharon McCone, saying she had finally found the form she wanted to write.

I read Marcia Muller early on, found her first book in a mystery bookstore in Houston (Murder by the Book) and pounced on it. It must have been about 1981, and I was toying with the idea of writing about a female private eye myself. I thought Edwin *was an excellent story and haunted the library until I found another Muller,* Ask the Cards a Question, *in 1982. Since then, I've eagerly awaited each new Sharon McCone each year.*

I met Marcia in 1988 and shortly afterward began a correspondence with her. We managed a few visits and telephone calls at mystery conventions, and in 1991, she and Bill came to Austin to sign books. The best scheduling turned out to be over Easter weekend, a holiday not conducive to author appearances and book signings. So my husband Elmer and I had a couple of days to show them Central Texas and the Hill Country during bluebonnet season, and the signing on Tuesday was a huge success.

The following visit took place recently, not face-to-face but via telephone and fax machines.

JG: In the recent release of the McCone short stories you mention how you came up with the name of Sharon McCone. Will you recount that for us?

MM: Sharon is for my college roommate and McCone is for the late John McCone, a former head of the CIA.

JG: Nothing unusual there—but I do like the name. It fits her. Was the first manuscript you wrote published?

MM: No. I wrote my first book at age twelve, and as an adult, I wrote another unpublished manuscript.

JG: Was that one a private eye?

MM: Yes—a Sharon McCone. I'd fallen in love with the mystery and with the private eye form after reading Ross Macdonald. I soon found Chandler and Hammett as well. Two American women authors I admired were Lillian O'Donnell and Dorothy Uhnak. They write strong, tough women characters—what I wanted to write.

JG: There's several years between *Edwin* and *Question*. How did you keep from being discouraged?

MM: By continuing to write. I think during that period, editors then thought McCone wasn't realistic enough, but later they realized there actually were female private detectives and people wanted to read about strong women characters. Speaking of discouragements, in college, my creative writing class teacher told me I'd never be a writer because I had nothing to say. And it was true; I was only nineteen. As a result, I went into journalism.

JG: Do you think Sharon and Kinsey and Delilah West and V. I. Washawski, the first contemporary private investigators, made mystery readers more aware of how the genre would change with the addition of strong women writers?

MM: Yes and no. I think what they did was make mystery readers who were interested in writing in the genre more aware and encouraged women to enter the field. For instance, Nancy Pickard has said she read us and was inspired to try her hand at a novel.

JG: Do you think women mystery writers were influenced by the Nancy Drew books?

MM: Those stories influenced all of us who read them. For me, it wasn't so much Nancy Drew as Margaret Sutton's Judy Bolton books. They were the cornerstone of what I read in children's literature. They were what made me read adult mysteries.

JG: The appealing thing about Nancy Drew is that she was an independent young woman and went out and solved these cases by herself, alone. That impressed me as a young girl.

MM: That's what impressed me about the Bolton books. I went back and reread them because I was doing an article for *Deadly Women*. I discovered similarities to Sharon McCone I hadn't known existed. For instance, Judy had a boyfriend who was a pilot.

JG: I think your characterizations are superb, and your plots *ain't* bad, either. Do you think knowing Sharon as you do makes things easier?

MM: Definitely easier. I can be writing a scene with her and don't have to concentrate on her reactions, on what she's going to do or think. Instead, I can concentrate on the other characters, on the setting, on the pacing, on the nuances. Half the time when I write dialogue between her and the ongoing series characters—whom I know equally well—it just flows. Very often she simply takes over.

JG: You just write it.

MM: I just write it. She knows exactly what she wants to have happen, and it's going to happen regardless of what I may have planned.

JG: Sharon deals with more realistic situations with each book you write. Do you think perhaps writers today are more perceptive of the "realistic issues" of life?

MM: I can only speak for myself. And to some extent, for Bill, because we have similar approaches to our fiction. I'm certainly more perceptive now than I was early on. Realism is important in the mystery novel. We ask our readers to believe in some fairly preposterous situations, such as the private eye finding murder victims over and over. The more firmly the books are grounded in reality, the more the reader is able to suspend disbelief. For that reason, I follow procedure rigorously. I've had private eyes and attorneys compliment me on the books' accuracy, which is very pleasing because I'm trying to give my readers as much of the real world as possible.

JG: How do you keep a story fresh for you and for Sharon? You never write the same book, that's one of your strengths, and I wonder how you do it?

MM: Actually, I did write the same book. If you look at the first three McCone novels, you'll see they have similar structure. I was very much into formula.

With the sale of the third one, Bill told me, "Maybe you ought to think about varying your plots?" After that, I broke away a little bit more with each book. I've discovered I have a low tolerance for boredom. I figure if I'm bored and going through the motions, the reader is going to get bored and will stop going through the motions of buying the books.

I try to do something different with each book—with the background, a different structure. For instance, in *The Broken Promise Land*, I brought in Sharon's assistant, Rae Kelleher, as a second, first-person voice.

In the book I have coming this summer, *Both Ends of the Night*, I open the parts with all dialogue segments between Sharon and her flight instructor; what they're talking about relates thematically to what happens in the following section.

JG: I wanted to ask you about the flying lessons, so this seems like a good time.

MM: The flying lessons have been fantastic. It's been like going back to college; I've had to learn weather, aerodynamics, radio communication, the internal combustion engine. And how to keep the damn thing straight on the runway. It's been a real growing experience, and it's given me an insight into a whole world that I didn't know existed. And the people in that community have been overwhelmingly supportive. The people at our little airport knew I was writing this book, and they were immensely helpful. My flight instructor read all the parts of the book that pertain to flying. She even corrected typos.

JG: How great. Will you continue?

MM: At this point, I don't know where it's going to take me. I don't see myself buying a plane and zipping around the country, but on the other hand, I'd be unhappy if I couldn't fly occasionally.

JG: It's quite a diversion from sitting in front of a typewriter, too.

MM: Right; and I saw things I didn't know were there. For example, I knew there were geysers in the hills east of here, but I didn't know until I flew over them that Pacific Gas & Electric has them harnessed to pumping stations. I told Bill about it, and he used it in his latest Nameless Detective novel.

JG: Hey, that's cool.

MM: "Nameless" says Sharon told him about it, of course.

JG: Sounds as if you're having a really good time. Let's talk next about how Sharon is dealing with her family lately. Is that going to continue?

MM: The family . . . it's a dreadful family—totally dysfunctional. The continuing story of the Savage family goes on; I go into how the children are dealing with their parents' divorce. I'd love to bring back her brother John; he's one of the few people who doesn't take any nonsense from Sharon. I don't know about her brother Joey; he's dumb as a post and not a very interesting person. But the parents and the other sister—they'll be back.

JG: I was going to ask if you do your own research, but it's obvious from the flying that you do.

MM: I do, but I also have an assistant who helps. She is on-line, so I can ask her to find out almost anything, and the next thing I know, I have a huge folder of information. She then zeroes in on the specific aspect of a subject that I need. But I do all my on-site research myself.

JG: Do you visualize a big plan in your head for the next two or three books?

MM: Not usually. Sometimes I panic when I'm about halfway through, because I haven't got the idea for the next one. But lately, I've come up with enough of a personal angle on the ongoing story that I can see where the series is going. I actually have the first scene of the book after the one I'm writing now written in my head.

JG: Okay. Now, the next two questions deal with your office—and what is your writing day like? Do you have a big, businesslike office? Or a messy one?

MM: I have a small, messy office. Sometimes I get it organized, usually after I finish a book or at the first of the year. It has a lot of strange stuff in it. There's a stuffed gorilla hanging from one of the beams.

JG: Well, that's different [laughter].

MM: I used to wish I could dress up in a gorilla suit on Halloween, rent a limo, and go around and pick up my friends from their offices for lunch. It was a weird fantasy that I never carried out. One of them gave me the gorilla.

And as to the writing day, I usually start out about eight-thirty or nine in the morning, work until about eleven-thirty, then go to the post office. Then I'll come back to work in the late afternoon and go on till around seven.

JG: Is it not great to have a superb writer husband to bounce ideas off and talk about writing?

MM: You bet it is. I've learned more from Bill than I probably did in all the six years of college. When I started out in the business, I was learning while actually making a living at writing, and I had to do both very fast. Bill's help was . . . well, I can't place a value on it. And of course now I've come along enough that I can return the favor. We kick ideas around. We read each other's work in progress.

JG: Do you accept his criticism well?

MM: I can usually take it because he never says anything that isn't justified and usually has an idea of how I can fix a problem. Sometimes I grouse and grump about it mightily and throw a fit because it involves work. I'm the world's laziest person.

JG: Aw . . . I don't know. I thought I was. But I'm sure when he criticizes, it's something that makes sense to you and he knows how to tell you.

MM: Right. He never says anything really nasty.

JG: Tell me about your fan mail. Do you get Crayola printing on Big Chief tablets? Or scented stationery?

MM: By and large, my fan mail is pleasant. Usually typed and businesslike and written on good stationery. More than half of it comes from men, and the only letters I don't answer are the occasional abusive ones.

JG: My next question was if you had any idea of the number of male and number of female readers, but you say your mail is probably more than half from men.

MM: I think it's about equal; the men just are more prone to write. More and more, I encounter couples who both read me. It's gratifying to see because it means that Sharon rings true to both genders. Since Hy Ripinsky has appeared, I've noticed the men identify with him.

JG: Any words of wisdom for aspiring writers?

MM: Sit down in front of the keyboard and write at least one page a day. Write every day. Write more than that, if you can. Keep at it; be patient. That's really what it's all about. It's a tough business, but people do break into it all the time.

JG: Okay, the fun questions: What do you wish you had written?

MM: Better than I have.

JG: Who do you like to read?

MM: That's one I can't answer because I don't want to leave somebody out.

JG: Bill Pronzini. He's your favorite author, right?

MM: Of course.

JG: What music do you like?

MM: Country. And classical and jazz.

JG: What's your favorite color?

MM: Depends on what it's on. Red on cars, yellow in kitchens. Quiet colors like blues and greens in decorating, and green and purple on me.

JG: With whom would you like to be stranded on a desert island?

MM: Bill Pronzini. He would keep me sane.

JG: If you could live anywhere in the world, where would you want to live?

MM: I'd like a second home overlooking the Pacific Ocean.

JG: What does your best friend say about you?

MM: My best friend is Bill. One of the things he frequently says is, "You're weird, sir."

JG: What do you do to relax?

MM: I work with scale models. I've finished a model of Sharon's home. I dig in the garden. Watch old movies. Swim, when the weather's right.

JG: What's a great evening to you? Dinner out? Bill cooking dinner for you?

MM: Actually, it's the two of us cooking an Italian meal complete with his famous garlic bread. And some nice music and a good bottle of wine. Maybe watching an old movie and ending up by soaking in the hot tub.

JG: Sounds good. What do you wish an interviewer would ask you, and pretend I just did.

MM: What I wish you would have asked me is: "What questions are you glad I didn't ask?" I would answer, "Where do you get your ideas? Why is Sharon McCone a woman? And when are you going to write a real book?"

JG: That pretty well sums it up. Tell me again the title of the next book due in summer of '97.

MM: It's called *Both Ends of the Night*, and the one after is called *While Other People Sleep*. The latter is one of Bill's titles.

JG: And *Both Ends* is . . .

MM: Mine.

JG: Great. And thanks; I appreciate you taking time from your busy schedule for this.

A MARCIA MULLER CHECKLIST

The Sharon McCone Novels

Edwin of the Iron Shoes
Ask the Cards a Question
The Cheshire Cat's Eye
Games to Keep the Dark Away
Leave a Message for Willie
Double (with Bill Pronzini)
There's Nothing to Be Afraid Of
Eye of the Storm
There's Something in a Sunday
The Shape of Dread
Trophies and Dead Things
Where Echoes Live
Pennies on a Dead Woman's Eyes
Wolf in the Shadow
Till the Butchers Cut Him Down
A Wild and Lonely Place
The Broken Promise Land
Both Ends of the Night

The Joanna Stark Novels

Cavalier in White
There Hangs the Knife
Dark Star

The Elena Oliverez Novels

The Tree of Death
The Legend of the Slain Soldiers
Beyond the Grave (with Bill Pronzini)

A Nonseries Suspense

The Lighthouse (with Bill Pronzini)

Two Short Story Collections

The McCone Files
Deceptions

Mickey Spillane

INTERVIEW BY CHARLES L. P. SILET

M ickey Spillane has been a best-selling writer since his first seven
novels, six of them featuring Mike Hammer, broke all records for
sales during the late 1940s and early 1950s and helped to launch
the paperback revolution. Over his long career, Mr. Spillane has
written for slick magazines, the pulps, comic books, radio, television, and
the movies. He was also a circus performer, a pitchman for light beer, and
an actor, once playing Mike Hammer on the screen. His original comic
book hero, Mike Danger, is now appearing in a series published by Big
Entertainment, and he has just written a new Mike Hammer novel. In the
following interview, Mickey Spillane discusses his career, crime writing, and
the frustrations of working for Hollywood.

CLPS: You began writing in the mid-thirties, but didn't you start with
the mystery adventure magazines?

MS: I started writing for the slicks, and I don't remember which one
it was because I contributed to a lot of the magazines in those days.
This was right after I got out of high school in 1935. I was broke,
and after I worked for the slicks, then I went down to the pulps. In
those days, writing was a little bit different than it is now, because
you had lots of slick magazines in the market like *Liberty*, *The Saturday Evening Post*, and *Colliers*, which published fiction. And you

also had your pulps published by Street and Smith, like *Dime Detective, Dime Mystery*, and *Amazing Stories*, which also took fiction but were a lot cheaper. There was a big market for short stories, for fiction of all types, and you wrote a lot under house names. This was an occupation; I'm a writer not an author.

CLPS: Which house names did you write under and for which publications?

MS: I wrote under some, but I don't remember what the names were. I worked for all sorts of magazines; I covered the field, wherever there was a buck. We didn't have agents, so we just went to work where there was an opening or there was a place where we could get in. I worked my way down to the comic books, and actually, I made more money out of the comics then anyplace else.

CLPS: Why did you decide to write mystery and adventure fiction?

MS: Well, they asked that little bank robber, "Why do you rob banks?" And he said, "That's where the money was." Mystery and adventure fiction was an open market, and that's where the best money could be made. Not now, though, I wouldn't say, but for a long while, that's where the best money was. You had better sales in the mystery/adventure field than anyplace else. Now, you know, they're selling books by the pound. That was a time when a woman couldn't get anything printed, but now mystery fiction is a big woman's area, so you can see that the market keeps changing. I was one of those who chased the market, and I still do.

CLPS: You mentioned comic books. How did you begin to write for them?

MS: Well, the brother of a friend of mine, Ray Gill, was into that field, and he was working for Funnies Incorporated on West Twenty-fourth Street in New York City. Joe, who's my buddy, went in to see Ray, and he asked if I wanted to try something for them, to try writing a two-page story for the magazine, and I whipped one right out. I liked writing for the comics a whole lot, and I really liked the artwork; it was just a lot of fun. And here I am, back in the business again with the new Mike Danger series for Big Entertainment!

CLPS: Did you work for a number of comics?

MS: I didn't write just one comic; I wrote for everything that came along. I was writing for *Captain America, The Human Torch*, everyone you could think of. See, we didn't work for an outfit that published the magazines, we were a studio that sold our product to publishers, and that's how my Mike Danger book had started. I saw the publishers were making all this money, so I said, "Heck, I'm going to publish one." I got some artists to help me do the drawings, and we wrote the original comic book, *Mike Danger*.

CLPS: When was that?

MS: That was just before the war in the early 1940s, and then the war came along, and I put the book aside when I went into the military. We all went into the military, as a matter of fact. Once I put the book aside, I never picked it up again, because, after I came out, I found a new market with the advent of paperback books, and I began to write specifically for paperbacks. They did not have original paperback books back then; everything was a reprint. So in order to get *I, the Jury* into paperback, I had to go through the hardback market, but strangely enough, it wasn't even that market that I sold it to but Rosco Fawcett, who owned Fawcett Publications at that time with his brothers. He was a distributor and not a publisher, but that was an advantage because getting books distributed was the hard part of the trade. Anyway, he read the book and thought it was a great book and wanted to market it. He went to New American Library, which was Signet Books, and told them that if they would publish the book in paper, that he would get it distributed, get it placed on all the racks. That was a good thing for them. In turn, Signet went to E. P. Dutton and said, "If you publish this in hardback, we guarantee to reprint it." Because of the immediate reprint setup, Dutton knew they were going to make money, so they grabbed the book and released it in hardback.

CLPS: *I, the Jury* was published in 1947.

MS: It didn't sell very well. Still, there were two editions of *I, the Jury* in hardback, but when it hit the paperback market, it went right to the top. There is a very funny incident connected with the book.

Rosco Fawcett had never had a big seller, and he wanted to really push this novel in a big way, so he ordered a million paperback copies of *I, the Jury* from Signet to blanket the market. It was published during the holiday season, which was the wrong time of the year for books back then. It's just the opposite now; the holiday season is a big time for books. Anyway, they put it out between Christmas and New Year's, when books didn't sell, and, boy, I'll tell you, it sold like a son of a gun. This was in reprint, not hardback. It was a really hot seller, but nobody had copies of the books. Everybody was calling in wanting more copies of the book, and the distributor didn't have any more. Rosco called Signet and asked, "What happened to the million copies we ordered?" And Signet told him that they thought it was an error that he wanted one million of them, so they printed a lot less. From what I understand, somebody got canned for that. Anyway, he came back out with another big printing, and it went right to the top of the charts.

CLPS: What happened to Mike Danger?

MS: The Mike Danger comic book just sat there until two years ago when Big Entertainment wanted to know if they could bring Mike Hammer out as a comic book, and I said, "No, he's still too valuable a character." We were going to make movies with him on TV and do a few other things. Then they asked about Mike Danger, and I said, "You bought it." Right now, I understand from them that the new series is doing very well.

CLPS: Several issues are already out.

MS: Yeah, we've got the only character in comics who doesn't fly. They all seem to fly nowadays.

CLPS: How comfortable are you with the sci-fi setting for the new series?

MS: It's selling, and that's what the public wants.

CLPS: How much input are you having with the Mike Danger books?

MS: Any input I want, but I don't want that much. I haven't got time for comic books, but I do a lot of promotional things for them, and we talk over story ideas and situations. Right now, I'm involved in doing a book on Mike Danger, which should be out later this year. It doesn't take long to write it; it's just that I have so many other things to do. Heck, I'm seventy-eight years old, and I don't feel like working that much. But I can't retire, because from what can I retire? I never had a job. I won't let me retire. It's a continuing job when you're a writer.

CLPS: Your books have had phenomenal sales—some two hundred million by last count—and even from the beginning, they did well; the first six or seven sold in the millions, in paper at least.

MS: The first seven were sold in the days when the price was twenty-five cents a piece. Man, I'd like to have those sales again; you know, at six bucks. But then, as you get older, you find out money is a tool. It's like a hammer; you can kill somebody with that hammer, or you can build a house with that hammer. It depends on how you use your tool. I've never been money motivated to that extent. I live kind of a plain life. I have a modest house and drive a Ford pickup truck. My needs are pretty simple.

CLPS: You have not only sold well here in the States, but you've done well abroad in translation.

MS: At one time, I was the fifth most widely translated writer in the world, ahead of writers like Lenin, Tolstoy, Gorki, and Jules Verne, and they're all dead.

CLPS: After all this enormous success, however, in 1952 you stopped publishing novels for a while.

MS: But I didn't stop writing; I was doing other things. I had movies going, I had TV going. We made the first big television show, *Mickey Spillane's Mike Hammer*, with Darren McGavin, and I had four movies being made. I was doing a lot of things, and I was making money, except I wasn't writing; I didn't have to write. People think that if you are a writer that you have to write, that it's a necessity that you keep on writing, and that's not true. I'm a writer; I work for money; its my occupation; its what I do for a living.

CLPS: You published a number of short stories in magazines during the 1950s.

MS: I was working for *Cavalier Magazine* and several of the other men's magazines that were Fawcett publications. I did a lot of that, so I was very busy. I used to have copies of everything I did then, but a few years ago, we got flattened by Hurricane Hugo, and I lost everything. I lost all my old junk; I had to run out and by new junk.

CLPS: What was the attraction of writing shorter pieces?

MS: Well, it was a lot of fun, and the whole field is interesting. I enjoy writing, but I wouldn't want to be tied down to a job doing the same thing over and over again. I would hate to be a reporter doing dailies. I wouldn't want to be a writer for Hollywood at all, where you got lots of producers, directors, studio heads, everybody on your back telling you what to do. I don't like that. So the shorter pieces were a different kind of writing for me.

CLPS: Let's talk about your movie experience because a lot of your novels were made into movies in the 1950s.

MS: The movies were pretty much terrible. They made my first four novels into movies, and they were pieces of garbage. This is a good story. What happened was the producer, Victor Saville, a British guy, wanted to make a lot of money fast, so he got hold of me, figured we could make some cheap pictures with something hot. *I, the Jury* was the one he started with. His biggest picture up to that time was *The Silver Chalice*. You remember that one? Well, he made it, all right, and it was one of his biggest films and one of the biggest flops he ever had, too. He lost all his bills doing that. But if he had made *I, the Jury* properly, it would have turned out to be like *Dr. No* with Sean Connery. Actually, I never really got into motion pictures. I've done a couple movies, but that's not my cup of tea. I still prefer to write books.

CLPS: Were you ever satisfied with anybody who ever played Mike Hammer on screen?

MS: Me. I did a good job. I played Mike Hammer in *The Girl Hunters*. It was in black and white, and we made it in England, but we got ripped off by Hollywood again. However, that's another story. When we made *The Girl Hunters*, Hollywood was trying to parlay my name and reputation into something and then to sell the rights to it. Ah, it's Hollywood baloney. But when we got over to England and were there making a picture, they ran out on us, and they wouldn't send us the money. Anyway, I made a deal with the British publishing house to reprint some of the things I did with Fawcett publications, with *Cavalier Magazine*, and they took my novelettes and made them into novels, sometimes two or three to a book. So I sold them, and we were able to make the picture.

CLPS: What did you think about the recent version of *I, the Jury* with Armand Assante?

MS: Oh, gee, that. You know, he's such a great actor, but they gave him this updated thing and that picture was pitiful. You know, I'm not a tall guy, and I played the part; and at least, I was as big as Biff Elliot. Biff and I are good friends, and he played Mike Hammer in the first picture, and everybody's bigger than him. When I was in charge of casting on the picture, I would not hire anybody who was taller than me, so I swaggered through the picture bigger than everybody.

CLPS: Didn't you play yourself in *Ring of Fear*?

MS: Oh, that was fun. I enjoyed that. I was working with Jack Stang. Jack and I just talked the other day; we're old buddies. That was a great picture, Sean McClory's first American picture with Clyde Beatty and Pat O'Brien. It had a great cast, a cast of thousands, and all those animals. We had a great time making that movie, and I became a circus buff after that, and I used to go out and do shows every year for a month or two.

CLPS: What was different about that one from the others, just your involvement?

MS: Well, the people in the circus were great. You know, these were not show people, as you think of Hollywood, these were *real* show people but in a different area, and I enjoyed them. I enjoyed doing the picture, everything, the whole company was great! We were on location in Phoenix, Arizona, and were away from Hollywood, so we weren't tied in with all that baloney again, and the usual movie colony stuff. It was a real pleasant experience. I went back and I rewrote that picture. See, that piece was written originally by somebody else, and it was a real fiasco and John Wayne and Bob Fellows, who were the money men behind the film—it was a Batjac production—knew they had the flop on their hands; it was terrible. They didn't know what to do to get it done right. The writers in Hollywood didn't want to touch it, because they didn't want to have their name put on something that was going to fall on its face. So Bob Fellows, who was the producer on the picture, said, "Spillane's a writer; maybe he can help us out." I was living in Newburgh, New York, at the time, and they called me on a Wednesday, I went out on a Thursday, and I worked Friday, Saturday, and Sunday. They gave me a little back office, but it was a nice office, on Sunset. I worked for two and a half days, and I finished the script. I remember on Sunday Andy McLaglen coming in and saying, "How's it going?" and I said, "I'm all finished." He thought I meant I was finished for the day, and I was sitting there having a cold beer and everything was done, all typed up and everything. And he says, "That's nice, but how long will it be till you're finished?" And I said, "I told you, I'm all done with it." MaLaglen's wife was with him, and she asked, "What do you mean, you're all done with it?" I said, "I'm finished with the whole project." Now, Andy was not a writer, but he was a good critic, and he looked at the pages and he said, "God, he is done, and this is great." Anyway, he called Duke and Bob and they couldn't believe it; they almost fell over. Two and a half days, they thought I was going sit there for two or three more months, and anyway we got the show back and put it together and they stuck me in the Beverly Hills Hotel and said, "Here, have a good time." But I went home to Newburgh, I didn't want to have a good time in Hollywood. They were looking all over for me, trying to find out whatever happened to me. Where I'd gone, since I was in the picture. And someone said, I think he went home, and I had gone home. They were too busy with the picture again to worry about me, but they got a hold of me in Newburgh and Bob told me, "What the dickens are you doing there?" So anyway, I came out to the picture again, and it was a roaring success. I just saw Clyde Beatty's ex-wife a couple months ago down in Florida, and she told me that she gave the negatives of the picture to her son, Clyde Beatty, Jr., who's out in California somewhere. I'd like to get a copy of that picture. I don't know where it'd go, in the motion picture archives or something.

CLPS: *Kiss Me Deadly* appears often on TV, but the movie considerably revised the novel.

MS: Oh, yeah, in France it's a cult type of thing. A lot of these movie guys just buy the titles; they don't buy the story. I have no faith in Hollywood, per se, you know. If you're going to do something, do it right, but the problem is half of these writers and actors—they can be good—but they have too many people coming in and saying let's do this and let's do that, and they pick the story apart on you.

CLPS: What do you think of the atomic bomb ending?

MS: Ah, it stank. My God, I thought the whole picture stank.

CLPS: You've had a better success on television.

MS: Oh, yeah, sure. I worked with Jay Bernstein. He's a star maker out there, and he was my producer in Hollywood. He did a good job, especially with the series starring Stacy Keach. We're making plans to get back into it again. When I say we, Jay's the one making the plans. He's right there on the scene. I have nothing to do with it. I let the guys who are there do it; you can't shoot a deer when you're a hundred miles away.

CLPS: What did you like about Stacy Keach's portrayal?

MS: He was a good actor—he's a great actor—and he did a real good job. He's well built; he handled the character well. You know, people will always complain about something with the Mike Hammer figure: its not rough enough, or it's too rough, but he played right down the middle pretty nicely, I liked what he did. Of course, unfortunately, he doesn't know how to wear a hat, but nobody knows how to wear a hat in Hollywood anyway.

CLPS: Why did you get back into writing novels?

MS: For the money.

CLPS: But you were making lots of money doing other things.

MS: Yea, but money gets used up, especially these days with taxes. If you're a writer, you get a check, it gets cut right down the middle, half of it goes to the CPA to be put into taxes, and I get the other half. You know, you could make a million, and you only get half a million now. You got to pay agents and all that sort of stuff. You get nickeled to death, so you keep writing.

CLPS: What was it like getting the Grand Master Award this last spring from the Mystery Writers of America?

MS: Well, I wish it came on a piece of green paper with my name on it.

CLPS: Did you feel as if you were finally getting recognized by the crime-writing community?

MS: Oh, no, I get recognized. I get recognized all the time and the people pay me for it. See, I don't belong to the club, and that's one of the reasons why I didn't get it a long time ago. I didn't care though; it didn't bother me. I looked at all the writers that were there, and I didn't know anybody. I knew some of the guys, when I was introduced to them, but nobody I could look at and say, "I know him, he's a writer, he's this and that." I was the only one who was recognizable, and it was a very strange place to be. Being a writer, I have lots of plaques and things that have been given to me. This is very nice, you know, but where you going to put them? I have a little Oscar. It was given to me, presented to *us* really, because obviously I wasn't the only one who got it, by Miller Beer. And on it says it was given to me, given to *us,* for having sold three billion (not million) cases of beer. That's an awful lot of beer. We took a beer that was little known and made it the second largest selling beer in the world, and not just light beer—though it was the first in the light beers— but the second largest selling beer in the world. The only beer ahead of it was Bud. You know, that's a heck of thing to do. When I got that, I said, "Some people got Oscars for doing a good movie, but they didn't sell three billion cases of beer." Barrels, cases? Anyway, that's my little Oscar, and right next to it I have the plaster statue of Edgar Allan Poe, the Grand Master Award, which is nice, too. This is a good award to get, but what it does, it gets you publicity and gets you advances on your next book, but it's also nice to be recognized by people in the business. Now, I've known a lot of the writers, but we don't hang out together. It's a strange thing.

CLPS: Is it in part because you live in South Carolina?

MS: Ah, no, I don't think so. How does one writer get to know another writer? I knew John D. MacDonald pretty well. I used to go down to see him when I went to Sarasota. I saw a couple other writers down there, but you're not that close, you don't really have much to talk about. Writers are kind of funny, you know what I mean? You get them on TV and, boy, they fall apart. They have to have a script; they're as bad as movie stars. But now even the movie people are pretty used to TV, and they can handle an open mike and camera with no problem.

CLPS: Why did you decide to move to South Carolina?

MS: I've been here forty-one years, and I like it, but I'm getting ready to move back up to New York State with my buddy George Wilson. George and I flew together during the war; we were both fighter pilots, and he lives in Granville, New York. I am getting crowded out here, and I need a place to work in wintertime. I love the winters. The winter is my big time for working, and I need another office so badly. Right next to his house, almost adjoining it, there's this old building that I've rented and I'm renovating it into an office so I can have a place to get away from the tourists. So I'm going to go up there in the wintertime.

CLPS: You'll be the only one moving from the South to the North in the wintertime.

MS: I am a reverse snowbird. In the summer I like to go down to Florida, and in the winter, I like to go up in the snow country. This is the way to avoid the tourists.

CLPS: You're getting too many down there?

MS: Oh, man, I live in a tourist area. You know, I'm right on the water, and when I moved down here, it was a great place for writers. I thought nobody would ever move down here; it was just too remote.

But they found us. I'm right next to Myrtle Beach, and they got a hundred golf courses there, and they're expecting up to fifty thousand more people next year. I can't work with this constant busyness. People knock on your door, and I appreciate them wanting to get an autograph, which I'm glad to do. I have a good rapport with the public. I'm glad to do these things; it's part of the business. If they think so much of your work that they want your autograph, give it to them; that's your way of saying thank you, and it works both ways. If you leave a good taste with the public, they will keep coming back. I tell everybody I don't have fans, I have customers; if you're nice to your customers, they'll keep coming back to you.

CLPS: I've read that your advice about writing, which seems to be write fast and don't revise. Is that an accurate statement?

MS: If you are a writer and you do a scene ten times, the last one probably will sound like the first one, and you're not going to get any better as you revise. The best stuff you put down comes right off the typewriter, *bam!* When I wrote my last book, I think I threw away four pieces of paper, that's all. I don't have a big garbage problem.

CLPS: You begin a story with the ending?

MS: Sure I do. Why do you listen to a joke? The biggest part of the joke is the punch line, so the biggest part of a book should be the punch line, the ending. People don't read a book to get to the middle, they read a book to get to the end and hope that the ending justifies all the time they spent reading it. So what I do is, I get my ending and, knowing what my ending is going to be, then I write to the end and have the fun of knowing where I'm going but not how I'm going to get there.

CLPS: How do you get from page one to the end?

MS: If I was to tell you that, it would take two weeks. If I knew that, I'd be writing a book every two weeks. I don't know. People ask how do you write a book: I say I sit down and put down page one, chapter one. Actually, I'd already have written the ending.

CLPS: A lot of writers talk about the crime novel as a kind of social commentary. What do you think about that?

MS: Baloney! Crime novels are a good way to make money. If it's a good story and if it's got action, it will sell. You don't have good stuff in a newspaper. The biggest thing that you read about is crime, and it's somebody else's trouble not yours, so you can sit back and say, "Oh, boy, I'm glad I wasn't there." But crime novels are where all the action is and all the movement is, and they get you involved. Crime novels are great, and every great novel is a book about crime.

CLPS: Is there anything that you've never done that you'd like to have done?

MS: No, I don't know, I do a lot of things. What we're talking about now is my occupation, and I can't do too much anymore, mainly because I'm too old. I mean, I'd like to go skiing again, but if I could ski, it would have to be on the chicken-little hill, and what I want to do is ski the big runs. I used to race automobiles, and I still fly. The things that you like to do physically someday you'll find yourself too old to handle. And I hate to just observe these things, I like to participate. I don't go to ball games, because you have more fun when you do things. I feel so sorry for guys who quit work after they've done some menial job all their life. Maybe they've worked in a shop, and then they retire, and now there is nothing for them to do.

CLPS: And you're just going to keep writing?

MS: Oh, yeah, sure. It's a good occupation.

CLPS: I have to ask this last question: Do you still use the Smith-Corona?

MS: Absolutely. I got nine of them, and whenever one breaks down, I cannibalize the others for repair parts. I use the parts, because you can't buy parts anymore, and I keep two really good ones operational. I also have one electric one that I use when I'm up working in New York State when I get oppressed by the weather, but I'm not much on electric typewriters; I prefer the manuals, and computers confuse me. I can't type any faster on a computer than I can on a typewriter.

Portions of the interview originally appeared in *Mystery Scene*, No. 52 (March/April 1996), 32, 63–67.

Ian Rankin

INTERVIEW BY JERRY SYKES

I an Rankin became a crime writer almost by default. In 1985, while studying for a Ph.D. in Scottish Literature at Edinburgh University and using the time to write novels and short stories, he came up with the idea for a psychological thriller. The novel, Knots & Crosses, began with a pun: noughts and crosses/knots and crosses (in Britain, tic-tac-toe is called noughts and crosses), the idea being that the hero would be sent little clues: knotted pieces of string and crosses made from matchsticks. At this time, Rankin was also reading a lot of literary theory and particularly liked the idea of playing games with the reader, the whodunit being the ultimate author/reader game. Even the name he chose for his hero, John Rebus, was a pun, a rebus being a picture puzzle.

When the book was published, Rankin looked in vain for reviews, only to be told that he should be looking in the crime section. Sure enough, the reviews were there. Rankin thought they'd made a mistake; he hadn't written a crime novel. But then the Crime Writers' Association asked him to join, and he realized that it was he who had made the mistake.

Two more novels followed, a Greene-ish spy story and a conspiracy thriller. (Rankin has continued to write thrillers under the name Jack Harvey.) But people wanted to know what had happened to Rebus. Eventually, Rankin came up with another slice of Edinburgh gothic, Hide & Seek, and decided to resurrect Rebus as protagonist.

It was this novel that defined the backdrop for the subsequent Rebus novels: an Edinburgh that exhibited a definite dual personality, the basis for this duality being firmly rooted in history. Up until the end of the eighteenth century, rich and poor would mingle together, either on the street or in drinking dens. They even shared the same tenement space, with the rich living close to the ground floor and the poor living closest to the sky. In human terms, the embodiment of this was Deacon Brodie. A respected citizen by day—a deacon of the city and a locksmith—by night he was a riotous and corrupt individual who employed a gang to break into the houses to which he himself had fitted the locks. Brodie is thought to be the inspiration behind Dr Jekyll and Mr Hyde, *a novel set in London but with Edinburgh in its soul. Public probity and private vice: these are the two sides of the Scottish character that Rankin explores in his Rebus novels.*

The third Rebus novel, Wolfman, *published in the States as* Tooth & Nail, *took him to London on the hunt for a serial killer. This book is probably the weakest of the series, with Rebus a fish out of water and the story a straightforward hunt for the killer. By the next novel, Rebus was back in his native city and Rankin back to blowtorching the veneer of respectability from the establishment: in* Strip Jack, *an MP is found in a brothel during a raid;* The Black Book *concerns the arson of a hotel frequented by judges, lawyers, and known villains;* Mortal Causes *investigates the funding and support of sectarian paramilitaries; and in* Let It Bleed, *Rebus finds himself in the very highest offices of the Scottish establishment itself.*

At the heart of the books, Rebus is a man who is as much a creation of the city as of the society in which he operates. This is probably best summed up in the opening line of The Black Book: *"It all happened because John Rebus was in his favourite massage parlour reading the Bible."*

JS: From the brief biographical details published in your books, you had quite a checkered career before turning to writing. Can you give us an overview of your background?

IR: Born and raised in a Fife mining village (five miles from where Val McDermid was growing up; eight miles from Iain Banks). Comprehensive school. Edinburgh University. Spent most of my time playing in a punk band, going to gigs, frequenting bars with exotic dancers. Worked on a vineyard in France, came back and got a job in a tax office. Back to Uni to do a Ph.D. on the novels of Muriel Spark, but used the time to write my own novels instead: three in three years (*Summer Rites*, which was never published, then *The Flood* and *Knots & Crosses*). Married in '86, moved to London. Worked as a secretary in the National Folktale Centre, then as a hi-fi journalist—there was more fiction in my reviews than in any of my stories.

JS: What would you say were your earliest influences?

IR: Comic books. But then when I was twelve, thirteen, you'd find me in the local library, especially when I found they'd let you borrow anything. I couldn't go into a newsagent's and buy adult magazines, I had a fight on my hands to persuade cinema owners I was eighteen, but no one stopped me reading *The Godfather*. My parents didn't mind, either, since somewhere along the way an old uncle they respected had told them, "It doesn't matter what he reads, so long as he's reading." The first crime books I ever got into were Ernest Tidyman's scrappy (but I loved them) *Shaft* series. These led to a love of American fiction in general, and eventually a degree in U.S. literature.

JS: Your first few novels were in a variety of genres. Was this a deliberate choice—experimenting with genres—or did you just choose plots that interested you?

IR: I had some stupid idea that I'd write a novel in every genre I could think of. What lay behind this was that I didn't know what kind of writer I wanted to be. I knew I wanted to be populist, but I'd spent seven years at university as part of the whole lit crit machine, and I wanted critical appeal, too. Then I found there's this stuff called Crit Appeal by Fabergé—you just splash it on and people start theorizing about your work.

JS: Given that the first Rebus book was intended as a one-off, were you happy to continue with the character? Did you change him in any way?

IR: I liked him straight off, but he's changed a lot. He's stopped aging, for one thing. I made him too old in the first book. Plus he used to listen to jazz and enjoy the company of cats, but then John Harvey came along, and he knew more about jazz than I did and his character had a too-similar name as it was, so *whammo*! John Rebus digs sixties rock and *hates* cats. What I like is, in the early books you can see the mistakes, because I was writing them too young. And as you progress through the books, the writing, the material, and the character all become stronger.

JS: The Rebus books are very detailed. Do you do a lot of research?

IR: I remember an early attempt at research. When I was researching *Knots & Crosses*, I wrote to the chief constable of Lothian and Borders asking if he'd answer a few questions. He told me to be at Leith Police Station on a certain date, certain time. A couple of bored-looking detectives were on hand to help me. They asked what the book was about, I said a child killer. What I hadn't realized was that a child had just been abducted in Leith and a murder room had been set up. So they took down my details and added me to their computer. I became suspect number 350 and spent more time answering their questions than they did mine. (Only years later did they catch the guy; they reckon he may have killed up to twenty young girls.) I reckon if I'm making a living writing about people, I owe it to them to get the facts right. There's a lot of serendipity involved in my research, which makes me think the books *want* to be written, the stories want me to tell them.

JS: There was a lot of wordplay in your early books; in *Knots & Crosses* and *Hide & Seek*, for example, the plots seem to hinge on wordplay. The later books have less wordplay and appear more realistic. Do you agree?

IR: I love wordplay; I'm a fiend for anagrams and puns. I had a school friend who used to learn songs backwards. He called me Nai Niknar. It sounded like I should be playing sax for Hawkwind. We had a lot of fun with language. And remember, when I wrote *Knots*, I was still a student, up to my oxters in deconstruction and semiotics. Literature was supposed to be a self-reflexive game, so I played it. The early books are filled with in-jokes and cross-references. But as I grew up, I suppose I learned that if you break the overall tone of a book just so you can slip in a good joke (or even better, a bad one), you may not be doing the book as a whole a good turn.

JS: In the books to date, Rebus has often worked alongside his fellow officers, but in the last book, *Let It Bleed*, he was very much on his own. Is that how you see him developing? Becoming increasingly marginalized?

IR: Rebus has what might be termed an attitude problem. He can hardly suffer himself (gladly or otherwise), never mind fools or those around him. I'm more interested in the lone detective as a *type* than in multicharacter procedurals, because in the former the detective stands for both author (working alone at constructing the book) and reader (working alone at interpreting it). In the latest Rebus novel, *Black & Blue*, Rebus becomes obsessed with a case—and obsessives, as James Ellroy could tell you, have very little time for other people.

JS: The new book, *Black & Blue*, is partially based on the true story of a Scottish serial killer, Bible John. There was a lot about the case in the news last year, with the police exhuming the body of a suspect for DNA testing. How did the revelations affect the book?

IR: I was on tenterhooks for about six months; then the police came over all embarrassed and admitted that all the DNA tests proved was that their suspect *wasn't* Bible John. The whole Bible John angle is only a subplot, albeit crucial thematically. What interests me about Bible John is the mythology that sprang up around him: For Scots he really is the bogeyman made flesh. Plus I wanted to investigate obsession. Cops who become involved with unsolved cases oftentimes find themselves obsessed. Their whole lives are spent in the shadow of this unknown killer. I wanted to take Rebus to that place. I think the book is more complex than previous offerings, while delivering a slam-bang story. It was funny, when the Bible John/DNA story broke, a lot of fellow writers wrote to offer advice. Larry Block told me not to change a thing. I think Val McDermid said I should invent a character called Testament Tam or Proverbs Pete. But I really wanted this novel to be set firmly in the real world. As Ellroy says, if you have the stones, you can rewrite history to your own specifications, and that's what I try to do in *Black & Blue*.

JS: I believe some other aspects of the novel are coming true as well.

IR: It's always been like this with my books. *Let It Bleed* concerned bogus training agencies. A couple of months back, a story broke in the news that just such an enterprise had been uncovered in Glasgow. In *Black & Blue*, there's the whole Bible John story resurfacing. Plus other sidelines are coming true or almost true. Much of the novel is set in a corrupt Aberdeen, and the papers seem to have been full recently of bent Aberdeen cops, club-owning mafioso, and oil-executive rapists. I should tell you it's happening again with the book I've just started writing. The whole thing's beginning to make my head nip.

JS: You regularly contribute stories to the major anthologies. Do you enjoy this form?

IR: If I could make a living writing nothing but short stories, I would. Between novels, I usually write three or four stories, a way of limbering up, of experimenting with narrative construction, point of view, character. The Rebus books are pretty well fixed in what's become a kind of stream-of-consciousness third person. In stories, I can write first person, second person, anything. I can put in more comedy than my novels would accommodate, more anarchy in general. I've won a short story Dagger and been short-listed for the Anthony, so I'm probably doing something right.

JS: Your first radio play, *The Serpent's Back*, was recently broadcast by the BBC, and the story was published in *Midwinter Mysteries*. Did you adapt the story for radio, or was it the other way around?

IR: I was reading up on eighteenth-century Edinburgh and came across these caddies: people who could be hired to run errands, find you a good boardinghouse or whore, or get you home safely after a night on the bevvy. And I thought: great characters, perfect for a mystery, because, like cops and private eyes, they had access to the high life and the low life, and could move with ease between the two. They were sleazebags with ambivalent (if any) morals, and would make perfect antiheroes. I wrote it up as a short story but wanted to take it further. A BBC producer liked it, so commissioned the ninety-minute play. The Beeb now want three more plays featuring the same central character.

JS: You're very prolific: one Rebus and one Jack Harvey book a year. Can you tell us something about your working habits?

IR: Protestant work ethic meets Calvinist guilt. If I'm not working, I'm not living. Also, when I get into a plot, I want to race to the end. I'm like that when I'm reading, and I'm like that when I'm writing. An average book used to take me four to six weeks to write, eight weeks of research and plotting preceding. So I could do two a year. This is no longer the case. I'm pacing myself, writing with more deliberation, and doing a lot more preplanning. I may write another Jack Harvey if I get a good idea for a thriller, but I'm concentrating on Rebus now. I think he deserves it. As to working habits: I've got an office in the house; no phone or anything; computer, books, hifi, that's it. I write to music: Joy Division, Jesus & Mary Chain, Bathers, Eno . . . Some people would not call this music. Six-hour writing day when I'm motoring; maybe ten good pages (3,500 words) by the end.

JS: Which authors would you say had influenced you?

IR: Probably every author I've ever read. Reading is a learning process when you're a writer. You pick up tips everywhere. Scottish writers: Alasdair Gray, William McIlvanney, Gordon Williams, Irvine Welsh, Muriel Spark even. Plus old Robert Louis. Scots gothic starts with him; I wish he were writing today. McIlvanney showed me that you could write genre fiction and still be taken seriously by the establishment.

JS: Who are your current favorite authors?

IR: I'm still not comfortable with the mystery form and admire writers who take risks with it. Lawrence Block can write a book with only the bare bones of a crime plot, yet make it gripping and memorable. James Ellroy takes risks with language: He's not the first writer to realize that words are imprecise tools, and that sometimes the more we write, the less we say. Other names: Earl Emerson, Derek Raymond/Robin Cook . . . Nicholas Blincoe is one to watch.

JS: You've won several awards in your career, the largest of which was probably the Chandler-Fulbright. What did this involve?

IR: You had to persuade a bunch of influential people that you were a coming star. So they gave me £10,000 and told me to go to the U.S.A. to spend it; that was the only real stipulation. My wife and three-month-old son Jack came along. We bought a VW bus and drove all over the place, nearly 20,000 miles. A one-off, a lifetime memory. I plotted *The Black Book* on the road and stole bits of that book's Heartbreak Cafe from a dive in New Orleans.

JS: You've just moved back to Scotland, I believe.

IR: That's right. I lived in France for six years, but now I'm back in Edinburgh. The first Rebus novel, *Knots & Crosses*, is the only one to have been written in the city, so it's slightly strange being back and writing about the place. In France, I lived in a farmhouse in the middle of nowhere. I was number one in a field of one: the only Scottish writer in the Dordogne. Here, I'm surrounded by bookshops full of other people's books—fuel for my inferiority complex.

Dominick Abel

INTERVIEW BY ROBERT J. RANDISI

RJR: Some simple questions first. What is your background in the publishing business, and why did you become an agent?

DA: I started in publishing in Chicago, in 1966, when I went to work for a magazine called *Christian Century*. It was like *The Nation*, except with an ecumenical orientation. Working there was a very interesting experience, but like most small magazines, it had a small staff and not much room for growth. I was copy editor/proofreader, with little chance of doing anything more substantial.

After about six months, I got a job as an assistant editor at what was then called Henry Regnery Company. (Years later, the name changed to Contemporary Books.) I spent seven or eight years at Regnery. It also had a small staff, but it was a company in transition from a small, very conservative literary house to a house with a much more general emphasis. As part of the new staff there, I got to do a lot of things—more than most editors get to do. I went from editor to senior editor to editor-in-chief to executive vice president. You have to realize that it *sounds* better than it was. There were only half a dozen people who reported to me. I think the title was more a reward for being around than a reflection of my responsibility.

I became an agent because I had a falling-out with management and realized it was time to move on. In Chicago, there really weren't very many other publishing jobs to move on *to*. There were a few trade houses, but they all had people sitting in the chairs I would have wanted. I decided to go into business for myself.

There was another big reason. I was feeling increasingly uncomfortable working for a publisher with whom I found myself in disagreement. I felt it would be a lot easier and more appealing to work for myself and for the writers I represented. When you're an editor at a publishing house, you're responsible to your authors, but naturally you're answerable to your boss, the publisher. When those responsibilities are in conflict, you're put in a very difficult position.

In any case, I set up shop in Chicago early in 1975. I think starting in Chicago was a pretty good strategy, because when I first hung out my shingle, I was something of a rare bird—that agent from out of town. When I visited New York, which I did frequently, people would see me all hours, and I would get a lot accomplished. And I was fortunate in signing up some good Chicago-area writers very quickly. I moved to New York in March of 1977 when my wife, Kathleen, got a job. She had been book editor of the *Chicago Tribune*. She was hired as executive editor of the Literary Guild.

RJR: If we could look out the window of your office, what would we see?

DA: My office is on the first floor, so you would see a typical Upper West Side Manhattan street. One-way traffic, some trees, brownstones across the street. In the summertime, you can see the flowers I have in my window boxes and the planting boxes that constitute my rather pathetic little garden. If you look around my office, in winter and summer, you won't see too many books, but there is a huge collection of Shawnee Pottery. (If you'd like to do an interview about the collection, I'm ready whenever you are.) There are books in the office, of course, but they're all downstairs and next door, in my assistant's office.

RJR: How many clients do you have who are mystery writers?

DA: I'm not big on counting my clients, since it gives me a number that doesn't mean much of anything. I have some clients who haven't written a book in years; some who maybe will never write another one. But they're still my clients. And I have clients, as you well know, who write several books a year. So it doesn't make much sense to count them up and say, "Well, I have fifty or eighty or a hundred clients." As far as mystery writers are concerned, I probably have thirty or forty. If you look at the last Bouchercon program, you'll get a fairly good listing. Bear in mind, though, some of those people use more than one name.

RJR: You did not start out to be the agent to the mystery stars. I know when I came aboard, in 1981, you already had Stuart Kaminsky, Sara Paretsky, and Jonathan Valin. How did it all escalate into the stable you have today?

DA: You're right. I didn't start out to be an agent for mystery writers. I started out to be an agent, period. And I still think of myself as an agent who has a *specialty* in mysteries and mystery writers. I have other specialties as well. I represent quite a number of people who don't write mysteries in fiction and a considerable number who don't write fiction at all.

My very first client, I'm proud to say, was Stuart Kaminsky. Stuart came to see me when I was still an editor. I told him that I was shortly going to be leaving Regnery and setting up an agency and suggested he come back and see me then. He did come back and brought me some pieces of nonfiction to sell. I sold several nonfiction works for Stuart, who at that time was a professor of film.

Then he showed up one day with a novel—a mystery. I liked it very much, and we placed it with St. Martin's. It was the first Toby Peters mystery, *Bullet for a Star*. Before that, the only fiction I had represented with any success was a short story. I sold it to the first place I submitted it, *Harper's* magazine. Even I knew that was a fluke. *Bullet for a Star* was the first mystery novel I sold. Once I started to sell Stuart's mysteries, I kept my eyes open for other mystery writers. When Stuart came across a promising student in the writing class he was teaching, he told her to see me about getting published. That student was Sara Paretsky. I've been working with mystery writers ever since. Coincidentally, this was around the time when mysteries were beginning to become more popular. I was fortunate in timing.

RJR: Have you always enjoyed reading mysteries, or do you just read them now because you have to? And if you don't read them for enjoyment, what do you read?

DA: I've always enjoyed mysteries, particularly American mysteries. Growing up in England as I did, I loved to go to the movies to see what I thought of as cop movies and thrillers. (Now I know that I was seeing the movies of the *film noir* period.) I liked to read Raymond Chandler and writers of that generation very much. America was a fantasyland that I thought about a great deal and mostly experienced through books and movies, particularly mysteries and thrillers. (I also loved Westerns, but that's a whole other story.)

I still read mysteries for pleasure. I vastly prefer ones written by my clients, of course, but I also read mysteries by other writers. But I have other literary interests, too. I like to read other kinds of general fiction. I often read classics. I've gone back to Dickens more than once. I'm not that familiar with really modern literary fiction, but I read plenty of older fiction. I don't read very much nonfiction for pleasure.

RJR: I have heard from editors and authors alike—even your own clients—that you are very intimidating. Is this by design?

DA: Yes, I've heard that, too, and no, it certainly is not by design. I think it's the English accent and the British reserve. But as you well know, Bob, my reserve can be broken down fairly easily. A few drinks and I'm a wild and crazy guy like anybody else. I suspect my reputation for intimidating people is more a matter of people's reaction to the fact that my take on life and relationships is perhaps more formal than other people's. But most of the time I think that a professional reserve is the *appropriate* response. Once in a while, I make a New Year's resolution not to be so scary, but then I go back to being my old intimidating self again.

RJR: The trend in the mystery genre has been heavily in favor of female authors, historical mysteries, and cats for some time now. What do you see as the coming trends?

DA: I think most things that become trends become trends naturally. Take legal thrillers. Legal mysteries became trendy because there were some books published that were very successful. So other people started to write them and publish them and they were successful, too. Eventually, you had a trend, but it developed organically, from the success of a few books. I think that's what has happened with historical mysteries as well. There have been historical mysteries forever. They're not a new trend. Obviously, there is interest in historical mysteries, but again, it's organic rather than deliberate. People did not sit down and say, "What's the new trend? Oh, let's publish historical mysteries."

Of the three that you mentioned, I think that the female authors category is the most interesting. God knows, there have been female authors writing mysteries for a very very long time, but female authors who are writing out of a feminist viewpoint are relatively new. They are there and have been successful because society has *demanded* that they be there.

I guess I've taken a long time to say that I don't have any idea what the new trend will be. I think that the only real trends, when it comes down to it, are good writing and good ideas, a good voice, good narrative drive, and good setting. Those are the qualities that agents and editors will always be looking for. If something comes along, if there's a new success for a certain kind of mystery, undoubtedly that will develop into a trend in the sense that other people will jump on the bandwagon. But I don't think it's a predictable quality. I wish it were. It would make all of our jobs easier.

RJR: Could you expound a bit for us on what you see happening in the publishing business these days, and especially how it will affect the mystery?

DA: I hate to say it, but in my opinion, nothing particularly good is happening in the publishing business. I think that the consolidation of houses and the consequent change in ownership have too often given us people at a very high level who don't have much experience in publishing and don't understand it. They regard publishing simply as a place where money is made. I believe that you just can't look at publishing that way.

Years ago, there was a study done about high-risk investments. At that time, the number-two form of risky investment, according to this study, was Broadway show production. Number one was trade publishing. I think there's still a lot of truth to that. Publishing is *not* a place where people get rich. Some people and some publishers get rich, sure, but there's not a whole bunch of money to spread around.

For the most part, book publishing has always been a marginally profitable business, at least as long as I've been in it, and yet greater demands than ever are being made that books be successful and that publishing houses be successful. Given the budgets that are involved now, if you take a little house with a small budget, the few thousand dollars that can be made on a typical first mystery is a nice little contribution to the overall picture of the house. Take that same book and apply it to the tens or hundreds of millions in the budgets of a *big* house, and a lot of managers will say, "What's the point of doing this book if the best we can reasonably expect is a very modest profit that amounts to a few tens of thousands of dollars? Why not take all of this money and invest it in something that might create a great fountain of money?"

And that, I think, is what we're experiencing today. We're seeing good mystery writers who publish a book or two or three finding it extremely difficult to continue to publish, because houses are saying, and editors are being compelled to say, "You haven't sold enough copies. You haven't grown enough in sales. We're going to set you aside and try somebody new." I think that is the single most significant development in the publishing world as far as mystery writers are concerned: the impatience of publishing managers with slow growth and the demand for a significant and specific return on investment.

At the same time, of course, the smaller houses are finding it harder and harder to compete for books and authors and to compete for shelf space in the stores. After all, the giant publishers have books of every kind. So the smaller houses are having a harder time selling their books and the bigger houses are not in the market to sell the small quantities of books typically sold by mystery writers.

Most specifically, I think there is the problem of reprint publication. With the consolidation of the industry, more and more houses and more and more reprint houses—paperback publishers— have been absorbed by or have themselves absorbed hardcover imprints. And so you have Delacorte/Dell and Dutton/Signet, for instance. When a publisher buys hard/soft, it can be good for the authors, of course. But it also means that the pool of available reprint slots for writers who are *not* bought hard/soft is getting smaller and smaller. If you do not have a hard/soft deal, you may not get published in paperback at all, because the paperback slots have been taken up by the books that were published in the first place by the hardcover arm of the paperback house. And as we all know, the engine that drives sales for all fiction writers is paperback. Even if an author has a hardcover publisher, if the publisher can't get the book into paperback, the author is forced to face the problem of a declining market share. If you don't have paperback publication, the sales don't grow. You have more difficulty getting books out and attention paid.

RJR: If you had the power to *make* something happen in publishing, something that would change the biz, what would it be?

DA: That's easy. If I ran the publishing world, publishers would continue to support writers who are not, at this time, huge successes but who are developing well. I think that's the single most depressing aspect of the business these days—that writers are thrown aside far too soon, far too readily, far too callously and unwisely. I would definitely change that. I would make managers of publishing houses realize that slow and steady wins the race. I would make them see that it makes sense to publish somebody who can develop because he or she writes well and solidly and delivers what is supposed to be delivered. If this writer is allowed to continue, in time he or she will find a market. Oh, another change I'd make is that all my clients would be number-one best-sellers.

RJR: You attend quite a few mystery conventions during the year. Why? What are the benefits for you?

DA: I actually don't go to very many. I go to Bouchercon because it's *the* mystery convention. I go to Malice Domestic because, well, for one thing I'm the agent for Malice Domestic. Before I was the agent, I went because it was the spring convention that filled the gap. Those are the only two I go to with any kind of regularity. I go to other ones when a client of mine is being honored or for some other special reason. And I never miss the Edgars, of course. The food at the banquet is so delicious!

But why do I go? I go because they are fun—or they can be. I like writers very much, and I admire them. I like to see them getting the credit they deserve, as they often do at these conventions. And I like to play poker. I *don't* go to conventions for the panels, because I often don't find them terribly interesting. In fact, I've been known to sneak off to antique malls during some of them.

RJR: Looking back over your career as an agent, have you achieved what you set out to achieve? Are you happy with where you are? And where do you see yourself going in the next five years?

DA: Geez, it sounds as if I'm almost dead. I am not a great believer in asking myself where I'll be in five years. I think it's smart to make tentative plans for the future, but basically, I believe in concentrating on *now*. Twenty-some years ago, I set out as an agent to make a living by representing writers whom I liked personally and I liked professionally because I admired their work. By and large, I've been fortunate in having an agency that gave me these advantages. So, yes, I think my agency has been a success. In five years' time, I hope I'll be doing the same thing I do now. I hope that my writers will be even more successful than they are now. I know that they'll be people I like, because life is too short to be involved intimately, as one is as an agent, with a client one does not like. I have no plans to change the agency itself. It's unlikely to get much larger in terms of clients, because I have a pretty full plate. The staff will probably stay the same, too. Thanks to computers, I can manage with just one assistant.

RJR: What do you do for enjoyment in your free time?

DA: I read. I follow baseball and play in a rotisserie league. (In fact, I'm the agent for The Rotisserie League.) I like to play cards. I'm a fanatic collector of Shawnee pottery. Kathleen collects old cookie jars, and together, we do quite a lot of traveling in search of the ultimate American pottery experience. We like living in New York City, and we do as much as we can to take advantage of the city. We go to the movies often, and we like the theater very much; we go to a lot of plays. In my free time, I visit bookstores and rearrange the shelves so that my clients' books are face out.

RJR: What is you favorite breakfast cereal?

DA: Wheaties, the breakfast of champions. What else?

Tony Hillerman

INTERVIEW BY JAN GRAPE

Mr. Hillerman has a busy schedule, and we were unable to manage a face-to-face or telephone interview, but I mailed questions to him, which he then answered prior to a signing and speaking trip to the West Coast and New Orleans.

I first met Tony at Bouchercon in San Diego in 1989. As a relative newcomer, having only one short story published at that time, my immediate reaction was one of awe. Yet this quiet, modest man listened to me as if I were the well-known best-selling author instead of him. None of our subsequent meetings have changed my opinion. And if you ever have a chance to listen to him speak informally about writing as I did at Left Coast Crime in Scottsdale a couple of years ago, you will come away feeling as if you might be capable of making the grade, too.

Tony Hillerman was born in a small village named Sacred Heart, in Pottawatomie County, Oklahoma, and grew up there during the depression years. Poor by today's standards, the family had no indoor plumbing or electricity until he was in his teens, but none of the children thought of themselves as being poor because everybody else was in the same shape.

He attended the first eight grades at a school for Pottawatomies and learned from an early age that Indians were no different from himself, simply fellow humans.

As a veteran from World War II, his fascination with the Navajo *culture began when he happened upon an Enemy Way Ceremonial being given for two Navajo marines just returned home from the war in the Pacific. He witnessed part of that ceremony.*

JG: I'm assuming that curing ceremony touched you in a major way?

TH: It made a strong impression. I remember thinking this was a mighty fine way to bring someone back from a war. Their whole family clans attended, and they were being cleansed from being among alien cultures. It brings your family and friends together, you're the center of attention, and you're given all these good wishes. All this positive energy is coming your way, and I thought, *Man, this is a great idea.*

JG: Tell me about your own World War II injury when you stepped on a land mine and had broken legs and were temporarily blind. How did it happen?

TH: I was carrying a stretcher, it was dark, and I was following another soldier through the mine field—stepping in his footprints—but the problem was, he had small feet and I have big feet. So I stepped on the mine, and it blew me into the air. I remember thinking, *Boy, this is really going to hurt when I land.*

JG: What effect did being blind for a few weeks have on you as a writer? Or did it?

TH: I didn't sweat it out too much. I guess I was young and healthy and thought I'd be okay, and fortunately, I was. I really hadn't given much thought about being a writer then.

JG: So, when did you decide to be a writer? I know you majored in journalism at OU, so the idea must have been there all along?

TH: When I got back to the States to recuperate, I went to see my mother in Oklahoma City. A newspaperwoman had written this newspaper article about me. She had read my letters and asked my mother to invite me to talk to her when I came home. So I go down and talk to this woman, and she tells me I ought to be a writer.

JG: She came up with this from reading your letters? Boy, those must have been some great letters.

TH: Yes, I wrote all these descriptions of landscape and what I was doing besides the combat stuff. I didn't want my mother to worry about me. I'd never thought about being a writer, but I didn't have anything else to do. My cousin, my best friend when we were growing up on the farm, had always wanted to be a surgeon, but he got his hand mostly shot off in the war. I went to see him in the hospital. He asked me what I was going to do, and I said, "I think I'll be a writer—a journalist." And he said, "Okay, I will be, too."

JG: Just like that, huh? Two journalists were born.

TH: Right.

JG: So you worked as a journalist for seventeen years and taught for twenty-one years and wrote a lot of nonfiction. And somewhere along the line, you decided to write fiction. Why?

TH: I wanted to write the great American novel one day. To see if I could finish a book and sell it, I started with a mystery: *The Blessing Way.* I didn't know if I could do characters or plotting very well, but I knew I could do descriptions. I chose the most beautiful setting I could think of. If the story was weak, at least the readers would enjoy the background. I'd write for a few weeks, then think it wasn't good enough to be published, and I'd put it back on the shelf. Until one day, after a couple of years, I got tired of it and I decided to write a final chapter and send it to my agent. I had an agent selling my nonfiction work.

JG: And what happened? She liked it?

TH: No. I called her, and I don't think she had even sent the book out to an editor. She said it wasn't a mystery and it wasn't mainstream and no one would know what to do with it. And I said, "So, what should I do?" And she said, "Dump it or rewrite it. Take all the Indian stuff out and make it a straight mystery," she added. But I didn't want to do that.

JG: So we nearly lost you at that point? But someone else must have liked it. Someone published it.

TH: About then, I read an article by an editor named Joan Kahn at Harper and Row in one of the writers' magazines. I liked what she said, so I wrote her a brief letter telling her a little about my book—that my agent didn't like it—and asked if she'd take a look at it. She said, "Yes, send it to me." I sent it, and I waited eleven days, and then I called her and asked what she thought. She said, "Didn't you get my letter?" And I said, "No." And she said, "We want to publish the book if you'll write a new last chapter."

JG: So the rest is history?

TH: More or less. That letter Joan Kahn sent saying they wanted to publish the book was a two-page, double-spaced one telling me what all was wrong and that I needed to do some major rewriting. It gave me a chance to expand the character of Joe Leaphorn.

JG: I like that name: Leaphorn.

TH: It's the only name that I made up entirely. All the others are authentic Navajo names: people I've known or people who ask to be in my books or I get them from the Navajo Communications Company telephone directory.

JG: I know you've answered this many times, but just how do the Indians—the Navajo people—feel about your books? Is their reaction positive or negative?

TH: Positive. My books are used in their schools, and I get letters from Navajo kids all the time. In fact, the Tribal Council gave me an award naming me a Special Friend of the Navajo.

JG: That's the only time it's ever been given, isn't it?

TH: Right, and the negative reactions have been minimal, but I once heard from a young Navajo woman who really thought a white man shouldn't be exploiting the Navajo.

JG: I never felt you exploited them, but then I'm not Indian. But if the other Navajos don't feel exploited, then that should take care of it. I know you've read and studied the Navajo and tried to be as accurate as possible in your work.

TH: After *The Blessing Way* was published, I realized I'd learned two things: one, that Leaphorn should be a stronger character; and two, that I didn't know as much about the Navajo culture as I thought I did.

JG: I get the feeling this is not your favorite book. Is that true?

TH: Mostly that's true. There are parts I like and parts I wish I could go back and redo.

JG: We all share that feeling sometimes. You did go ahead and write your non-Indian novel, *The Fly on the Wall*. Did you plan to make John Cotton a series character?

TH: No, I didn't. My plan for that one was it would be a big, important book. It didn't turn out that way, but I still like it. It's still in print, and I get letters now and then from newspaper reporters commenting on it.

JG: Tell me about switching your main characters, and do you recommend this to other writers?

TH: I'll answer the last part first. Sometimes circumstances force you to do things you might not have planned, but no, I wouldn't necessarily tell writers to do it.

And about switching characters: two reasons. One, because I wanted to write about the Checkerboard Reservation where various religions—like Methodist and Baptist and Native American and Roman Catholics and Mormons and fundamentalists—all live and where a melting pot of peoples—Mexicans and Lagunas and Zunis and old Anglo ranchers—are all mixed up in one area. I thought the idea of these religions and cultures rubbing up against each other would make opportunities for what I wanted to do. But Joe Leaphorn didn't fit in there. He was too urbane and sophisticated and old to be amazed or even interested. I tried to write a younger Leaphorn before he got so cynical, but I wasn't comfortable with that either.

Leaphorn was more mature in my mind, and I couldn't fit the younger version to my mental image.

JG: Thus Jim Chee was born.

TH: Yeah. Jim Chee, a younger man but with a more traditional background and an authentic Navajo name. That was one reason I changed characters.

JG: And the other reason?

TH: Came from not reading a contract closely enough. I'd signed a movie/TV option for *Dance Hall of the Dead*. As the contract was written, they bought the continuing rights to the continuing characters by renewing the options. I now owned two-thirds of Joe Leaphorn, but they owned his right leg. I felt I'd been screwed. I didn't want to continue feeling that way, so I retired Leaphorn.

JG: And then somewhere along the line, you decided to put your Navajo policemen together in a book. Brilliant idea.

TH: I wish I could take all the credit for that, but I can't. I was doing a signing at a bookstore—in California, I think—and this woman was talking to me while I was signing. She asked me why I changed my character's name.

JG: She thought you'd just up and changed your character's name?

TH: Yeah, and I tried to tell her how different Leaphorn and Chee were, and she said she couldn't tell them apart. There was a moment of stunned silence while I tried to pull her dagger out of my chest. The funny thing is, you ignore the nice things people say—you think you deserve that—but when anybody says anything critical, oh, man . . . you know. So I couldn't get this out of my mind. Are these guys that much alike? They seemed totally different to me, but I wondered if I'd been kidding myself.

JG: So you put them in the same book?

TH: I wanted to look at them side by side. So Chee was the main character in *Skinwalkers*, but I dumped Leaphorn in there, too. So that lady, whoever she was, gets the credit, and it turned out to be a good idea.

JG: I can see the growth of Leaphorn in the later books with Chee. And I think in many ways, Chee is a stronger character. Do you think the growth of the author is the reason?

TH: Yes, you're right. Until your brain cells begin to die too fast, if you have an interest in something, you continue to learn. With every book I wrote, I was learning.

JG: I personally enjoyed *The Fallen Man* a lot—better than *Sacred Clowns*, I think. Yet I enjoyed the humor in *Clowns*. How about you? Do you like one over the other?

TH: It takes me months after a book is finished to be a judge. I think I prefer *Clowns*.

JG: Do you have a favorite of all you've written?

TH: Yeah, it's *The Thief of Time*. Generally, I think I'd like to go back and rewrite parts of each one—make them better—but in general, it was more clear and had less draggy places than some of the others.

JG: I was impressed with *Finding Moon*, too. I've heard you'd wanted to do this story for a long time, can you tell us why?

TH: During the bloody fracas in the Belgian Congo, I thought it would be a great setting in which to show a character developing. See how a character reacts in the chaos of a collapsing society. By the time I knew how to write it, that awful episode had been forgotten. So I used Vietnam.

JG: What's happened to the movies of your books? I think I read somewhere the first one, *Dark Wind*, had not been released in the U.S. Are they working on another one, or is it a forgotten project?

TH: *Dark Wind* was a disappointment. *Skinwalkers* may be produced in 1997. Who knows?

JG: To keep yourself charged and energized in your writing, are you planning to do a Navajo book and then alternate with something else?

TH: I'm working on another Leaphorn/Chee book. After that, I don't know.

JG: Does the new Leaphorn/Chee book have a title?

TH: Probably *Wrong Eagle*.

JG: As a grandparent myself, I enjoyed hearing how your grandchildren use you and your books as show-and-tell material at school. And I wonder how your adult children feel about this person known as Tony Hillerman?

TH: We all get along very well.

JG: When Aaron Elkins won his Edgar for *Old Bones*, I sent him a note of congratulation. He wrote back that Charlotte still makes him take out the garbage. Does your wife, Marie, still make you take out the garbage?

TH: Worse, she makes me take walks.

JG: Do you have any words of wisdom for aspiring writers?

TH: First, you have to like it yourself. Don't just try to please an audience. Second, don't let other writers read your manuscript. They'll give you advice on how they would write it.

JG: Do you still get rejected?

TH: Not lately.

JG: Who critiques your work? Your editor or agent? Or do you have a close friend who's a good reader?

TH: My editor. And my wife.

JG: Who do you like to read?

TH: I read mostly nonfiction.

JG: What famous book do you wish you had written?

TH: *Red Sky at Morning.*

JG: Who would you like as companion/s on a desert island?

TH: My wife.

JG: If you could live anywhere in the world, where would it be?

TH: Albuquerque, New Mexico.

JG: What type of music do you like?

TH: The old masters and the ballad singers of the sixties and seventies.

JG: What's your favorite color?

TH: Never thought of that.

JG: What would your best pal say about you as a person?

TH: That I'm amiable.

JG: Tell me a secret about Tony Hillerman (a like, dislike, pet peeve, great joy, etc.).

TH: Thunderstorms provide a great joy, reminding me of God's glory. My pet peeve is hypocrisy.

JG: You're always giving interviews. What do you wish someone would ask? Then pretend I just asked you that question, and answer it now.

TH: Since you asked, I think the so-called "War on Drugs" is a terrible mistake. We tried it with that worst killer of all drugs, alcohol. Prohibition was a total failure. Now we repeat with the lesser drugs and get the same results: a huge increase in crime, corrupt police, contempt for foolish, unenforced laws. Either legalize drugs or amend the Constitution to make unilateral mandatory blood tests legal. Then fine or jail the buyers and dry up the market.

JG: Thank you, sir, we appreciate your time.

HILLERMAN BIBLIOGRAPHY

Fiction

The Blessing Way (1970)
The Fly on the Wall (1971)
Dance Hall of the Dead (1973)
Listening Woman (1978)
People of Darkness (1980)
The Dark Wind (1982)
The Ghostway (1984)
Skinwalkers (1986)
A Thief of Time (1988)
Talking God (1989)
Coyote Waits (1990)
Sacred Clowns (1993)
Finding Moon (1994)
The Fallen Man (1996)
Boy Who Made Dragon-fly (for children)

Nonfiction

Hillerman Country
The Great Taos Bank Robbery
Rio Grande
New Mexico
The Spell of New Mexico
Indian Country

Bill Pronzini

INTERVIEW BY ROBERT J. RANDISI

RJR: Let's start with a hard one. What do you feel is your place in the P.I. genre? Leader? Follower? Innovator?

BP: There's no way to answer that without sounding overly modest or overly immodest. Besides which, writers are not very good judges of their own work, and that goes double for anything it may have to offer beyond simple entertainment. I'll say this much: I came into the field as a follower, writing what I loved to read growing up; I have never had any aspirations to be a leader of any kind nor any exaggerated opinions of myself or my work in such a capacity, and while I like to think I've helped to establish the modern school of humanist detective fiction, in which the protagonist is a multidimensional character whose world is of greater importance than any one book's plot ("the confessional school" was one critic's derisive phrase), I don't consider myself an innovator. As to my place, whatever it may be, in any aspect of crime fiction—history will be the judge. If I'm still read fifty or a hundred years from now (assuming anybody still reads books in fifty or a hundred years), then I'll have made some sort of significant contribution; if I'm not, I won't have.

RJR: Continue this lineage of the P.I. story, or reorganize it: Carroll John Daly, Dashiell Hammett, Raymond Chandler, Mickey Spillane, Ross Macdonald . . . ?

BP: Carroll John Daly, Dashiell Hammett, Raymond Chandler, Mickey Spillane, Ross Macdonald, Marcia Muller (or Sue Grafton or Sara Paretsky, lest I be accused of undue bias). There is no question that the most important new direction in the past twenty years is the widespread reader popularity and critical acceptance of the female private eye. Purists such as Lawrence Block, who once said that women shouldn't be writing about tough-minded, self-sufficient women detectives because it violates the private eye tradition, may not like it, but the female P.I. is here to stay. More power to 'em, I say. Personally, I'd much rather contend with Sharon McCone and her creator than with Nameless and his first thing on any given morning.

RJR: You and the Nameless series have had several starts and stops in your careers. In fact, a few Christmases ago, you told me it might be time for both of you to hang it up, yet here you are, back again. [Note: At the time of this interview *Illusions* was being published.] To what do you contribute your continued longevity?

BP: Any number of factors. Such as:

Mule-stubbornness. Critical, editorial, and/or peer misunderstanding or dismissal of my work only makes me more determined to hang around. As an irritant, if nothing else.

The thought of having to try to find a job. After thirty years as a professional writer, I'm virtually unemployable at any level above pizza deliveryperson.

A hyperactive imagination.

A willingness (up to a point) to adapt to changing markets and changing reader tastes.

An aversion to writing the same book or same sort of book twice, even within the framework of the Nameless series. Trying as many different kinds of stories and genres as I feel comfortable with is challenging and helps me grow, stretch, become a better writer.

Corollary to the above, a willingness to take risks in plot, character, style. *Shackles* is one example: a private eye novel that is about as far removed from the traditional variety as it is possible to get, yet is still traditional in spirit. Another example is a recent nonseries novel, *A Wasteland of Strangers*, which is told entirely through the first-person viewpoints of more than a score of small-town citizens.

Luck. This, maybe, most of all.

The retirement question: Yes, there was a time when I gave some serious thought to pasturing Nameless. This was a couple of years ago, after more than a dozen of the New York editorial mavens decreed that the old fellow (and by extension, his creator) had had his day—never mind consistently strong hardcover sales, excellent reviews, and a loyal readership. Very frustrating period. Fortunately, Kent Carroll of Carroll & Graf didn't go along with the majority opinion and rescued Nameless just as he was about to begin munching grass on the south forty. Judging from sales figures on the two Carroll & Graf titles published to date, Kent hasn't had cause to regret his decision.

Will Nameless ever retire? Maybe, someday; depends on the vagaries of publishing and whether or not I run out of stories to tell about him. Will I ever retire? Not if I can help it. Cut back some as I enter my dotage, yes, but that's all. Writers write. What else would motivate me to get out of bed in the morning?

RJR: Talk a bit about your non-Nameless books. Which are your personal favorites? With which were you the most successful in achieving your goal when you started writing it?

BP: A lot of people seem to think *Blue Lonesome* (1995) is my best nonseries book; it made the *New York Times* Notables list for that year, which was gratifying (the more so because my work and I went through a ten-year period in the eighties and nineties in which we were completely ignored by the *Times*). I'd rank it as one of my own favorites, along with *The Running of Beasts*, a 1975 collaboration with Barry Malzberg, and *A Wasteland of Strangers*. But the truth is, I don't feel I've written a really first-rate novel yet, and I doubt I ever will. (*Shackles* and *Blue Lonesome* probably come closest, with the fewest flaws of any of my series and nonseries books.) Though of course I intend to keep on trying.

RJR: In the past you have collaborated with Collin Wilcox, John Lutz, Barry Malzberg, and your wife, Marcia Muller. Who do you wish you could have collaborated with? And would you ever collaborate again with someone other than Marcia?

BP: With the exception of a mainstream novel, *The Cambodia File*, which I did with Jack Anderson, and which was a monumental headache from start to finish, I've always enjoyed collaborating. For one thing, it eases the loneliness of the long-distance writer. For another, it's easier for two heads to work out a complicated plot than it is for one. And the third and main reason is that collaborating allows two writers to create a third voice: a blending of styles and visions of each to create a composite that is different, if only subtly, from each alone. For that last reason alone, I'd love to have collaborated with Chandler, Woolrich, McBain, and dozens of others just to find out what the third voice would've been. I suspect that in one or two cases, it might have been something special, but that in most, the work wouldn't have equaled that of either individual.

Would I collaborate with anyone other than Marcia at this stage of my career? Probably not. She and I have done some fairly good fiction together, because we know each other's work so well and because we have similar philosophies; we don't argue, at least not much, during the process. Recently, we perpetrated a collaborative short story for an anthology of original tales by married writers, and we coedited an anthology of our own, *Detective Duos*, for Oxford University Press. We'll probably do other shorts together, though no more anthologies (which are not as satisfying as fiction). We've discussed writing another McCone/Nameless adventure, but I doubt it'll happen, since we have different publishers with different agendas.

RJR: You were inspired by many writers before you, and you have inspired many writers who came after you—Marcia and myself, included. Who do you think are the authors today who will inspire a future generation of writers?

BP: Again, I doubt there's any way to make an accurate prediction. Generally speaking, it seems to be the megabucks best-sellers who inspire modern professionals and newcomers; everybody wants an immediate ride on the golden mare. The current hot trend is the John Grisham/Scott Turow–style legal thriller. Tomorrow . . . who knows? As to whether or not best-sellers such as Grisham and Turow will continue to inspire writers in this or the next generation, my best guess is no. I think we'd be hard-pressed to find a single contemporary writer who would own up to being influenced by the likes of Gene Stratton Porter, Harold Bell Wright, Florence Barclay, Clarence Budington Kelland, or Ross Lockridge. Yet they were all huge best-sellers in their day, Porter having authored five of the biggest blockbusters prior to 1945.

RJR: When you first started writing, there were no annual mystery fan conventions. (Yes, you started that long ago.) Over the years, there has been a proliferation of them. Who do you think these conventions are important to?

BP: The early conventions were of primary interest to fans. I attended the second Bouchercon, which was held at an Oakland airport motel, and there were maybe five other writers and no editors among the seventy-five or so attendees. Nowadays, Bouchercons draw upwards of two thousand people annually, a large percentage of whom are writers, editors, agents, and media representatives. A lot of business is done at Bouchercon and other conventions, so I'd say that presently, they're just as important, if not more important, to professionals.

RJR: This is a slightly different question than the first one. How do you think you are perceived by others in this business? How would you like to be perceived?

BP: Judging from the difficulty I had in finding a new publisher for Nameless and the open attitude of some critics and publishing personnel, I'd say I'm largely ignored or dismissed as just another prolific hack. As if the mere fact of being prolific has anything to do with the quality of one's work. Does this frustrate and anger me? Yes, particularly in view of the fact that at least a dozen writers who have published far more than me—in some cases, such as Ed McBain and Lawrence Block, up to three times as much—are seldom if ever subjected to the same criticism. Does it make me bitter? Yes. But not for the reasons you might think. I write because it's what I do; I can't help it if words come more quickly to me than to someone else. I don't publish first drafts; I couldn't if I wanted to, because they're invariably terrible. I rewrite extensively because I care about my work and because it's the only way I know to make it better—just as constant writing and revising are the only ways I know to make myself a better craftsman today than I was yesterday. One thing for sure: I'm a far better writer now than when I sold my first story in 1966; I'm a better writer than I was five years or even one year ago. Anyone who judges me and my work without reading what I've published recently is doing me an injustice. I'd like to force-feed novels such as *Blue Lonesome*, *Illusions*, and *A Wasteland of Strangers* to the "prolific hack" critics; they might not like what these novels say, but if they possess even an iota of objectivity, they'd be hard-pressed to dismiss any one as hackwork.

Enough ranting. I'll be good now.

What do I want out of this business? Respect, especially peer respect. That's all.

How do I want to be perceived? As a writer who works damn hard to make himself as good as he can be, and who is succeeding.

RJR: If a young writer came to you today and said he wanted to write P.I. fiction, what should he read first? What would you tell him? If it was a woman, what would you tell her?

BP: I'd tell the young prospect to read *all* the major writers in the development of P.I. fiction, beginning with Hammett and working forward to the present, and not limiting selections to the big names only. That's what I'd say, but I'll bet I could give that advice to a hundred wannabes and maybe one would follow it. There's little sense of history among today's writers, successful professionals as well as newcomers. If a book or story was published more than five years ago, they're not interested. The reason for this is money, of course. There's a great deal of money to be made in crime fiction today, and it doesn't seem to matter to those who covet similar rewards that only a very few writers are getting rich, and the ones who are, are doing it by writing their own work, not by copying others or following or trying to anticipate trends. Too many people keep trying to be the next Elmore Leonard, the next Sue Grafton, which is why there are so many exploitative, overblown, and just plain bad novels. Professionals and newcomers both would be a lot better off in the long run if they were willing to pay their dues, earn their shot at the big time through understanding of their chosen field and development of their own talent.

RJR: If you could make a living writing either novels or short stories, which would you choose, and why?

BP: Short stories. Ideas are easier to come by (for me, anyhow), they're fairly simple to plot now that I've published some 250, and best of all, the creative process from conception to completion is relatively brief. Novels require a lot more work and a lot more patience. The best works of fiction I've written, I think, are short stories. If there were enough modern markets for shorts to allow me to earn a living from writing them, then I would probably do novels only occasionally. Having said that, I would still rather write a really first-rate novel than a really first-rate short story. Greater difficulty, greater satisfaction.

RJR: Speaking of short stories, why have you edited so many anthologies over the years? Do you intend to continue?

BP: I've done so many anthologies because they're relatively easy to compile, since I have a large collection of books and magazines and have read widely in different fields; because I enjoy shepherding good stories, particularly by little-known writers, back into print; and because they paid well enough in lean years to keep my creditors at bay.

No, I doubt I'll edit many more. As I mentioned, I've just finished one with Marcia on detective teams, and I recently compiled one with Ed Gorman called *American Pulp* that focuses on stories from the fifties and sixties, but those were special cases, and two of only three anthologies I've been involved in since 1990. Unless someone makes me an offer I can't refuse—not too likely in the anthology market these days—*Detective Duos* and *American Pulp* will probably be my last. I'd rather spend my time writing novels and stories of my own.

RJR: What are some of the more important developments in the P.I. genre over the past twenty years?

BP: I pretty much answered that question earlier, I think. The female private eye novel is *the* most important development in the subgenre in the past twenty years. The second most important is the influx of ethnic writers and ethnic detective characters, most prominently African-Americans such as Walter Mosley and Easy Rawlins, Gar Anthony Haywood and Aaron Gunner. It may well be that Mosley's name will follow Marcia's or Grafton's or Paretsky's in the lineage list in the second question. In any case, gender and ethnic diversity is one of the things helping to keep the field fresh, and it also helps to open up possibilities for new writers with new approaches and ideas.

RJR: If you were breaking into the writing business now, how would you go about it?

BP: One of the saddest facts about the current genre-fiction marketplace is that there are so few training grounds left. By that I mean magazines that regularly buy short fiction (only *Ellery Queen's Mystery Magazine* and *Alfred Hitchcock's Mystery Magazine* are left in our field), and book publishers willing to buy modest first novels and continue to buy subsequent efforts while an author learns his or her craft and builds a readership. Nowadays, with the intense and unreasonable emphasis on fat, best-seller–type novels in all categories, a new writer has to be very good to start with (or else very lucky). I had a pretty raw talent when I started out in the late sixties; what saved my butt were the training grounds that were much more prevalent back then. Frankly, if I were trying to make it as a professional fiction writer today, using the tools I had in 1966, I'd either fail completely or at best have a much less successful and no doubt shorter career than I've enjoyed—and books such as *Shackles* and *Blue Lonesome* would never have been written. The really tragic thing is that many young writers are at the same stage I was thirty-some years ago, and most of them will never make it far enough to write novels that might well be *better* than any I've done or will do.

As to how I'd go about breaking in, first and as already noted, I'd read everything of significance in the area I wanted to work in; study plot, structure, characterization, internalize the methods successful writers use to achieve their effects, and forget everything else about their work; then sit down and tell my own stories in my own way. And I'd keep on doing my own work, whether it sells or not. I'd believe in myself and what I was writing; that's what is important, not any of the trappings (money, fame) that come out of the work if they come at all. I'd write every day, even if it was only a paragraph or two. You can't be a writer if you don't write!

RJR: Pick an era to have lived and written in, and tell us why you chose it.

BP: This may surprise you, but my first choice is the present. I like what I'm able to write now. I like the complete freedom of expression in genre fiction today: no restrictions in style, subject matter, character type, or development. If I had to pick another era, it would be the thirties and forties, of course, when pulp magazines were the main form of popular fiction; I'd have been right at home contributing to *Black Mask*, *Dime Detective*, and the like. On the other hand, the pulps were a restrictive ghetto; one needed to produce a vast amount of fiction at one cent and two cents per word in order to pay the bills, and that left most pulpsters with little time, energy, or inclination to do more ambitious work. Too many talented writers in those days never progressed to their potential for that reason.

RJR: Okay, somebody asks you what three books of yours they should sit down and read, three books that would really tell them what Bill Pronzini is all about. What's your answer?

BP: Three Nameless books: *Shackles*, *Illusions*, and *Sentinels*. Three nonseries novels: *Blue Lonesome*, *A Wasteland of Strangers*, and *With an Extreme Burning*. These titles contain everything I am and am trying to do as a fiction writer—so far.

RJR: Finally, where are the mystery and P.I. genres going in the next ten years?

BP: I'm not so sure there will be a P.I. subgenre in another twenty or thirty years. The form may, in fact, be a twentieth-century phenomenon that is unadaptable to the technology-controlled and -altered society of the future. That's a long-range prediction, and one I hope is dead wrong. In the short run, I think we'll see a spate of high-tech, high-concept P.I. stories dealing with computer crimes, industrial and political espionage at home and abroad, that sort of thing—books this old technophobic traditionalist will never read. I think the old-fashioned male private eye will be around for a while, too, though the multidimensional ones like Nameless, who appeal to a broader range of readers of both genders, stand a better chance of survival than the ultratough, antiauthority, hard-drinking, and woman-chasing loner, who has pretty much had his day. And I think the female P.I. will be around as long as her male counterpart, maybe longer, though again, there'll be quite a few less than there are now.

Mystery fiction in general? Well, as long as there are books being published and people to read them, we'll have crime fiction of one kind or another, whether it's packaged as such or not. (The line separating genre suspense and mainstream fiction has so blurred that publishers find it all too easy to package one as the other.) General reader interest isn't likely to wane enough to kill the form. About the only things that can kill it, in fact, are the conglomerates who control so much of publishing and their increasingly irrational emphasis on huge profits, and—ironically enough—the Great God Technology, with future advancements, directions, and changes that our generation can't even imagine.

Elizabeth Peters

INTERVIEW BY DEAN JAMES

I n 1966, a young writer named Barbara Mertz published her first novel, The Master of Blacktower, *under the pseudonym of Barbara Michaels. Two years later, she published her first novel under the name of Elizabeth Peters,* The Jackal's Head. *In "real life," Barbara G. Mertz earned a Ph.D. in Egyptology from the famed Oriental Institute of the University of Chicago, and she published two very popular nonfiction works on the political history and the daily life of ancient Egypt. In the three decades since the appearance of her first novel, Barbara Michaels has become a best-selling writer, and Elizabeth Peters's books fly off the shelves as well. Michaels became known primarily as a writer of romantic suspense in the tradition of writers like Mary Stewart and Phyllis A. Whitney. Often mixing elements of the supernatural with more mundane terrors, Michaels can spin a web of suspense that keeps her readers sleepless. The books of Elizabeth Peters, on the other hand, are more akin to traditional mystery novels. Although her early novels were also cast in the romantic suspense vein, Elizabeth Peters soon invested her work with a healthy sense of humor and some rather innovative notions about the abilities of women and their relationships with men—ideas that were quite radical for the mystery and romantic suspense fiction of the time. From their very beginnings, two of Peters's mystery series characters, Jacqueline Kirby and Vicky Bliss, defied the conventional wisdom that any single woman in a mystery novel had to marry a hero at the end of the book. If either of these women ended up with a man at the end of a novel, it was by her choice and on her terms; and if there was no man around at the end, well, that worked, too. Several years before Marcia Muller launched the rebirth of the female sleuth with her novel* Edwin of the Iron Shoes *(1977), Elizabeth Peters and Barbara Michaels were busy writing about liberated and intelligent women confronting and tackling challenging situations with their own capable hands. The very first Guest of Honor at Malice Domestic, Barbara Mertz has won many honors in her career, including a lifetime achievement award from Bouchercon, an Agatha Award for Best Novel for* Naked Once More, *a Grand Master award from Mystery Writers of America, and an honorary doctorate from Hood College, as well as the unabashed adoration of her legions of fans, both male and female, around the world. She took time out from a busy writing schedule, immersed in the continuing adventures of Amelia Peabody Emerson, to allow "Elizabeth Peters" her say in her own inimitable fashion.*

DJ: What writers and/or books influenced the type of fiction that you wanted to write?

EP: If I wanted to be pompous, which I often do, I would say (truthfully) that every writer I've ever read has influenced my work—and then I'd give you a list, starting with Plato. The strongest influences, obviously, are from writers of thrillers and mysteries. I never read Nancy Drew, went straight to Agatha and Dorothy, Chandler and Ellery Queen—and to the fantasy writers my dad favored. It may have been Lovecraft and the other Weird Tales crowd who began my interest in horror stories. And of course there were H. Rider Haggard and John Buchan, from whom I borrow unashamedly.

DJ: When did you first realize that you were funny? And was there a conscious decision to make humor an important part of the Elizabeth Peters books?

EP: Am I funny? I hope so. As one of my characters once remarked, "Laughter is one of the two things that make life worthwhile." (Actually, I would make that four things—adding gin and chocolate.) In fact, I had a hard time convincing my then-editor that I could get away with humor in a mystery context. *The Camelot Caper* (1969) was the first book in which I let myself go, and the poor man was extremely dubious about the whole thing. People seemed to like it, so I was allowed to proceed from there. I still don't understand why he reacted as he did. Male writers had been producing comic mysteries for some time. I guess maybe it was, at that time, a new venture for women.

DJ: Is there any truth to the rumor that you are the illicit love child of H. Rider Haggard and Dorothy L. Sayers?

EP: Make that illicit *grand*child, if you don't mind.

DJ: Did readers and critics notice, back in the 1960s and 1970s, that Peters heroines like Vicky Bliss and Jacqueline Kirby weren't the standard-issue suspense-novel heroines?

EP: Some readers did; I can't remember that any critic was perceptive enough to notice I was being innovative, brilliant, and groundbreaking. The first Vicky, *Borrower of the Night*, which was published in 1973, was, I believe, the first liberated gothic. I can't think of an earlier mystery in which the heroine turned down both ardent suitors and blackmailed another guy into giving her a job. (This is where we miss dear Ellen Nehr, isn't it? She probably could think of one.) I'm proud of that, and I am still slightly annoyed at being overlooked by feminist critics. Thanks for asking, Dean!

DJ: Did you feel you were taking any risks by writing about such unusual women in a convention-ridden genre? Weren't you pretty much a "lone voice crying in the wilderness" for most of that time period?

EP: Thanks for asking that one, too. I don't believe I thought of myself as being a lone voice—though for a good many years, I guess I was—or of taking chances. I did my thing, and luckily for me, I found an audience of receptive readers who have been incredibly supportive and loyal. And, at the risk of sounding vain (something I constantly avoid) I think the books can be enjoyed on several different levels. It's only *very* clever critics like yourself who notice my subtler techniques.

DJ: In your career, there have been some significant changes in mystery publishing. What do think are the best changes? The worst?

EP: The great thing that has happened with mystery publishing is the expansion of the definitions and limits of the genre. The classics of the first golden age were almost all puzzles: whodunits. The second golden age produced writers as diverse as Reg Hill, Joan Hess, Charlotte MacLeod—the list is endless, and the additional richness such writers have contributed is vast. The worst thing? Take your pick: the excessive concentration on publicity, especially book tours, which I hate—it takes time away from writing, which is, after all, the point of the whole thing, and puts an additional burden on the beleaguered author—or the recent focus on blockbuster best-sellers to the detriment of good, solid, so-called midlist writers. We're losing potential talent because publishers want instant gratification and big profits, and they aren't willing to let a writer develop at his or her own pace.

DJ: Has Elizabeth Peters traveled to all the marvelous and exotic places that her characters have in the books?

EP: Yes, lucky creature, she has. And plans to go on doing so as long as her strength holds out. When it fails, she will be carried around in a litter. [Ed. Note: May I go ahead and put in my application right now as chief litter-bearer?]

DJ: What are the most endearing characteristics of your three series heroines, Vicky Bliss, Jacqueline Kirby, and Amelia Peabody Emerson?

EP: Hmm, well, some people would claim they have no endearing characteristics. All I can do is give you my opinion. In some ways, Jacqueline is the least sympathetic of the three; she is inhumanly competent, sharp-tongued, and cynical. I like her because she *is* sure of herself and not about to take any crap from anybody. The same thing could be said of Vicky and Amelia, but they have weaknesses Jacqueline hasn't demonstrated—and it is their weaknesses I enjoy as much as their strengths. Vicky is overconfident and too quick to leap to conclusions. "Sometimes I am wrong," she admits—and that's endearing, I think—not only that she is wrong sometimes, but that she can admit it. Amelia seldom admits she is wrong, but the perceptive reader will notice that she is very insecure on some levels, and the discrepancies between what she says and what she does make her, for me, both comical and attractive. Of course, the main thing about all three is that though they are ardent feminists, they all *adore* men. Especially certain men.

DJ: What are their most exasperating qualities?

EP: My dear, they have no exasperating qualities. I modeled all three to some extent on myself.

DJ: Is any of them more difficult to write, for some reason, than the others? Jacqueline and Amelia are particularly strong-willed, I think. Vicky is stubborn, too, but in a different way.

EP: It all depends on the mood I'm in and on the plot possibilities that come to mind. Some plots demand certain characters. I do Vicky when I'm feeling sentimental and romantic—or when a delicious scam comes to mind—but I guess Amelia is the one I find easiest to write about. Which leads us on to—

DJ: Amelia seems the nearest and dearest to your heart these days. Why? What is it about her that appeals more to you as a writer?

EP: It's true that at the moment I am more engaged with Amelia; I think it is in part because my interest in Egyptology has reawakened. It was always there, to some extent, but I've made three trips to Egypt in the past five years, and every time I go, I become more hypnotized by the country and the subject. The second reason is that I had, recently, one of those breakthroughs that sometimes (only too rarely) occurs with a writer. I now have clear in my mind the general plot outlines for the next four books, even the titles. This has never happened to me before. I can hardly wait to see how it is all going to work out.

DJ: What are the particular challenges in writing the Amelia books? What are the easy bits, if any?

EP: The challenges are also the rewards. Avoiding anachronisms and getting the background details right is a lot of work, but I enjoy that kind of nit-picking research. Perhaps the greatest challenge arises from the fact that I pinned the books and the characters down in time. I didn't do that deliberately, because at the beginning, I didn't intend to write a series. If I had intended to, I might have finessed the dates and the ages of the characters, and—above all else!—not given Amelia and Emerson a child who was bound to get older with each passing year. Ramses is twelve in the latest book [*The Hippopotamus Pool*]. He will be sixteen in the next, nineteen in the succeeding volume, and so on. I have to make him a believable (well, more or less) adult and yet retain his distinctive characteristics. The same is true, to a lesser extent, of the other characters. It's enormous fun! The easy bits relate to the relationship between Amelia and Emerson. I can write their dialogue when I'm half asleep. (No comments, please.)

DJ: The latest Amelia novel, *The Hippopotamus Pool*, introduces a new character, David, whom we all hope to see again. Will we see further complications to the Ramses/Nefret relationship in upcoming books? *The Hippopotamus Pool* also brought back Evelyn and Walter Emerson; will we get to see more of them?

EP: You will indeed see David again. One of the things I enjoy about these books is the cast of supporting characters. I've gotten to know many of them quite well; I think about them, worry about them, and wonder what is going to happen to them. With Evelyn, for instance, it seemed to me quite reasonable that—devoted mother though she is—she would be a little envious of Amelia's adventurous life, so I gave her a parasol and a chance to have a few adventures of her own. I use these characters as I need them, but I have a certain fondness for them. Kevin O'Connell, the young journalist, has been frustrated in love several times; I think he needs a wife, and one day, I may give him one. Abdullah is getting old; what am I going to do about the dear fellow? (I have an idea.) Ramses and Nefret . . . I know how that relationship is going to turn out, but there are a good many complications for them and me to work out before the culmination. And what about Sethos, the master criminal, my favorite villain? Is he really dead? *Who is (or was) he, really?*

DJ: What's next for Elizabeth Peters?

EP: You should have a pretty good idea, from the above, what is next for Elizabeth Peters. I want to do another Vicky one of these days—not only because she and John still have a long way to go before they can straighten out their relationship, but so that I can play a particular joke involving a certain famous fictional detective who specializes in art thefts. However, my major concentration for a while will be on Amelia and company. I am having almost as much fun with these books as some of my readers appear to have, and although I know in general terms what is going to happen, I can't wait to see *how* it will happen.

DJ: As a scoop, Elizabeth Peters gave us her titles for the upcoming new volumes in the adventures of Amelia Peabody Emerson and crew:

Vol. 9: *Seeing a Large Cat* (Warner, 1997)

Vol. 10: *The Ape Who Guards the Balance*

Vol. 11: *Serpent on Your Brow*

Vol. 12: *Thunder in the Sky*

[Ed. Note: There are no publication dates yet for these, but fans will be awaiting them eagerly. Just like me.]

Minette Walters

INTERVIEW BY ADRIAN MULLER

W ith just five novels to her name, Minette Walters has become one
of the big names in crime fiction. She burst onto the scene with
The Ice House *in 1992, winning the Crime Writers' Association's
John Creasey Award for Best First Crime Novel. Her two subse-*
quent titles, The Sculptress *and* The Scold's Bridle, *respectively won the
Edgar Allan Poe Award from the Mystery Writers of America and the
CWA's Gold Dagger Award, both for Best Novel of the Year. Her fourth
novel,* The Dark Room, *was a huge hit, and the author's fifth,* The Echo,
*went straight to the top of the British best-seller lists within a week of being
published.*

*Walters's work has been compared with Agatha Christie, P. D. James,
and Ruth Rendell, placing her firmly in the English tradition of suspense
writing. In this interview, the author talks about her writing and her interests in crime and fiction.*

Minette Walters was born Minette Caroline Mary Jebb in Bishops's
Stortford, Hertfordshire, in 1949. Her father died when she was nine
years old, and she and her two brothers were brought up by their
mother, Colleen Jebb. The family's only income was the small state
pension they received, and to supplement this, Walters's mother used
her artistic talent to paint miniatures from photographs sent by people

who had seen her advertisement in the *Times*. "We had very little money," says Walters, "and I often wonder how we would have managed if my mother hadn't been so gifted. She taught me that women can do anything when they put their minds to it." All three children won scholarships to boarding school, in Minette's case to Godolphin School where girls were encouraged to go on to university.

Before going to university, Walters took a year off and traveled to Israel in a group of young men and women. They were taking part in a six-month voluntary service scheme called The Bridge in Britain. The scheme was set up by Greville Janner, a member of parliament, and was designed to strengthen the relationship between Israel and the United Kingdom. The author speaks fondly of that time abroad. "I always say that if I had to choose between my right arm or give up that period between school and university, I'd give up my right arm without a second's hesitation. It was the most formative time of my life because I'd spent five years in an all-girls' institution, and I was suddenly offered unlimited freedom. You grow up very quickly in those circumstances. Also, I developed a hatred of all forms of prejudice, which exists everywhere and is almost always based on ignorance."

On her return to England, Minette Walters attended Durham University, where she obtained a degree in French. She attended few lectures but wrote many short stories without ever having anything published. "It was weird, surreal material, she remembers, very postmodernist." After a succession of temporary jobs to pay off her overdraft from university, she joined IPC magazines as a subeditor/journalist where she eventually became editor of a romantic fiction publication. In a roundabout way, this job would lead to Walters's career as a crime novelist.

"I shared an office with another editor called Patrick Cunningham, who had won several prizes for short-story writing, and I complained endlessly about the quality of stuff that was being submitted to us. I was reading upwards of two hundred manuscripts a month. That's a lot of reading!" Fed up with her complaints, Walters's colleague challenged her to write a romantic novelette herself. "So I did, and ended up writing thirty. It was good training, because in those days, the discipline of romantic novelette writing was very tight—thirty-thousand words maximum, no sex, no strong drink, and only chaste kissing—and it was a challenge to create realistic plots and characters from unrealistic ingredients."

All of these novelettes were published under pseudonyms, which still remain well-kept secrets. "I wrote them for money," says Walters, "and they each took me approximately two weeks to write. I'd rather be remembered for what I do now."

Patrick Cunningham was also instrumental in persuading her to try her hand at writing something in a different genre. "He told me that I was wasting my talent, because I had the ability to write anything I wanted to. He, more than anyone else, persuaded me to have a bash at something different, although it was some time before I actually did so."

Before starting on her first full-length novel, Minette Jebb left IPC to work freelance, married Alec Walters in 1978, and had two sons to whom she is devoted, although she adds with a laugh, "They temporarily destroyed my career. Babies and writing don't mix, not for me anyway. I need peace and quiet if I want to work." So it wasn't until her youngest son started full-time education that Walters began work on *The Ice House*.

The suggestion that Minette Walters write something that could win a prestigious literary award was a thought she never considered. "The only thing that ever interested me was whether I had the ability to write crime fiction," she says. "I'm very fond of the genre, and I'm also very interested in criminology and psychology. I have read vast quantities of true crime books, and I wanted to blend all these interests together."

Explaining why motivation is at the heart of her writing, Walters says, "I take a handful of people, explore why one of them has suffered a violent death. Where," she wonders, "does the level of anger and dysfunction, which must exist in order for this most traumatic of acts to occur, come from? It fascinates me."

Walters's first contact with crime fiction was, like that of so many other readers, through classic mystery authors such as Agatha Christie. Though she is eager to avoid the "general dumping on Agatha," as she puts it, she agrees with fellow writer Michael Dibdin that the queen of crime's success was responsible for hijacking British crime fiction for a very long time. "Publishers," she says, "just weren't interested in putting out something that did not conform to the Christie format. Consequently, only authors with similar styles, like Ngaio Marsh and Margery Allingham, were published."

About the latter author Walters adds, "I think Margery Allingham was a brilliant writer, but sadly, she is not as well-known as her contemporaries. She really was remarkable, because her stories had a much more violent streak than Christie's or Marsh's."

Returning to the subject of Agatha Christie, Walters says she initially considered Miss Marple a "more realistic character" than Hercule Poirot, but now believes that David Suchet's television portrayal of the Belgian sleuth has turned Poirot "into a deeply compassionate man, transforming the character into something very convincing."

For Walters, Christie's strongest point was the writer's powers of social observation. "Something that nobody nowadays ever gives Christie credit for is her sharp portrayal of English middle-class life in the thirties, forties, and fifties. I always say that people should read Agatha Christie if they want to know how people of that period talked, dressed, and ate—it can all be found in her books in meticulous detail."

Walters repudiates the general attitude in Britain that crime fiction has little literary value. "It's not pukka to write crime fiction," she asserts. "It's pulp, according to the great and the good, but I would defy anybody who says Ruth Rendell doesn't write literature. Rendell and P. D. James inherited Agatha Christie's mantle and gave it a modern twist. I feel Rendell's books paved the way and allowed me to write my novels, which are also one-offs. I frequently wonder if I would have been as fortunate if Ruth Rendell hadn't already established this principle."

The author enjoys reading all styles of crime fiction but concentrates her defense on that of the traditional genre. She does not agree that these novels merely exist to pose a mystery. "I think analytical and puzzle-based novels treat social issues in a different way. Mine tend to concentrate on a claustrophobic environment, often with a family at the heart of them." Quoting a statistic that 70 percent of all murders occur within the family environment, Walters is convinced that infinitely more damage is done in a domestic situation. "That is where I differ entirely from a hard-boiled novel," she says, "because instead of bringing the action out onto the streets, I'm taking it right into this enclosed environment, be it a family, a village, or both."

The claustrophobic village, and a family of sorts, are at the heart of *The Ice House*. In the opening pages, the murdered body of an unknown man is found in the building of the title, a structure used to keep food cool in the days before fridges. This ice house lies in the grounds of a mansion owned by Phoebe Maybury. Phoebe lives a secluded life with two female friends, Diana Goode and Anne Cattrell, all the subjects of malicious village gossip due to the unsolved disappearance of David Maybury, Phoebe's husband.

Walters explains the origins of her first novel. "I'd been thinking about a plot where I could isolate three women within a community, making their relationships very introspective because nobody wants to talk to them. Clearly murder was a great way to achieve this, making people suspicious of them and the circumstances in which they lived. I was interested in exploring whether women would support each other in such a situation. In *The Ice House*, this was very much the case."

A further theme, also frequently revisited in Walters's books, is the difficulty caused by noncommunication in relationships, especially those between men and women. In *The Ice House*, this is most prominently the case between Anne Cattrell, an acerbic journalist, and Sergeant Andy McLoughlin, one of the investigating policemen.

"What I do in these relationships is to try and show that both sexes are deeply vulnerable when it comes to emotional involvement. The idea that relationships are ever easy is crazy. This whole concept of love at first sight, I simply don't believe in it. I'm sure it does happen on the odd occasion, but I truly feel that relationships only work when mutual respect is established between two people. One way of doing that is to have them challenge each other. Then, once you've got a mutual respect, I think you automatically get mutual liking, and liking is so important in a relationship. You really *do* have to like the other person if you intend to spend a lot of time with them!" With a laugh, Walters adds, "Fancying someone rotten, that part of it passes."

The author frequently upsets readers when they ask her if she thinks Cattrell and McLoughlin went on to marry. "I tell them that I think it is highly unlikely. They probably would have such a row after six months, that they would just split up."

Walters does not feel she could sustain a series, believing that, by the end of her books, she always has written all that can be told about the characters. "What I might do one day," she admits, "is revisit a character readers wouldn't necessarily expect me to write about. Somebody like Phoebe Maybury for instance."

Walters remembers the commotion when it became apparent that none of the characters from *The Ice House* would appear in her subsequent novel. Lots of publishers offered her more money, but only if she agreed to write a series. "I had already done about 75 percent of *The Sculptress*," she remembers, "when I got these frantic calls from my agent saying, 'Minette, you've got to write a series!' Thank God *The Sculptress* was as well-received as *The Ice House*," she says, laughing. "Of course, when that was published, I was constantly asked, 'Are you going to write a series with Roz and Hal?'"

Roz is Rosalind Leigh, who together with Olive Martin and Hal Hawkesley are the three main characters in *The Sculptress*. Rosalind, coping with a personal tragedy, is persuaded by her agent to write a book about Olive Martin. Olive is in prison, convicted for murdering her mother and sister. During her research, Roz manages to secure the reluctant cooperation of Hawkesley, Olive's arresting officer, which leads her to discover new evidence suggesting that Olive may be innocent. In her search for further proof, a fragile relationship develops between Rosalind and Hal. The inspiration for *The Sculptress* came from an incident Walters had as a prison visitor, a voluntary activity the author started long before her career as a novelist. "I was assigned to see a new prisoner," Walters says, "a mountain of a man who told me he was on remand for rape. It really was quite terrifying," she says. "There I was, sitting in this tiny little room with this extraordinary man who was four times my size. I was very aware that he could quite easily kill me—there would have been absolutely nothing I could have done about it. Then, once we started talking, it turned out he was completely and utterly charming, one of the nicest people I've ever met."

Before the case could come to trial, it became clear that the man was not guilty, and the charges were dropped. Yet the incident gave Walters pause for thought. "It disturbs me that we judge each other by what we look like," she says. "We all do it, and I don't think we'll ever stop, but I began to wonder: *Supposing those charges hadn't been withdrawn and he had gone to court. Would he have been found innocent when the immediate impression he made was so unpleasant?*" Walters developed the idea into a plot, changing the sex of the prisoner along the way, and was awarded an Edgar for her efforts.

Three years later, *The Sculptress* became the first of Walters's books to be adapted for television by the BBC. It stayed close to the book and successfully kept the ambiguity of the novel's ending. "I still get letters asking me whether Olive Martin was guilty or not, but I feel it is up to the reader to be the jury," says Walters, refusing to comment on Martin's culpability. However, she will admit that her protagonist "was certainly clever enough to have done it."

Unlike some writers, who are dismayed by inaccurate adaptations of their work, Walters is thrilled with the results of the television production. "I thought the series was very good," says Walters, "because it made exciting television. They caught the atmosphere extremely well. I was a bit concerned that Pauline Quirke, who plays Olive Martin, would just be so good that the others would find it very difficult to match up, but I thought Caroline Goodall as Rosalind Leigh was fantastic. She looked the part and sounded great. She was perfect, absolutely excellent." In fact, Walters praises all those involved with the production, which explains her agreeing to collaborate on a television sequel to *The Sculptress*. "I'm not going to write it," she stresses, "but I'm giving them the ideas so that a script can be developed."

As to why her second book made it to the screen before her other novels, Minette Walters offers various explanations. "For some reason, I think *The Sculptress* was conceived as a much more easily visualized book than *The Ice House* or *The Scold's Bridle*. Perhaps because, in a funny sort of way, it is the most conventional. It is more conformist and has these acceptable parameters that perhaps don't exist in the other novels. Having said all that, we're getting absolutely as much interest for the film rights to the other books."

Since Walters was so happy with the dramatization of *The Sculptress*, she is delighted that the BBC has gone on to produce *The Ice House* and *The Scold's Bridle* as well.

Minette Walters's third novel, *The Scold's Bridle*, was also published to great acclaim, this time winning a CWA Gold Dagger. The book is named after a barbaric cage which, once fitted on their heads, would silence unruly women in medieval times. However, it is very much the present when Mathilda Gillespie is found dead in her bath crowned with such an instrument. The scene of death suggests it might be a bizarre case of suicide. Sarah Blakeney, Mathilda's physician, is not convinced and suspects foul play. In her quest for evidence, her philandering husband is just one of the frustrations she must deal with. When the doctor is named the sole beneficiary of the Gillespie fortune, Mathilda's bitter daughter and granddaughter start a smear campaign against Sarah. In contrast to the supportive environment in *The Ice House*, in *The Scold's Bridle* Mathilda and descendants illustrate a very different picture of sisterhood. Walters explains the change. "In this instance, I was interested in what happens to people when they come from a family where there have been several generations of bad parenting," she says. "What effect does that have on the current generation? I thought that situation would be most interesting in a family where there were only three women, because I think women can be the most appalling verbal abusers. They are much worse than men in the sense that they don't physically beat up people, but they use their mouths instead. It's probably because it's been our only weapon for so long. We are physically weaker than men, but the old gab, that's the easiest way to dig the sword in when you don't have the physical ability."

In *The Scold's Bridle* Walters creates an explosive environment by bringing together three generations of women, all of whom are damaged through destructive relationships with men. The damage manifests itself through a cycle of repression, with the women not allowing each other to be happy, free, or contented. "When I started looking for something that could symbolize this kind of repression," she recalls, "I remembered the scold's bridle I had seen as a child in a museum in Reading."

People are often surprised when Walters says that Mathilda Gillespie is one of her favorite characters. "I know she was deeply pernicious," the author says, "but I am very fond of Mathilda. I weep for Mathilda because there was never any redemption for her." This was one of the author's reasons for including the entries from Mathilda's diary in *The Scold's Bridle*. "Trying to create a dead person is very difficult, which is why I wanted to give Mathilda a voice. The dead cannot speak for themselves. Everybody else is filtering information about them through their own eyes and words, so usually what is revealed are only snippets of truth."

In Walters's next novel, *The Dark Room*, the reader joins heroine Jane "Jinx" Kingsley in piecing together the incidents that led up to the car crash that left her the victim of amnesia. Recovering in a clinic, Jane discovers that, prior to the accident, her fiancé jilted her for her best friend, both of whom have subsequently disappeared. When two bodies are discovered, the police suspect that Jane's amnesia might be a cover for something more sinister.

In this book, Walters decided to concentrate on a single woman. "In *The Dark Room* I wanted to see what might happen if everything is taken away from a woman," says the author. "In other words, what would happen when you take away her memory. I put Jane in a situation where she has to rely totally on what she knows about herself because she is too frightened to confide in anyone else. The result is that she fights her corner alone, and I was interested to see how she would do that. It rapidly became very clear to me that the only way she could do this was to not talk to anybody." Walters feels that, these days, people cannot allow themselves to be vulnerable because once someone reveals a weakness, the general tendency is to start investigating for further personal details. "Society is getting worse and worse, so people are even less inclined to confide in others because there's too much fear involved. That is something else I wanted to include in *The Dark Room*," the author says.

Within days of being published, *The Echo* found its way to the top of the best-seller lists, giving Minette Walters her fifth consecutive hit.

The novel was a departure from her previous work in that it concentrated on male characters and lacked the romance of her previous work. It is journalist Michael Deacon's interest in the death of Billy Blake, a homeless alcoholic, that inspires *The Echo*. Deacon's interest in the case has been piqued by Amanda Powell, the woman in whose garage Billy's body was found. It is with the help of Barry Grover, a photo-librarian; Terry Dalton, a homeless teenager; and Lawrence Greenhill, a retired solicitor; that Michael is able to solve an intricate mystery.

"After all my novels dominated by women, I wanted to redress the balance with this book. The thing that offends me most about modern society—and I really use the word *offend* lightly—is that a man has to think twice before he goes to help a child in case somebody turns around and accuses him of abuse. The idea that society is flooded by rampaging pedophiles is absolutely absurd, that men are now afraid to show affection or interest in the well-being of children, shocking. In *The Echo* I wanted to show that most men are extremely pleasant, dependable, and perfectly trustworthy, and long may it be so!"

Walters would like to see her novels illustrated with more dynamic media. After her first book, which included a village map, Walters's subsequent novels have become increasingly more elaborate, incorporating text from diary entries, newspaper cuttings, and police reports. "Computers are doing infinitely more exciting things than books are at the moment, and I see no reason why books shouldn't try and retrieve a bit of this imagination." Walters says with some frustration, "Books are presented in just one particular format. What I would love to be able to do is write a fiction novel in the style of a true crime book. I would like to include photographs of a body, or a pathologist's hand drawing of where the body was found, or maybe scrunched up notes with fingerprints on them. I would love to have the whole thing look like a police file in book format."

While it might involve considerable expense to publish a book incorporating these ideas, Walters feels something has to change if publishing is to meet the challenge of the new media. "It's a bit like the fun element in modern art which, like life, is a bit of a black joke," the author suggests. "I like the idea of fun in life, and I feel the same way about publishing. I get the most enormous pleasure out of reading books, and I think it could be even more fun if they had such a visual impact that it would be exciting to turn the page and find something strange and new."

Minette Walters once commented that her favorite review describes her work as "about as cozy as careering down a winding English road in a sports car whose brakes have failed." She liked the comparison because it hinted at pace, twists, fear, suspense, and style, all of which are essential ingredients in a good page-turner. They are also all the ingredients found in the novels by Minette Walters.

BIBLIOGRAPHY

The Ice House. London, Macmillan, and New York, St. Martin's Press, 1992. (CWA John Creasey Award)

The Sculptress. London, Macmillan, and New York, St. Martin's Press, 1993. (MWA Edgar Allan Poe Award; Macavity Award from Mystery Readers International)

The Scold's Bridle. London, Macmillan, and New York, St. Martin's Press, 1994. (CWA Gold Dagger)

The Dark Room. London, Macmillan, 1995; New York, Putnam, 1996.

The Echo. London, Macmillan, and New York, Putnam, 1997.

John Harvey

INTERVIEW BY JERRY SYKES

John Harvey's first Resnick novel arrived like a message in a bottle: a broken bottle brandished in anger on a Saturday night; an empty bottle knocked over on a threadbare carpet. Finally, here was a writer to drag the British into the eighties and make them face up to what was going on right outside their front doors. Gone was the lone inspector and his trusty sergeant solving every murder within the city limits; in was the bunch of ordinary men and women trying to make some sense out of the moral wasteland that surrounded them. The book quickly established Harvey not only as a crime writer of the first rank, but also as a chronicler of the here and now.

The Resnick novels provide a picture of life in Britain in the depressed post-Thatcher years. Written in a clipped, rhythmic prose laced with dark humor, the books combine a strong sense of place and atmosphere with stories that center around the pubs, streets, high-rises, and shopping centers of the city and the ordinary, everyday people who inhabit them and the ordinary, everyday crimes they commit, and carry the reader along on the broken rhythms of the city.

At the center of the books is Detective Inspector Charlie Resnick, a disheveled, overweight man with a love of jazz. A dour, sensitive character, he often appears uneasy with the world, cold and distant; but at home with his cats and the sounds of jazz in his head, his soul comes alive, and the *reader gets to see the true nature of the man. Not to say that Resnick is the only member of the Nottingham police force in the books; Harvey has also created a wide spectrum of characters that reflect the true demographics of his chosen city.*

To date, there have been eight Resnick novels, each displaying in harsh focus aspects of the society in which he operates: Lonely Hearts *features a serial killer who chooses his victims through the small ads of a newspaper;* Rough Treatment, *which tells of a burglar caught up in an affair with one of his victims;* Cutting Edge, *the harrowing tale of a patient who wakes up during surgery;* Off Minor, *a moving story of a couple whose child has been abducted;* Wasted Years, *in which the imminent release of a violent criminal who swore revenge on Resnick forces him to take stock of his life;* Cold Light, *in which one of Resnick's squad is kidnapped;* Living Proof, *in which a visiting American crime writer is subjected to threats; and the latest,* Easy Meat, *in which the pressures of a single parent bringing up three children are put under the microscope.*

The extent to which Harvey sees his books as living, breathing slices of life was revealed recently when, in his radio adaptation of Cutting Edge, *he changed the identity of the killer from that in the book, as if to say, "Who knows how anyone will react, at any given time, under any given circumstances?"*

JS: You started your writing career in the mid-seventies writing pulp paperbacks. Can you tell us how you got into that?

JH: I got into writing through another writer called Laurence James, who I was at college with. He had written a number of biker books, and the publishers wanted another one, but Laurence didn't have enough time to write it. He knew I was fidgeting with my teaching job and wanting to leave it to do something else, so he said, "Why don't you try and write a biker book." I'd never ridden a motorbike in my life other than a little Honda 50 and didn't know any Hell's Angels, so he lent me his books. I saw that they were like Westerns with motorbikes; the basic narrative was the same as a Western. So I bought myself a kind of teach yourself how to be a Hell's Angel book and wrote a sample chapter and an outline with Laurence's help and sent it off to the publishers. They wrote back commissioning the book and offered me £250 for a 50,000 word opus called *Avenging Angel*. Then I was commissioned to write a second book, and I thought that was great, so I resigned from my teaching job and thought: *Hey, I'm a writer!* That was it, basically.

The thing that really set me going, though, was when Laurence took me along to the launch of Star paperbacks and introduced me to all the commissioning paperback editors in London. As a result of that, I pitched various ideas to all of them and some of them actually, incredible as it seems, commissioned me to do work. So I wrote books about mercenaries, I wrote books about anti-Nazi groups in Germany, and then one day, Corgi rang me and said they were looking for someone to write a Western series and would I be interested? Hah! I'd have been interested if they'd said they were looking for someone to write a series on Cistercian monks. Over the next three years, I wrote about twelve or thirteen Westerns a year.

JS: Were they all written to formula?

JH: The advantage of writing formulaic fiction is that it *is* formulaic. But there are only a certain number of basic Western plots, so the fun was in ringing the changes in them. By the seventies people like Robert Altman had started subverting the genre, making early postmodernist Westerns. We could see there was a lot of fun to be had with this, playing with the basic formula, turning it upside down a little. We would quote from our favorite movies, rip off scenes from movies that we loved, and use them again and again. And not just movies. I kept using the scene from *Richard III* where Richard woos Anne over her husband's coffin and persuades her to marry him. I used that in several Westerns as I thought that it was a great scene.

JS: As well as the Westerns, around this time you also wrote a few crime novels.

JH: I wrote four wretched private eye novels about a detective called Scott Mitchell. They were sub-sub–Raymond Chandler, an early attempt to write an American-style thriller in a British setting.

JS: Were they as successful as the Westerns?

JH: No, they sold very few copies. They were only ever published in this country, but you can still find, as I discovered to my chagrin, remaindered pristine paperback copies going for ten cents in Woolworth stores in the suburbs of Chicago.

JS: I believe *Mystery Scene* is going to republish one of your Westerns.

JH: They are going to republish the tenth Hart The Regulator book, *The Skinning Place*. I've always had a fondness for that one, partly because it's got a good poem by a friend called Alan Brooks in it, which is where the title comes from, and partly because it's got a really nice chapter that I like because it's about family conflict, so I'm really happy about that coming out.

JS: After a few years, you moved away from writing fiction and into TV and radio.

JH: Yes, I only published a few books over the next few years. However, when I did return to writing fiction, I found the script work I did for TV and radio had taught me different skills to do with narrative that I hadn't had before, and it also improved my dialogue. Plus I also read things that inspired me when I came to write the first Resnick book. I'd read huge chunks of Elmore Leonard, Ross Thomas, and also a lot of nongenre writers, like Jim Harrison and Thomas McGuane, which helped me. The other thing that helped, without any doubt, was that I wasn't having to write a book a month anymore, so when I sat down to write *Lonely Hearts*, I could have the luxury of having three or four months of writing the first draft. That might not seem like much to some people, but after writing a book a month, it is a huge amount of time.

JS: Where did the idea for Charlie Resnick come from?

JH: I've got no absolutely clear idea. But very early on, before I started the first Resnick book, I spent a long while talking to a really nice man and a good writer—who sadly died before the book was published—called Dulan Barber, who was intensely thoughtful about what went into a book and about people's work. I spent a number of days with him just talking about the story and talking about the character.

I knew that I wanted him to be a policeman and I knew very early on that I thought it would be interesting if he was of Polish descent, which was possible because there is a large Polish population in Nottingham, which is where the books were going to be set.

My first sighting of him was this big, bulky man in an overcoat walking away from me down the hill into the city from the police station that I knew he was going to be in. I didn't see his face and his face is never described in the books. I didn't have a face for him until Tom Wilkinson played him on television; I'd never seen Resnick's face up until that point. Never. But I knew his size and shape and something about him. So he was there partly from discussions before I started writing but actually didn't really emerge until I started writing about him.

JS: How about the other characters?

JH: *Hill Street Blues* and the TV series I wrote about the probation service called *Hard Cases* were very strongly in my mind when I was setting up the books. I knew I wanted to have multiple story lines and, although I wanted Resnick to be the central character, I didn't want him to be the only protagonist, the only police character. I wanted to try and present a range of the sort of people that might reasonably be found in the Nottingham police force: I had a woman, I had an Asian policeman, I had a fairly sexist, racist policeman, and I had a couple of fairly normal, tolerably boring policemen as the squad working with him. One of the things that I've always been terrified about in writing novels is getting bored, so I always want to be able to skip around from one point of view to another. That's because my imagination works basically cinematically, so in my mind I'm always cutting from one scene to another and it's much easier to do that if you have got a number of characters.

One of the functions Resnick has in the narrative is to hold all those threads together, and that's the reason that in every fourth or fifth chapter there is a section with Resnick at home, to provide a kind of home base for the reader, so that just as Resnick is going home and maybe relaxing a bit, so the reader can as well. Because when the reader gets home with Resnick, the action slows down, and everyone puts their feet up and has a cup of coffee and a sandwich and listens to some music. It's a kind of still point every now and again in the book that allows a little résumé of the story up to that point, before you go hurtling around again.

JS: Do you think that these chapters emphasize his character, especially with the jazz? I get the feeling he identifies with his jazz heroes.

JH: I think it does. I think it shows something about his sensitivity and the romanticism of his nature. There's also a kind of sensuous side to him that finds its way out through food and music and not, sadly, a lot of the time, through physical relationships with people. I think the jazz is important because it shows you elements within him that don't necessarily surface during the rest of his working day.

JS: Talking about jazz, there are a lot of edgy rhythms in your prose.

JH: One of the people that Resnick listens to most is Theolonious Monk, and if you know Monk's piano style, it is very edgy and fragmentary, jagged phrases and phrases that are not finished. I don't usually write to music, but if I ever have music on when I'm writing a Resnick novel, it's Monk. It seems suitable both to the speech rhythms of the book and to the edginess of the subject matter. But I also think there's a sense that you make it slightly less than comfortable because you don't want people to be able to switch their brains off while they're reading.

JS: The minor characters are as well developed as Resnick and the other police characters. Do you think that this is important in crime fiction, where often the only thing you are told about a victim is that they *are* a victim?

JH: I think it's essential. I'm unhappy about crime fiction that puts people on the page just to be violated. I do write sometimes about people that are emotionally or physically violated, but I want them to have some kind of life also so that we see them as living, breathing people and so we care about what happens to them. I also want to try and get some understanding of why people might commit crimes, sometimes violent crimes, and for me that's a challenge and one of the things that makes the books interesting to write.

JS: The crimes in your books are often committed out of socioeconomic circumstances rather than, say, grand gestures like a serial killer playing games with his hunters.

JH: What I'm interested in doing is writing novels about some of the harder edges of life in contemporary urban Britain. A lot of that involves crime, and I hope it gives the books a kind of veracity because

I do think a lot of crime has to do with unemployment, the lack of opportunity, the lack of hope. That has probably a lot to do with what happened in the eighties where we moved away from what was basically a fairly compassionate society into a society that was more motivated by greed and the desire to own and protect what you own.

JS: In your latest book, *Easy Meat*, the fruits of those years are visited upon one family. Is that what you intended to explore?

JH: It's a continuation of what I've been writing about. It looks at a single-parent family, at a woman who's had a hard and pretty difficult life herself, trying to hold together a family of teenage kids. Although I think the book is more about some of the problems of maleness in our society, especially if you are a young working-class male. I was moved to write about those things by things that I'd read about, not only in the national newspapers, but also in the Nottingham newspapers, about the problems of keeping kids in care and in remand, the kind of bullying that goes on when kids are in care, and horrific instances of fourteen- and fifteen-year-old lads killing themselves or trying to kill themselves because of the pressures. I also wanted to write about sexuality and young men. There was a really nasty outbreak of male rape in London just before I moved back to London from Nottingham. There were several instances of men being raped on the underground and on Hampstead Heath, two of which I think ended in the victim dying. I wanted to try and write about that as well because it appeared to me that all of those things seemed to come together. So that's how *Easy Meat* came about. It's not just about men though, it's about the mother and sister as well.

JS: The book also finds Resnick in a stable relationship. Is this something you've been planning for a while?

JH: When I wrote *Wasted Years*, what I was doing was making Resnick confront in detail the breakup of his marriage, clearing the decks so that he would at some point be able to start a proper relationship again. And then he has a kind of needy, false start, the one-night stand in *Cold Light* with Dana, which takes him totally by surprise and frightens the shit out of him, because she's a witness, apart from anything else.

JS: I think that was the thing though; it was because she was a witness and he behaved unprofessionally.

JH: But I think also it was just one of those things that happens as they occasionally do when two people who are both very needy suddenly find themselves in the situation where sex can happen.

I had a long bus ride on the way back from Seattle Bouchercon with a friend of mine—Pat Kehde, who runs a mystery bookstore—and she was telling me that although she likes the books a lot, Resnick needed to get out of this rut he was in and have a relationship because he was getting boring—the same old stuff.

From that point on, it was very conscious on my part that I wanted him to have a relationship, but I had to wait until I could find the right kind of character in the right situation, and it seems to me that the relationship in *Easy Meat* is okay. I wanted to create someone who would be an equal to him but also someone who I could fit in to the narrative so that there would be a reason for them meeting and a reason for them to carry on meeting. I wanted to work her properly into the story, and I think in *Easy Meat* I was able to do that. She carries on beyond *Easy Meat* and will be in the next book, and their relationship, in fact, will be absolutely central to the book I'm about to start, which is called *Still Water*. If there was a focus on male sexuality, homosexuality, and problems of gender in *Easy Meat*, then there will be a focus in *Still Water* on problems of power and sexuality in heterosexual relationships.

JS: I was wondering how Resnick was going to deal with his emotions in this relationship. Do you think it's going to create more problems for him? I think the title may give it away: *Still Water*.

JH: *Still Water* . . . yes, well . . . it won't run smooth beneath the surface. One of the problems that they have will be a very common problem in relationships about how do you equate issues of power and dominance and submission within your sexuality, and how do we deal with those things. Those are problems that every couple has, I think, to a greater or lesser degree. But what I want to do is to address those problems within their relationship and also to deal with those same issues in the crime plot so that reverberations are going through the book around that central issue of power and domination.

JS: You've said in the past that you are only going to write ten Resnick novels. Is that still the case?

JH: There are only going to be ten Resnick in Nottingham novels. But I've always said that I wanted a novel where Resnick goes back to Poland, which I would like to do at some point as a one-off. Ten Resnick novels are basically ten years of my working life; it will be the main thing that I've written in ten years, especially if you add the two TV scripts and two radio scripts.

JS: Apart from the Resnick in Poland, is there anything else you have in mind?

JH: Both my American and British publishers seem interested in publishing a book of short stories that would follow on from the ten novels. They'd all be Resnick stories, some of which have been previously published, but some of them would be new. They'd all be about characters that appear in the novels, like footnotes to the characters. One of the stories that's already been published tells you what happened to Ed Silver, the jazz musician who's in *Cutting Edge*. And I've just done a story featuring Grabianski from *Rough Treatment* called "Bird of Paradise." I think it's the best one I've written so far.

What I like to do is try out characters in stories before writing the novels, so that all the stories relate to a particular novel. So, for the short story collection, what I thought would be a good idea would be to write a linking commentary showing how each story related to the novels, a sort of key to the novels.

Sharyn McCrumb

INTERVIEW BY CHARLES L. P. SILET

S
haryn McCrumb is the author of three series. The Jay O'Mega books,
Bimbos of the Death Sun *(1987) and* Zombies of the Gene Pool
(1992) are hilarious send-ups of the si-fi world of fandom and the
authors who feed on its adulation and groupies. Her Elizabeth
MacPherson books, now eight in number, have attracted a wide audience
of traditional mystery readers. Funny and poignant, the series has been as
far ranging in subjects as they have been in locales, Southern weddings in
Georgia, Highland festivals, and isolated islands off the Scottish coast. As
the series has darkened, it has become more bizarrely humorous, and the
latest, If I'd Killed Him when I Met Him . . . *features a wildly comic*
character who has just murdered her ex-husband and his new trophy wife,
an enterprising born-again preacher who hears the voice of God, and a
woman who wants to marry a dolphin.

The novels that are currently attracting the most attention, however,
are the Ballad Books, a crime series set on the edge of the Appalachian
Mountains and featuring a small-town police officer, Spencer Arrowood.
The first three books of the new series have been published, If I Ever Return,
Pretty Peggy-O *(1990),* The Hangman's Beautiful Daughter *(1992),*
and the latest, She Walks These Hills *(1995), and although they are all*
very different in theme, they all explore the densely interrelated lives of a
small Southern town against the haunting and mysterious background of
the Appalachian Mountains.

Sharyn McCrumb's fiction has received broad acclaim from both readers and critics alike. Her novels have either won or been nominated for most of the major awards in the mystery and crime field, including Edgars, Anthonys, Neros, Macavities, and Agathas. Both The Hangman's Beautiful Daughter *and* If I Ever Return, Pretty Peggy-O *were named notable books of the year by the* New York Times, *and* If I Ever Return, Pretty Peggy-O *made several other lists for the year's best fiction.* The Hangman's Beautiful Daughter *and* Lovely in Her Bones *were both winners of the Best Appalachian Novel of their respective years.*

CLPS: How did you get interested in writing crime and mystery fiction?

SM: I didn't. I was supposed to be a Southern novelist, and as an undergraduate, I took courses from Max Steele and Sylvia Wilkinson at Carolina. Reynolds Price used to come over from Duke and do what he could for us. I was supposed to write that coming-of-age novel in which a bright, perceptive child will grow up to be the author. About the time I was ready to do that, minimalism came into contemporary fiction. Coming from a race of storytellers, I could not figure out how to write a book in which *not much happens to people you don't care about anyway.* So I wrote in the style that I know best, which is sort of a continuation of nineteenth-century narrative, I suppose. The way Jane Austen handled it or Dickens, which is: I will tell you a rattlin' good story if you insist on having one, but if you will read this with your brain in third gear, you'll find that I'm saying something else, as well. You could read *Bleak House* as a murder mystery. You could also read it as an indictment of the legal system of Victorian England. I turned in my first book, *Sick of Shadows*, which was sort of Jane Austen, except that it was a send-up of Southern weddings. It was a comedy of manners and social satire, but because I killed somebody and because I didn't have an MFA or work in New York, the publisher decided it was genre fiction and asked me for another one. It has taken me a while to try to get people to see that there's something else going on in my books. I want a readership that will look for other things. When people come up and say, "I figured out who done it," in say, *The Hangman's Beautiful Daughter*, I want to say, "Did you figure out who did it in *To Kill a Mockingbird*?"

CLPS: Talk about yourself for a minute as a Southern writer.

SM: I come from a race of storytellers, but there are two Souths: Magnolia and Mountain, and I am a blend of both.

My father's family—the Arrowoods and the McCourys—settled in the Smoky Mountains of western North Carolina in 1790, when the wilderness was still Indian country. They came from the north of England and from Scotland, and they seemed to want mountains, land, and as few neighbors as possible. The first McCoury to settle in America was my great-great-great-grandfather Malcolm Mc-Coury, a Scot who was kidnapped as a child from the island of Islay in the Hebrides in 1750 and made to serve as a cabin boy on a sailing ship. He later became an attorney in Morristown, New Jersey; fought with the Chester Militia in the American Revolution; and finally settled in what is now Mitchell County, western North Carolina, in 1794. Another relative, an Arrowood killed in the Battle of Waynesville in May 1865, was the last man to die in the Civil War east of the Mississippi. Yet another connection (we are cousins-in-law through the Howell family) is the convicted murderess Frankie Silver, the subject of my next novel, *The Ballad of Frankie Silver*. Francis Stewart Silver (1813–1833) was the first woman hanged for murder in the state of North Carolina. I did not discover the family tie that links us until I began the two years of research prior to writing the novel. I wasn't surprised, though. Since both our families had been in Mitchell County for more than two hundred years, and both produced large numbers of children to intermarry with other families, I knew the connection had to be there. These same bloodlines link both Frankie Silver and me to another Appalachian writer, Wilma Dykeman, and also to the famous bluegrass musician Del McCoury.

The namesake of my character, Spencer Arrowood, my paternal grandfather, worked in the machine shop of the Clinchfield Railroad. He was present on that September day in 1916 at the railroad yard in Erwin, Tennessee, when a circus elephant called Mary was hanged for murder; she had killed her trainer in Kingsport. (I used this last story as a theme in *She Walks These Hills*, in which an elderly escaped convict is the object of a manhunt in the Cherokee National Forest. In the novel, the radio disc jockey, Hank the Yank, reminds his listeners of that story as a prayer for mercy for the hunted fugitive.) I grew up listening to my father's tales of World War II in the Pacific and to older family stories of duels and escapades in Model A Fords.

With such adventures in my background, I grew up seeing the world as a wild and exciting place; the quiet tales of suburban angst so popular in modern fiction as Martian to me.

Two of my great-grandfathers were circuit preachers in the North Carolina mountains a hundred years ago, riding horseback over the ridges to preach in a different community each week. Perhaps they are an indication of our family's regard for books, our gift for storytelling and public speaking, and our love of the Appalachian mountains, all traits that I acquired as a child.

I have said that my books are like Appalachian quilts. I take brightly colored scraps of legends, ballads, fragments of rural life, and local tragedy, and I piece them together into a complex whole that tells not only a story but also a deeper truth about the culture of the mountain South. It is from the family stories, the traditional music, and from my own careful research of the history, folklore, and geography of the region that I gather the squares for these literary quilts.

Storytelling was an art form that I learned early on. When I was a little girl, my father would come in to tell me a bedtime story, which usually began with a phrase like, "Once there was a prince named Paris, whose father was Priam, the king of Troy. . . ." Thus I got the *Iliad* in nightly installments, geared to the level of a four-year-old's understanding. I grew up in a swirl of tales: the classics retold; ballads or country songs, each having a melody, but above all a *plot*; and family stories about Civil War soldiers, train wrecks, and lost silver mines.

My mother contributed stories of her father, a sixteen-year-old John Burdette Taylor, a private in the 68th North Carolina Rangers (CSA), whose regiment walked in rag-bound boots, following the railroad tracks from Virginia to Fort Fisher, site of a decisive North Carolina battle. All his life he would remember leaving footprints of blood in the snow as he marched. When John Taylor returned home to Carteret County, eastern North Carolina, at the end of the war, his mother, who was recovering from typhoid, got up out of her sickbed to attend the welcome home party for her son. She died that night.

My father's family fund of Civil War stories involved great-great-uncles in western North Carolina who had discovered a silver mine or a valley of ginseng while roaming the hills, trying to escape conscription into one marauding army or another.

There were the two sides of the South embodied in my parents' oral histories: Mother's family represented the flatland South, steeped in its magnolia myths, replete with Gorham sterling silver and Wedgwood china. My father's kinfolks spoke for the Appalachian South, where the pioneer spirit took root. In their War Between the States, the Cause was somebody else's business, and the war was a deadly struggle between neighbors. I could not belong completely to either of these Souths because I am inextricably a part of both. This duality of my childhood, a sense of having a foot in two cultures, gave me that sense of *otherness* that one often finds in writers: the feeling of being an outsider, observing one's surroundings, and looking even at personal events at one remove.

So much conflict; so much drama; and two sides to everything. Stories, I learned, involved character and drama, and they always centered around irrevocable events that mattered.

Cultural identity, I learned from my dual-culture childhood, is optional. The point of those novels is not to reveal whodunit, but to satirize a pretentious segment of society: in *Highland Laddie Gone*, for example, the Scottish wannabes at the Highland Games are lampooned. The last novel in that series, *If I'd Killed Him when I Met Him* . . . is a synchronically structured mediation on the dysfunctional nature of contemporary relationships: i.e., there is a war going on between men and women these days, and in this book, Elizabeth MacPherson becomes the war correspondent. These satirical novels reflect the culture of my mother's South: the mannered society and appearances and social position.

CLPS: Where did Elizabeth MacPherson come from?

SM: She was not intended to be a series character. I wanted to write *Sick of Shadows* because I thought it would be very funny to have a character who was a sociology major because of course no one would hire her and then she could go around and have interesting adventures indefinitely. I started with a plot on that. MacPherson books start with a plot and the Ballad books start with themes. I thought: "Wouldn't it be funny if someone were painting a picture beside a lake and was murdered, and the painting was taken, and if you knew what was in the painting, you'd know why the murder was committed." I got fifty pages done on it. It was satirical, but in terms of plot, I didn't know what was in the painting, which made it difficult to finish the book. Then I read a newspaper article that gave me the idea about repressed memories. It was exactly the same case: a North Carolina case from the late seventies, on which Lee Smith based her book *Family Linen*. If you read her book and my book, you'll see no similarity, but if you read about the case and then read both books, you'll realize that we were both starting from the same point and then going left and right with it.

CLPS: How did you go on to the next book in the series?

SM: Well, I think it helped when I started really getting serious and knowing what I wanted to say and having time to say it, which was when I finished grad school and when the children were born, when I finally got to settle down and clear the decks. That is something that Emily Brontë and Jane Austen never had to worry about. I began to see why they didn't get married. It took me until 1989 to start writing *Peggy-O*, although I got the idea in 1986, but it was just a question of having five consecutive minutes to be able to think. I also think that the early books are very light and funny. I don't know that I could write *Highland Laddie Gone* again. It's very good for just Oscar Wilde satirical silliness, but I think, as with physics, there's almost an age limit to when you could think like that, and that once you pass thirty or so, you do one of two things: You either start parodying yourself and go on to such silly novels that they become cartoons, which I didn't ever want to do, or, like Jonathan Swift, you direct your tendency to be a smart aleck toward things that actually anger you. *If I'd Killed Him when I Met Him* . . . is a very dark book, and that's more Swift than Wilde.

CLPS: Let's talk a little bit about your latest Elizabeth MacPherson, *If I'd Killed Him when I Met Him* . . . First of all, it's a great title; it's also an extremely dark novel, but also in some ways a very funny book. What would you say to somebody who said that you really seem down on men?

SM: There's a song that came out in the spring of '94 by Johnny Cash, who's a great favorite of mine, so I'm not going to bad-mouth Johnny Cash here. I like him. In the sixties the Kingston Trio did a song called "Delia's Gone," and I remember when they did it that it was a fairly innocuous song. It sounded in their version like this guy's girlfriend had left him, and he's sitting in the bar drowning his sorrows over having been left. And the chorus of the song mentions "one more round" and "Delia's gone," like they're all going to get drunk with him. When Johnny Cash does it, the song takes on a whole different meaning because he emphasizes the death of the woman and uses the word "round" to refer to a round of ammunition. What do you think of that? It's got a whole new meaning. I mean, especially that last verse, which talks about *doing your woman like Delia got done.* A little advice for boyfriends like O. J.: That song has been playing on American Top 40 for a year or so; *Newsweek* reviewed the album, with a big picture of Cash, and nobody said diddley. That kind of thing has been in the canon for centuries. Almost every folk song, such as "The Banks of the Ohio," is about murdered women. I just thought it was time somebody shot back. Have you noticed that the war has escalated? I live in the Bobbitt state, so this may have come to my attention before you all noticed it, but about the time that Lorena and John had their unpleasantness, I went out to California on a book tour, and there were bumper stickers that said, "Do you know where your ex-wife is tonight?" They were referring to Betty Broderick in San Diego, who is the model for Eleanor Royden, and she really did shoot her lawyer husband and the new wife, and she was not particularly sorry. She was not as articulate as I made Eleanor, but she could have played the part. I just thought, "Let's put all this out on the table." I guess my overall message was: Relationships don't work.

CLPS: Let me shift gears just a bit and have you talk about your two science fiction books. What possessed you to write *Bimbos of the Death Sun?* I'm glad you did, but I just wondered why.

SM: There again, I wasn't thinking of the canon for posterity. David, my husband, was in graduate school, and he was a war gamer when we started. So this was perhaps cheaper than therapy. I had been observing these people for some time. The little local science fiction club had a convention at the Econo Lodge, and they could only afford to bring in one writer, so they brought in Margaret Weis, who writes The Dragonlance series, which I think is with Bantam now. Anyway, it's full-fledged science/fantasy stuff. Now they had to bring her all the way from Wisconsin, but they couldn't make her speak for eight straight hours, so they were scurrying around trying to find other ways to fill up the time. They said, *"You've* published a couple of books." And I said, "Well, not science fiction." And they said, "Yes, but you published something. Why don't you come and give a reading." I guess so that Margaret could go to the bathroom. This is when I taught journalism and for a while was film librarian at Virginia Tech. And I thought, *Wouldn't it be funny if one of the engineers at Tech had written a science fiction novel and sold it to a sleazy paperback house. Suppose they had changed the name of the novel, given it a flashy title, and then sent him to a convention like this.* So I wrote the first two chapters of *Bimbos* and read it out loud for them. Margaret Weis liked it much better than they did, because she had lived through this kind of experience before she became famous, and she asked if she could have a copy of it. I got her photocopies and sent her off, thinking she was going to pass them around the office, and she did, but the office was that of her publisher. They called me about seven months later and said, "We want to publish your book." And I said, "What book?" They said, "*Bimbos of the Death Sun.*" I asked, "Have you talked with my agent?" And they replied, "Oh, my God, you have an agent?" I guess they thought I was a sophomore sci-fi writer, and so that's how that came about.

CLPS: When did you decide to do *Zombies of the Gene Pool*?

SM: Well, you know the first book was saying, "Get a life," for which I became the Salman Rushdie of science fiction, with a price on my head in Federation credits. It was telling all those people under thirty to get a life. But I kept observing fandom and a good half of fandom were a bunch of fifty- and sixty-year-old guys who were still mimeographing their little fanzines, doing diatribes about American foreign policy, which they're mailing out to eighteen-year-olds, while they themselves are older than the U.S. secretary of state. I thought this was sad. What do you say when it's too late for you to get a life? So *Zombies* became a darker book because what's funny in an eighteen-year-old is fairly tragic in a sixty-two-year-old. The second was: "Here's what'll happen if you didn't take my advice in the first book."

CLPS: Is that why you changed directions in the Ballad Books?

SM: It's what I always wanted to write. When I was in graduate school, my focus was on Appalachian literature and culture, and so I studied and got more deeply into the culture. *Peggy-O* was partly an Appalachian book and partly a look at that baby boomer generation, the class of '66, facing their own mortality twenty years later. I really liked what I had said about Appalachia, although that book, really, could almost have been set in Kansas and not lost very much of the flavor of it. The experiences were common to boomers everywhere. But with the second book, I wanted to get more specific about the region and talk about the environmental dangers exemplified by the river, and the whole idea of liminality, which is what I was doing in *Hangman*. Liminality is anthropology as opposed to English. Victor Turner, the anthropologist, has a theory that there are threshold states in everything; for example: Twilight is neither day nor night; it's something in the middle. But he says culturally that there are threshold states. In *Hangman*, the liminality lies between life and death. In every thread in that narrative, I examine how many ways one can be somewhere on the threshold between life and death. First, there is the groundhog who isn't dead. But when it's hibernating, it's not alive in the sense that it's running around eating and behaving as other animals do. So it's in a liminal state. The river is not dried up, but since nothing can live in it, and because it's causing cancer deaths and it looks like tobacco spit, you couldn't call it a viable river. Naomi Judd is a celebrity, but what happens to a celebrity when they're no longer in our faces anymore? She's living happily on her farm outside Nashville, but she's gone from MTV and she's gone from radio and so on, so she's in that liminal state of not being dead physically but being gone. And in the novel, Josh Underhill killed his family and himself, but his sister Maggie is still getting phone calls from him. Laura Bruce is pregnant, but the child is dead, so there's that liminal state again. Over and over, you've got that. Did you figure out why the groundhog was named Percy? Persephone. Because when she's hibernating, it's winter, and when she comes back, the world goes into spring, which makes Nora represent Demeter.

CLPS: You have an old woman seer, Amelanchier, in one of the Elizabeth MacPherson books, and now you have Nora Bonesteel. What about such magic figures? Tell me a little bit about that character and why she fascinates you.

SM: It's in the blood. Once at the Appalachian Studies conference a bunch of my friends who had been presenting papers at the conference—they're professors at other universities—got together for a party that evening in the little cabin that I'd rented for the weekend. After the first bottle of wine, everybody (they were all Ph.D.'s, but also all of them were from the mountains) had a family ghost story. Not the "Golden Arm" or something clichéd but something that had happened to them or to someone in their immediate family. They weren't especially scary stories, just the typical ones. Grandmother is in the kitchen washing dishes and she looks out the window over the kitchen sink and sees her son John walk across the lawn. He lives in Cincinnati, and so she's wondering why he drove in to surprise her. She puts down the dish towel and runs out, and his car is not in the driveway, and he's not there. He's not in the barn. When she comes back in the house, the phone is ringing, and it's Cincinnati telling her that Uncle John died exactly when she saw him in the yard. Every mountain woman has got a variation of that story. I do, too. My editor, who's from Tucson, was the only woman present without a ghost story. Apparently, they don't have such stories in Arizona, especially in big cities. One of the Appalachian professors said, "Well, honey, ghosts just don't have call waiting." The two men in the room didn't remember any ghost stories, either, and the same woman said, "Well, your family has ghost stories, but you don't know them. Let me tell you how to find them." She said, "You know, on Thanksgiving, the whole clan gets together at a relative's house. After the meal is over, the men go out and watch football on television or go out on the front porch and talk about stuff, while the women clear the table and start scraping the dishes and getting everything put away in the kitchen. In the kitchen first they tell childbirth horror stories, and that gets all the rookies out of the room. And then, when the amateurs are gone, they get down to it. If you can't stay past all the childbirth horror stories, you have never heard the family ghost stories." And she said to the two men, "Ask your wife; if she helps with the dishes, she knows the stories." I said that night to Susanne Kirk (my editor), "If I had it to do over again, the one thing I left out of *Peggy-O* is some kind of experience like that." And I even know who would have had it and when. Remember when Spencer and Peggy went up the mountain to see those two old people, which was really going back into the past, and the old woman up there, Aunt Till, was talking about Spencer's brother? She would have known when he was killed in Vietnam, but I didn't say it. *Peggy-O* was a book that took place in the summer, it dealt with the past, and it was from the men's point of view. Spencer Arrowood will never see a ghost as long as he lives. As long as he sees things from the male perspective. So there were just no ghosts to be had. In the next book, I reversed it. *Hangman* takes place in the winter; it deals with the future, and it is told from the point of view of women. It is the culture from both sides. They're really mirror-image books. I mixed it with *She Walks These Hills*. In *She Walks These Hills*, the time is autumn, it's male and female, and past and present are really running together to where one becomes another.

CLPS: *The Hangman's Beautiful Daughter* continues your tradition of dark books.

SM: I wrote that book starting each night about midnight so that it would be dark and cold and quiet. Because I had to feel it. The other thing that I use to obtain mood in that series, which apparently I'm the only person who does, is music. Every one of those Ballad books, besides being named after Ballad, has a sound track. I listen to music to get to know my characters. Every one of my characters has a theme song. Spencer Arrowood's is a Don Williams song called "Good Ol' Boys Like Me," which you've probably never heard. The last verse, which really typifies him, talks about him hitting the road, but that it doesn't matter how far he goes, he will always be a good ol' boy. This is a good ol' boy who isn't stupid, and I wanted to establish that early on, which is why in *Peggy-O*, when Peggy makes a condescending remark about the question "that was in another country and the wench is dead," she says, "Shakespeare" and Spencer replies, "Marlowe."

CLPS: Let's talk about your latest book.

SM: It's called *The Rosewood Casket*, and it's about losing the land. With our generation or maybe our parents' generation, in the early part of the twentieth century, there were so many people who had farms in the family. If not your parents, then your grandparents or your uncle. Somebody had a farm that was family land. Then families were split up by World War II, and the young people all went off to jobs in the cities. You didn't get back to the farm very often, maybe just a day or two every five years, but it was there; it was *the* family farm. Now all those old people that could stay on that farm are dying, and the next generation is faced with what's going to happen to the farm. Nobody's going to give up their life and go home to be the new guardian of the farm, but do you really want to sell it to a developer who's going to put two hundred houses on it? In the novel, four sons have come back to east Tennessee because their father is dying, and he wants them to build his coffin. They're shut up in a little wood shop, squabbling with each other and reliving their childhood while they build his coffin, and they have to come to terms with losing the land. Of course, one of them wants to keep the farm intact, one of them wants to sell it to the developer because he needs the money, and so on.

CLPS: So you'll continue the Ballad books?

SM: That's what I want to be remembered for. They're being taught now in a number of colleges and universities. I'm trying, in fact, to compile a list of places where they're being taught. And I've got a teacher's guide that I've put together with, for one thing, a wonderful essay by Susan Wittig Albert about the series, talking about liminality and my use of synchronic structure. In normal narrative fiction, what is used is diachronic structure which is: A happens and then B happens, a linear thing. But with Ballad novels in particular, I use a synchronic structure: a number of parallel things happen. You're supposed to get one particular point. Remember the song, "Where Have All the Flowers Gone?" What you're supposed to remember from that is, "When will they ever learn," so if you forget the young girls, or the young men, or the soldiers of the graveyard, you've still got five different chances to get the message, "When will they ever learn." The Ballad novels keep giving you different examples of their meaning, always with the same point in mind. Look at *The Hangman's Beautiful Daughter*. There are so many liminal states that, if you miss the groundhog, you might get the pregnant woman, or the river, or Naomi Judd, or the phone calls from the dead, or Nora talking to the living and the dead. There are so many ways you can get it. Or the environmental message. In *She Walks These Hills*, look at the journeys: Every single one of those characters is making a journey home in either a spiritual or a physical sense. And if you miss it with Harm, you might get it with Katie or Martha or Jeremy.

CLPS: What challenges do you set for yourself as a writer?

SM: In the short story of mine that won the Sherwood Anderson contest, I wanted to know if I could kill the main character in the first sentence. (She's not present except that everybody else talks about her.) She's the most dominant force of the story, but you never meet her. In *Missing Susan*, which was really a satire on the crime genre, I wanted to see if I could tell you who the murderer was in chapter one and not have the crime committed until the last chapter. I also wanted to have you sympathize with the murderer and be praying that the victim would be killed. This is a complete reversal of what people are usually trying to do in mysteries. That was a challenge. It's not easy to get people to sympathize with murderers, I think. In *She Walks These Hills*, I wanted to see if I could write about a character who has a fifteen-minute memory span. Every single time a scene featured Harm, he had to figure out where he was and what time it was. He's always looking for clues in nature. The corn is tasseled; the leaves haven't fallen. Because he's always disoriented. That was hard. It's fun to see what I can do and also to see if I can tell a story well enough to get the message across. The thing that will probably forever keep me out of what I call "tenure" fiction is that they tend to be preaching to a very small audience of the converted. On the other hand, Charles Dickens changed the child labor laws of England with *Oliver Twist*. Now, he could have sat down and written a very earnest pamphlet with footnotes, but the only people who would have read it would have been the people who already agreed with him. Instead, he took people who didn't even know that they had an opinion and made them cry for a little boy who existed only on paper. And, by God, those laws got changed. I thought, *Let me see if, with the Ballad books, with all of them, I can change how people feel about Appalachia.* If I could do the same thing Tony Hillerman has done for the Navajo. He pretty much wiped out the stereotype, and I think if people know more about the culture of the mountains, perhaps I could do something to change that stereotype.

CLPS: What have you not done that you would like to do?

SM: Well, in case you start a publishing house, I want to write a book that is a first-person narrative told by Mark Twain. I've been doing Twain research. I've been to Hannibal and been to Hartford just really getting the atmosphere. I've been on a Twain kick. I have three shelves of Twain criticism and all his books. But I want to do it with him telling the story. And I'm going to have to maybe get a little farther away from crime fiction before I write it, because I don't want people to say, "Well, who are we going to kill in this one?" This is definitely not a whodunit. I want to write novels, because I'm a storyteller.

Portions of this interview appeared in *The Armchair Detective*.

Sue Grafton

INTERVIEW BY CHARLES L. P. SILET

ue Grafton routinely has *two* New York Times *best-sellers: one on the
paperback list and one on the hardback list. Her latest, "M" Is for*
Malice, *is number thirteen in a highly successful series that began in
1982 and which Grafton plans to run out to 2008 or 2009 when she
reaches the letter Z. She won't answer if you ask what comes after that. The
central character of this alphabetic cycle is Kinsey Millhone who, along with
Sara Paretsky's V. I. Warshawski and Marcia Muller's Sharon McCone,
helped to open up the hard-boiled detective novel to female P.I.'s. In the
process, these women have set in motion what one critic has described as a
"feminist counter-tradition" in crime fiction.*

*Grafton would probably take exception to the label because she does
not see crime writing as gendered and because she enjoys playing the game
with those male authors who have traditionally dominated the genre. But
Kinsey Millhone certainly approaches her criminal investigations from a
different perspective than did the detectives of the classical period. Grafton
feels that detective fiction inherently delivers a social critique, and she was
quoted in a* Time *magazine piece of a few years ago as saying that women
are "looking for a mirror not an escape" when they read crime novels. So
it's no wonder that Kinsey Millhone provides a strong role model in an age
of increasing female activism.*

In the following interview, Sue Grafton talks not only about Kinsey

Millhone but also about mysteries and the place of the crime writer in the larger context of American fiction.

CLPS: I know *how* you got started, but why do you continue to write mystery novels?

SG: I *love* mystery; it is my favorite form. It is sublimely difficult, and for my money, it encompasses everything that is interesting about writing because you need a strong story, strong characters, and mood and atmosphere. It is also the perfect vehicle for social commentary. Mysteries are about the psychology of crime and the psychology of human nature. It is a form so difficult that I know I'll never conquer it. So it's the perfect place to keep throwing myself into the abyss. When I read mainstream fiction, often I am dissatisfied because there is a sort of spine missing. I think, *Where are we going with this? What's the point? Get down to the punch line.* So for me, it is the most challenging of literary forms.

CLPS: Do you find any particular restrictions?

SG: The restrictions are what makes it interesting. It's like writing a sonnet; if you do it well, it's better than free verse because you hit the mark. I love the restrictions. I always liken it to playing bridge in that when you play bridge, you're always dealt thirteen cards, but within that framework you *never* know where a hand is going to go. The mystery novel has its structure and its refinements also, and it's both something really exciting and maddening.

CLPS: What makes your books different from other crime novels?

SG: I haven't got a clue. That's the department for the critics. I try never to make pronouncements about my work because that requires me to step outside my body and make judgments about myself that are so self-serving. I mean, it would be ludicrous to comment. So I don't answer the question. Some people ask, "How do you explain Kinsey Millhone's appeal?" Beats me. That's not my department. My job is to write the books, and other people can make pronouncements about them. It keeps me from being schizophrenic, you know.

CLPS: Is there a difference between crime novels written by men and by women?

SG: I don't think so. I have always operated on the principle that writing has no gender, that it's not about gender. It doesn't matter. The talent is what matters and the work. It is dangerous to categorize because as soon as you do, somebody will astonish and amaze, and that's what makes it wonderful. I certainly think there's room for everybody. As for trends in the mystery, I don't know anything about that, either, because I think you need to write the book you need to write. If they told me as of tomorrow the hard-boiled female private eye was going out of fashion, I'd write them anyway because it isn't about trends, it's about what I want to do for my life. Even if none of them sold again, I would still write them.

CLPS: Is there a difference between female P.I.'s and male P.I.'s?

SG: I think in the past there has been. If you look at the traditional Raymond Chandler, Mickey Spillane, and Shell Scott detectives, they tend to be hard-drinking, heavy-smoking, womanizing bullshitters. Then women came along, and the times changed. So in the 1990s we watch our fat and cholesterol intake, we give up cigarettes, and we don't have the whiskey bottle in the bottom drawer. But in some ways, those are fairly superficial characteristics. I think women have brought a dimension to the mystery novel, to the hard-boiled private eye, that has made it easier for the guys to work, as well. We've demonstrated that you can move away from macho posturing. Even so, some of the women posture, too. You get into imitating the guys and strutting your stuff. But I think the best of books don't fall into any of those pits.

CLPS: Is there always social commentary in crime or mystery novels?

SG: I think by definition there is at least a comment about police procedure, attitudes toward crime, and the legal system. I think that there are writers who make more comments than others. There are the writers who like to use the mystery novel as a way of promoting a point of view. I try not to, because I'm not trying to persuade anybody of anything. If you have an agenda, the danger is that you will distort a story to prove your point, and I'm always leery of that.

CLPS: Where did Kinsey come from? I understand where the crime novel idea came from, A, B, C, and so on, but where did the character come from?

SG: She is a projection of my own nature. When I began, I didn't even know what a private investigator did. I know nothing about police procedure, nothing about criminal law. So I began with the writing of *"A" Is for Alibi* to teach myself as much as I could. I was also having to teach myself how to write the detective novel, and when it came down to the prime character, I thought, *Shoot, I'm playing that part myself, thank you, folks.* Playing myself was at least something I knew and felt comfortable with, and I thought if I could use myself as the heroine, then that's one thing I didn't have to labor over. It felt easier to me, more familiar. We're not identical, but we are much the same. She's younger, and so her life looks different. She was born in California; I was born in Kentucky. We've both been married twice, but I'm married for a third time, and I don't know if she'll ever marry again. She has no kids; I'm more domestic than she is. But I think in some essential way, we see the world the same. I'm sure she cusses more than I do. I'm sure I'm much more ladylike than she is.

CLPS: Why don't you get her more involved, emotionally, in relationships?

SG: Because I don't think it's very interesting to write about. I think her strength as a private investigator to some extent is her neutrality or detachment. Certainly there are many occasions when she gets emotionally connected. In *"A" Is for Alibi*, she crosses the line, she gets involved with Charlie Scorsoni, and it was a mistake, and she *knows* it was a mistake. She knows when you're dealing with murder, you can't afford to have emotional connections with the people involved, because you don't know who did what to whom. I think, too, that readers need to understand that these books are about her professional life. So if they complain to me that she doesn't have enough friends or she doesn't get laid often enough, I reply that we don't know what she does between books; that's her own private business, and the books are about her professional life. Traditionally, the private eye has been a loner, he has been that knight errant, so to that extent, Kinsey has been a continuation of the tradition of the hard-boiled male private eye.

CLPS: Of the classic detective writers, who influenced you the most?

SG: Probably Raymond Chandler and Ross Macdonald. I've *never* been that fond of Dashiell Hammett. I think Raymond Chandler was a wonderful poet of the dark side, and I think Ross Macdonald had that quality, too: the ability to evoke things, to create, with very few images, whole worlds and whole realities. Those are writers that I admire for their skill and their brevity and their point of view. With Ross Macdonald, you got to a point, though, you could tell he was writing one book really, and the same things would surface over and over again. When he does it, they call it a "leitmotiv"; when I do it, they say I'm repeating myself.

CLPS: Were you ever a Nancy Drew fan?

SG: I was. I started with Nancy Drew and all matter of things. I also read Mickey Spillane really early, because my father wrote mystery fiction, and we bought a lot of trashy detective novels. My parents thought that children should be allowed to read anything, which I think is a great, great premise. They must have sat holding their breaths when I read *I, the Jury* at about age eleven or twelve, but they kept their theory in effect. Here's how it worked. We'd go up to the corner, and we'd get these paperback novels, and my mother would read them and she'd mark them in pencil "dirty," "dull," or "good." And of course, my sister and I would go straight to the "dirty" ones. But she knew that after we read enough of them, we'd get bored because they were so predictable and there was no mystique attached. Then we would drift over to the good ones. That was a perfect way to grow up.

CLPS: Your series has been going on since 1982, about fifteen years, but yet in the novels you have covered only about four years, I think. When do you make decisions about moving time forward?

SG: Oh, it came about accidentally. *"A" Is for Alibi* took place in May of 1982, then *"B" Is for Burglar* took place in June of that year, and *"C" Is for Corpse* took place in August. I didn't understand at that point that the series would go on as long as it has, and now I'm trapped in it in a way. I mean, I think it's better to keep the sequence going than to get into one of those maneuvers where suddenly it's 1994 but Kinsey's still thirty-five.

CLPS: You just didn't want to age her?

SG: I don't mind aging her. I liked following her as closely as I did, and I certainly want to keep her in an age range that seems believable to me. So she'll age one year for every two and half books, and when I get to Z, she'll be forty. That's perfect. We should all be forty.

CLPS: Forever?

SG: Yes, that's right.

CLPS: Do you work to a plan?

SG: Yes, that's how I decide from book to book where we're going to be in time. Generally, I do two books in each of these fictional calendar years. So, for instance, *"K" Is for Killer* takes place in February of 1994, because I knew I wanted to do a book at night. The days are really short in February, and it just seemed like a wonderfully gloomy time. In *"L,"* Kinsey will have had a birthday, that will have come and gone. So I keep track of when books are set, and I look for new moody times of the year to deal with.

CLPS: Tell me about the past in your fiction.

SG: Actually, it's real simple. The reason I bring the past into a book is often it is the perfect way to conceal what is going on. Dealing with the past gives you a little bit more clever way to obscure your purpose. Also, private investigators are not generally involved in a homicide. That is the proper jurisdiction of the police. They don't like private investigators messing in their work. So it's not realistic or appropriate for Kinsey Millhone, girl gumshoe, to set out to solve yesterday's murder. Something that happened twenty years ago, if that gets brought back to life, nobody cares that much. A homicide file is always open, it's always considered an active case. But murders, violence, and crimes are piling up so fast these days that the police, while they will go back to occasionally work or develop a lead in a past crime, they're not as inclined to bristle on those issues. So investigating past crimes means the case has faded away from an active homicide investigation. So some of what I do is just try to put Kinsey in situations where she is not treading on toes in an active homicide case. So, if for instance Lorna Kepler has been dead for ten months, the police are less protective of information about the case, and they're probably more inclined to say to Kinsey, "Oh, hell, we'll let you look at what we got; you go have a go." Whereas, if it's been a week, they're going to be very, very unhappy if she's messing around with their business, and rightly so. The past is a nice device for getting a story moving in a way that seems realistic.

CLPS: Where do you come up with plot ideas?

SG: You just look at all kinds of things; I don't know. I invent that as I go, generally.

CLPS: Do you go to newspapers for ideas?

SG: I'll go to them for side issues. The true crime is so silly and so ludicrous that it's usually not very workable for fiction because in the real world, people will kill each other for a pair of tennis shoes, and most mystery readers do not find that satisfying.

CLPS: Do you want to talk a little bit about *"K" Is for Killer*?

SG: Okay, one of the problems I set myself was that I just wanted to write a book that took place at night; that was part of what interested me. I see it as Kinsey's descent into the underworld, and I see it as a world that is populated with night demons and strange creatures who can transform themselves from male to female to male and the inexplicable happens.

CLPS: You do reverse day for night.

SG: I am very much a day person. I'm probably sound asleep at nine every night, so it's fun for me to get into my pickup truck and drive around Santa Barbara late at night and see what the world is like. I got curious about who's up at that hour, what happens to you, what do they think about, who are those people who do the night work, how do they feel, and what does it look like. I realized that nights are very different from one another. I always thought night was just dark and faintly chilly, but really, there is weather, there is all manner of differentiations between one night and the next. In the story line itself threaded throughout *"K"* is the image of water, a symbol of the unconscious. It was a book in which I really thought about these things. Often you write a book and include things without doing so consciously. For instance, in *"F" Is for Fugitive*, I reached the end of the book before I understood that it was about fathers. The whole book was about the relationship that we have with our fathers, but I hadn't seen it until I got to the end. Sometimes I'm conscious of an effect that I want or an area I want to explore, and sometimes I realize I have done it in spite of myself.

CLPS: Let's talk a little bit about *"L" Is for Lawless*.

SG: Somebody said to me just recently, "I wondered if that wasn't your tribute to Elmore Leonard?" You know, maybe so, because it was not a whodunit, but it was a caper novel, which is exactly what Elmore Leonard writes, and I am his number-one fan. I thought that it was fun to try a book that wasn't the traditional whodunit. I get to a point that I think, *Who cares who done it. Do something else for a change.* I enjoyed the adventure of that book, both in terms of the research and in terms of the story line. Again, it was a way of trying something new. A lot of readers didn't like it, but that's true of everything I do. The process is about my learning my craft, about my challenge to myself. Some books are more successful than others, and you can't predict that in advance. You have to do as well as you can with every single book, and then you can't sit around worrying about public taste.

CLPS: What about your latest, *"M" Is for Malice?*

SG: This is such a mystery to me. People have said to me, "Oh, that was such a fabulous book, and she's just grown so much as a person." I don't even know what they are talking about. I wrote the book as well as I could, and I'm happy with it. I don't even know what they see. People project. One woman, who has been a fan of mine for years, wrote, "Oh, my God, I saw the picture on the back of the book. What happened?" She said, "Is it your health failing, did something happen to your husband? I could tell exactly the point in the book where whatever it was happened." So I wrote back and said, "Darling, those pictures were taken two years ago. Nothing happened in the middle of the book. I'm in good health; I'm lifting weights; I'm having a blast." She was projecting. It isn't anything in me. Somehow, it triggered something in her, and she thought I had met my maker or something. Often you get people reacting in ways that are just mysterious. I can't control that, and if you can't control it, there is no point in worrying about it.

CLPS: Is *"M"* somehow darker, do you think?

SG: I don't think so. I did fall in love with this character, Guy Malik. He was a character I really cared about, and I was sorry he had to die. Everybody else was sorry he had to die, but that's the way it goes sometimes. Maybe that's part of what they are reacting to. But homicide is like that: it's not the bad people who die, it's the good people who die.

CLPS: Do you want to talk about *"N"* at all?

SG: No. I'm just getting into that, and every day is a new adventure. Some days I think, *Got it. Got it.* The next day I go, *Nope, not yet.* But I am making good progress. I just worry about spooking myself.

CLPS: Is the pace of one book a year hard for you?

SG: Killing, killing, killing, but I'd like to slow down now. I was late turning *"K"* in. I thought *"K"* was for *Kidnap*, but I couldn't make that work. I worked on it for four months, and junked it and started again, so that threw me way off. I usually turn in a book the first week in September; *"K"* I turned in the first week of December. They scrambled around and got it out on time, but I suspect it would have been a better book if I had a little more leisure to look at it. Why are we writing a book a year? I don't get this.

CLPS: Are there commercial reasons for doing it?

SG: Yes, but if you look at people like Amy Tan, she wouldn't do a book a year and everybody goes, "Oh, this is la-di-da literature." I would like to believe that a mystery novel is literature, and that we can take the requisite time and attention and care for the book.

CLPS: Do you have a non-Kinsey book you'd like to do?

SG: Perhaps, way, way, way, boys and girls, in the future. When I am done with this. For the moment, she is a fairly jealous little person, and she doesn't allow me to think about anything but her. She's tough. It suits me just fine that our relationship is as it is. I try to do right by her, and so far she's doing right by me.

CLPS: How do you keep the series fresh?

SG: Part of my objective in life is to do exactly that. I never take the easy way out; I never relax my grip on reality; I never assume that I'm over the hump; I never presume that my reader will follow me wherever I go. I do unrelenting research and unrelenting revisions on the work I've done, and I am constantly casting about for some new way to approach homicide and the mystery in the construction of these books.

CLPS: Do you set a specific goal with each of the novels?

SG: Each generally has a problem that I am setting for myself, and sometimes I can articulate that better than others. For instance, as I mentioned, in *"K" Is for Killer*, the challenge I set for myself was to see if I could write a book set entirely at night.

CLPS: You mentioned research. How do you go about researching a Kinsey Millhone book?

SG: Somebody had mentioned to me "the slabs" down in the Mojave Desert. The minute I heard about it, I thought, *I have to see what that's like*. I made a trip down there, and I realized that I could fold it into the book I was writing. So I went down there, took a lot of pictures, made some inquiries. Actually, I made two trips down to make sure I got the information I needed. Then I made that part of the setting in *"G" Is for Gumshoe*. Research can be anything from location scouting to a chat with a coroner. I just took a tour of the new morgue here in Santa Teresa. I talk with cops, attorneys, private investigators. I have a lot textbooks in my personal library that I consult. I'm always coming up against my own ignorance. I think one of the things that keeps the series fresh is the fact that I have to learn the stuff every time out. I don't retain the information. That is just not how my brain works. So every time I tackle something that has to do with California criminal law, I have to look it up all over again. It's fresh to me, and I go, *Wow, what an amazing thing.* I hope by the time I get to *"Z" Is for Zero*, I have got some of this stuff. In the meantime, I am always careful that I don't take myself for granted. Where I make errors is not in issues where I know I'm ignorant; it's with issues where I think I know what I'm talking about. That's sometimes fatal.

CLPS: What are the limits to your research?

SG: Any piece of information that is critical to making the book work, I do first, and then many other things I do as I go along. You could spend your life doing research. It's really fun, and you're safe, you know? No one can criticize you when you are in the middle of doing research. It is when you finally get around to putting your ass on the line out there that things can suddenly run amok. You can research up to a point, and then you just have to plunge in and do the job.

CLPS: How important is setting for you?

SG: It isn't as important in some books as it is in others. For instance, with *"M" Is for Malice*, that book was set here in Santa Teresa, and I knew that turf pretty well, so I didn't have to do any location work at all. Other times, I decide that I am bored with Santa Teresa and I go somewhere else, and then I have to set out on a little journey to see what I can uncover. So it varies. It depends on the book itself.

CLPS: Do you have a particular process for developing a story once you get it going?

SG: Inevitably, what I do is to open a journal for each book I write. The journal is like a long letter to myself in which I wring my hands, I whine, and I talk about how dumb I am and how I'm never going to figure it out and how my career is over. You know, just the little day-to-day reflections in the average day in the life of a writer. I just talk myself through it. As I go on from day to day, I talk about what a scene is meant to do as I approach it. I try to figure out what's making me uneasy, where I need to do research. If a line of dialogue occurs to me, I go ahead and lay it in. So sometimes I work ahead of myself, because I'll think of a scene and I'll say to myself, "Oh shoot, I know just how that goes." Anything out of thin air, I grab. I sort of construct the book like a patchwork quilt.

CLPS: So you don't block it all out ahead of time?

SG: No. I often know the future in a book, but I think it is so boring to do it in a linear fashion. I'm always afraid that I'll just fall asleep. So it seems more entertaining to discover the book as I go. I have a sort of master plan. I know, in general, where I'm going, but I've noticed that anytime I try to outline, it looks great on paper, but it means absolutely nothing when it comes to the actual writing of the book. I'll lay in an outline: Kinsey discovers the compelling clue. But I get there and I think, *What clue? How did she figure that out?* Then I realize later that I have just fooled myself. I have felt so productive, I have imagined that I have actually conquered a problem, and I haven't done it at all. So I might as well wait till I get there and see what it is about at that point, because by then, I may know something about the book that I didn't know when I was at the outline stage.

CLPS: Are there subjects that you won't tackle?

SG: I am not really interested in writing about little children getting maimed, mutilated, and killed. I would never do a serial killer book. I just think that is just so tedious. There are too many of them, and how many ways can you do that? Generally, those are the books about women getting mutilated, stamped, and killed. Oh, stop it already! It just doesn't interest me. There are lots of people out there making a handsome living at it, so they can have it.

CLPS: What about violence?

SG: We live in a violent world, and in fact, what is homicide but a piece of violence? So I don't say yes or no to that until I get there. It depends on what the book is and what is required. I don't shy away from it if it is necessary. That's how I make my living, talking about violence, but if you are asking about graphic or gratuitous violence, I prefer to think I avoid it.

CLPS: Is there a line one doesn't cross?

SG: I think there is a sense one has of good taste, if homicide can be considered in good taste. I have a very clear sense of what I consider okay and not okay. Some readers might disagree, because I think we all have a different attitude about that sort of thing. I write for myself, and I can't be accountable for everybody's attitudes. So if people don't like what I'm doing, they are very happy to write me letters and tell me that.

CLPS: Do you hear regularly from fans?

SG: Always. What I've noticed is for every book I write, about eighty-seven people write to say "fabulous," about ten write to tell me I did something wrong, and then there's three who tell me I should just give it up, get a day job, that I have just done the worst piece of shit they have ever read. I write back to everybody. I feel if someone has taken the time to write to me that I owe it to them to reply. Sometimes they are so insulting that I think, *Phooey on you, too.* Most of the time I think, *Oh, well, you don't have to agree with me, that's okay, I don't like you much, either.* I suppose if everybody liked what I was doing, I would take offense because it would mean that I was so bland and generic that even grannies liked me. Although I don't intentionally set out to offend anybody, at least it means that I'm cutting close to somebody's bone.

CLPS: Kinsey gets physically hurt more than occasionally in the books. How does this affect her?

SG: I try to keep that aspect of her life reasonable. I don't think she should get her nose broken in every book. I don't think it should be ridiculous. She lives in a hazardous world, and her profession is sometimes hazardous. I try not to make it ludicrous that she would suffer one kind of injury or another. I sort of vary it. I don't want every book to end in fisticuffs. So I pay very close attention to how the last book has been constructed to try to set it up so that the book after, the one I'm working on, doesn't duplicate the feel of something I've already done. Generally, I think in a mystery novel, what it comes down to in the end is a very physical contest. It's good and evil. It's the black hats and the white hats. It is about taking on what everybody else bypasses.

CLPS: In spite of the fact that Kinsey is aging very slowly, is she growing as a character?

SG: I don't make a deliberate calculation in that regard, any more than I think we do to ourselves. I would like to hope that each of us is growing and developing as the years go on, but I don't think we sit around thinking, *Gosh, what can I do to develop this year?* Life comes along, we experience it, it affects us one way or the other, we either rise to the occasion or we don't. I hope we learn something, whichever way it comes down. I hope she is growing and developing, but it isn't a conscious choice I make. I don't sit and map it out and then have a checklist. So, for instance, I wrote about her family in *"J" Is for Judgment*, and I'm still kicking myself for having done that. It seemed like a good idea at the time, but now people are very smitten with the notion of her family, and I'm bored to tears. So once in a while, if it seems appropriate, I write about it, but people say to me, "But, wait, I thought you would write about that in that next book, and I read it, and you never said a word about them." Well, it wasn't relevant to the story I was telling this time. You create these monsters without meaning to, and people get very exacting about what they expect you to do next. I have to be careful what I unleash.

CLPS: Kinsey works alone. Why don't you give her a close associate?

SG: In those books where there is the pal or the partner or the love interest, often those scenes don't interest me. I skip right over them. *Oh, God, here comes the witty repartee. Here comes the bedroom scene.* I think, *Well, let's just get on with the story, folks.* It's like Elmore Leonard says: He tries not to write those parts nobody reads. Let's just skip the parts nobody reads. You also then have these obligations to these other characters. Even Henry sometimes becomes oppressive to me. I already wrote about Henry in the last book. How come I have to write about him again? Can't we just let Henry rest, this book? But people write me letters telling me how much they were looking forward to seeing some more about Henry. If it interests me, I do it, and I think if the books are fresh, what keeps them so is because I'm fresh. If I'm not interested, you're not going to be interested. I don't just paint by the numbers. I try to keep moving, and sometimes I do something that is not according to the reader's expectations.

CLPS: In the past, you've done quite a bit of work for television. Would you ever go back to it?

SG: I'm so clever; I got out. I am the envy of all the people I know who still work for television. They ask me, "How did you do that?" I had to work really hard to get out. It is very seductive work because you are always getting paid what seems like huge sums of money. So you try to get out, and then your bills need to be paid and you think, *Well, one more. Just one more.* Finally, I understood that the only way out was to just quit doing the one more. I reached a point by about *"G" Is for Gumshoe* where I could afford to get out.

CLPS: Did you learn anything writing television scripts?

SG: It taught me a lot. Now that I don't work there, I could say some things about Hollywood, but I always try to be fair, because truly, Hollywood taught me a lot. They are lessons, as I've said later, that I'm not sure I wanted to learn, but they were important lessons. For instance, I learned how to write a dialogue scene, how to get into a scene and get out of it. I learned how to write an action scene. I learned how to structure a story, which is critical. I never knew how to do that before. So Hollywood was invaluable to me, and it never was the writing in that town that bugged me; it was the way business was done. I just got to a point that I couldn't tolerate it anymore. To have somebody else take their "fine gold pencils" to my work was obnoxious. I finally got to a point where I realized, *If you don't like the game, don't take the money.* I didn't want to turn into one of those terrible people who sits around bitching about Hollywood but is still working for them. Nobody was forcing me to do it at gunpoint. I was thrilled to get out.

CLPS: Will the books ever get made into movies?

SG: No, no. Because, you see, I invented Kinsey Millhone as my way out; I would never sell her back to them. I would have to be nuts to do that. I don't want them to have any power in my life. I don't want them to own any piece of me. As long as they have no cut of mine, we can be great pals, but I will never give those people power over me again. The perfect way to do that is just to mind my own business, keep writing my books, and let them do what suits them.

CLPS: Why don't you do more short fiction?

SG: I haven't done short fiction for many years. Short stories are really hard. If one occurred to me, I'd do it. I think they're fun. At least you get in and get out in shorter than ten months. There is great virtue to being able to do a finished piece of work in that amount of time. But you have to have an idea appropriate to a short story. My mind just works in different ways these days. If I could think of a short story, I would do one in a New York minute, as they say.

CLPS: Do the books just keep you tied up?

SG: Yeah, they'll ask me to write a story for a summer issue of some magazine, but I don't have the time or the ideas or the energy. Everything I own, everything I am, goes into these books.

CLPS: Does your success and that of some other female crime writers mean that there is something approaching parity for men and women in the field?

SG: It looked like it to me, but if you say that, they act like you're antifeminist or something. I know a lot of women are taking jobs away from a lot of the guys. I have heard that there are guys who can't get contracts renewed because the women are in there taking the money, getting the deals. If that isn't parity, I don't know what is. The truth about any business is that if you earn them money, you got parity, Bubba. There isn't any conspiracy that I can tell. The conspiracy is to earn money for people, and you will have as much equality as you can handle. I'm not a fan of the notion that anybody's out to prevent women from getting somewhere.

CLPS: You routinely make both the hardcover and paperback bestseller lists, so you're obviously doing very well with the public. What about the critics?

SG: I've stopped reading reviews. I think I'm still doing okay with the critics, but basically, I don't care. My job is to satisfy myself, and by the time the critics come along, my job has been done, and I've done it as well as I can. So, if the critics decide that a book doesn't suit them, it has nothing to do with me; I've moved on. I like to see how a book is going to do, and I always wish my books well, like little boats I push out into the stream. But I'm back at my machine, trying to set up the next impossible task for myself. I find that the good reviews are no more helpful than the bad reviews. The bad reviews are upsetting. It's upsetting to any writer, I think, to read the review that says, "Weak plotting, poor construction, bad pace." You know, whatever they say. It's hard enough to write if you're feeling real cocky.

CLPS: Do you see yourself extending the boundaries of crime fiction? Playing with the conventions?

SG: I don't think so, do you? Did something happen I don't know about? One always tries playing with the conventions, because it is fun to see how far you can push the form. But I don't see it as a terribly formulaic genre to begin with. I think the crime novel is a huge umbrella that covers many kinds of novels: espionage, techo-thriller, even serial killers have become a separate subtype. Those categories spill over into each other. So it's always possible to try it a little bit differently, to come at it from a little bit different direction. That's what makes it fun.

CLPS: Is there ever a question you wished an interviewer would ask you but they never do?

SG: I'm thrilled you didn't ask how I came up with the alphabet. There are some questions I think I'm going to die if I ever have to answer again. One is, how did you come up with this notion of the alphabet? The readers are always asking me. They'll ask me nine hundred times when I do a signing, "What are you going to do when you get to Z?" Or they'll say what's Z for? I usually say Z is for *Zero*. I *used* to say Z is for *Zero*, then I'll do numbers. I don't say that anymore. See, I won't finish this series until the year 2008 or 2009. Nobody knows what they're going to be doing in the year 2009. In fact, I may know more than most about where I'm going to be in the next fifteen years.

Portions of this interview appeared in *Mystery Scene*, No. 43 (1994), 40–42.

Anne Perry

INTERVIEW BY ADRIAN MULLER

*I*n 1979, Anne Perry's first novel, The Cater Street Hangman, *intro-duced Thomas and Charlotte Pitt, the protagonists of one of the two Victorian series of crime novels to be written by the British author. Ten books later, the second series debuted with investigator William Monk and nurse Hester Latterly in Perry's* The Face of a Stranger. *By this time, Perry had become a best-selling writer, finding huge popularity, especially in the United States.*

Then, in 1994, the film Heavenly Creatures *was released, drawing attention away from the author's writing and focusing it instead on events that had occurred some forty years earlier. The film was a highly stylized account of the murder, by Juliet Hulme and Pauline Parker, of Pauline's mother. A journalist discovered that the then-fifteen-year-old Hulme had grown up to become Anne Perry, the well-known crime novelist, and since then, press coverage has tended to focus on the more sensational aspects of the author's past.*

This interview concentrates on the writer Anne Perry, author of his-torical crime novels with skillful plotting and complex characterizations.

Anne Perry was born Juliet Marion Hulme in London in 1938. Nearly dying of pneumonia at the age of six, Juliet was sent to stay with family friends in the Bahamas after her parents had been told their daughter would not survive another British winter. It was not until 1948 that she rejoined her parents in New Zealand, where her father had been appointed rector of Canterbury University College in Christchurch.

When she was thirteen, Juliet met Pauline Parker at Christchurch Girls High School, and a close friendship developed between the youngsters. The threat to this friendship ultimately led to Juliet's and Pauline's convictions for murder, and the adolescent girls were sent to separate prisons, never to see each other again.

Upon her release, shortly after her twenty-first birthday, Juliet Hulme was given a passport in the name of Anne Stuart, Stuart being the name of her maternal grandmother. She was put on a plane to Britain, and back in England, she went to live with her mother, now married to Bill Perry. It was when she decided to take on her stepfather's name that the future author became Anne Perry.

Twenty years later, after writing numerous manuscripts in different genres, Anne Perry produced her first crime novel, which was then immediately accepted by an American publisher. "Writing is the only thing I ever really wanted to do," she remarks when asked about her perseverance. As for the origin of the plot, she says, "My stepfather had an idea for a book about who Jack the Ripper might have been. I wasn't curious about who the Ripper was, and I hope they never find out—it is much better as a mystery—but," Perry continues, "through that suggestion, I became interested as to what might happen to a group of people when they find themselves under an enormous pressure by the investigation of murder. It comes closer and closer to home, and then they suddenly realize it could be somebody they know, even somebody they care about in their own family. That is when the relationships start to fracture," the author says, "and everything has to be reassessed. That is how I came to write *The Cater Street Hangman*."

It is initially the death of a servant that brings policeman Thomas Pitt to the Ellison household. Then, gradually, as the investigation in *The Cater Street Hangman* progresses, a romance develops between Pitt and Charlotte Ellison, the middle daughter of the family. The subsequent marriage between the upper- and working-class protagonists allowed for the diversity of Victorian norms and values to be covered in the books that followed.

As fond as Anne Perry is of the early Pitts, she feels she didn't hit her stride until she changed publishers in 1990. "My first American publisher only took things after I had written them," she explains. "They never commissioned anything in advance. Consequently, you will find that in my first ten books, I played things fairly safe. Then I moved to Ballantine, who really allowed me to know that they believed in me. They commissioned books in advance, which allowed me to feel that I could break out and put more of myself into my work, to start packing the punches. That is when I started the Monk series. You'll find, I think, quite a jump in quality when I changed publishers," Perry concludes.

In the first of the Monk novels, *The Face of a Stranger*, a man wakes up in a mid–nineteenth-century London hospital to find that an accident has robbed him of his memory. He soon discovers that his name is William Monk, and that he is a policeman by profession. Gradually, throughout this book and its subsequent installments, he regains bits of his past, not always liking what he finds. It is also in *The Face of a Stranger* that William Monk first meets Hester Latterly, a fiercely independent nurse. Together with Oliver Rathbone, a barrister who first appears in *Defend and Betray*, the three became the leading characters in the Monk novels.

In light of the revelations about Anne Perry's past, there has been speculation that Monk's history—memory loss and his ensuing discovery that he had not been a pleasant person—was the author's attempt to allow herself to examine her own experiences in some way. Perry denies that this is the case. "It was not in order to examine myself," she says. "It was in order to examine others looking for 'monsters,' and then allowing them to discover that there are no monsters, there are only people." She adds, "We don't necessarily like all of ourselves, but bit by bit, we learn to understand and then, when you understand yourself, one hopes you can transfer that understanding to other people."

As an author, Perry is most happy when she hears that her books have helped other people. "Somebody said to me the other day that one of the reasons she enjoys reading the Monks is because, as Monk discovers a little more of himself in each story, she feels she discovers a little more of herself, as well. Now that," Perry enthuses, "is what I love. That reader has caught what I'm really trying to say. You discover yourself through discovering others. Then perhaps you reverse the process and discover others by discovering yourself."

Feedback from her readers is important to Anne Perry, and she finds her trips to the United States very rewarding. "My American publishers are very good and bring me over every year for a promotional tour of four to six weeks. I don't visit every state in the union," she says with a smile, "but certainly quite a few of them." While she is there to publicize her latest novel, the trips are also of great value to the author because they give her the most direct contact with her readers. "I hear what people think, and what they read in what I write. It's very, very encouraging."

It was on such an occasion that she was paid a memorable compliment. "A man in San Diego told me that he taught at a high school, and that my books were required reading for his course. I thought, *Oh, that's nice,* and I asked him whether he taught history or literature. He answered, 'Ethics.' Now that's the payoff! There I am, one hundred years old, wondering what I did with my life, and I shall say, 'Yes, that was something.' "

Anne Perry does not have a specific audience in mind when she writes her novels, saying that she really writes for anybody who wants to read. "I think it was Bernard Shaw who said, 'Heaven is like a concert hall with a great symphony orchestra playing,' " Perry says. "You can let anybody in, but you can not make everybody hear the music. You are never going to reach everybody. Ideally, I think a book should be a good enough story to draw in anybody who can read and has imagination, but for some there are layers and layers and layers. Only a few are going to get the very deepest layer."

Though the two series share Victorian England as a setting, there are numerous distinctions between them. The Monk books take place around the middle of the nineteenth century, and the Pitts some forty years later. There is a difference in tone, as well. "The Pitt books," Anne Perry explains, "are set in a slightly lighter period. There was a lot more glamour and fun in the nineties, and the stories are socially and politically orientated. The Monks are darker and tend to have legal, medical, and military backgrounds. They nearly always have a trial in them, and they also have this edgy relationship between Monk, Latterly, and Rathbone."

It is unlikely that Anne Perry will ever let the main characters from her two series cross each other's paths because the author is not willing to predetermine the future of Monk, Latterly, and Rathbone. She does not rule out, however, that older cast members from the Pitt novels may make an appearance in the Monk series.

Perry is equally undecided as to how the relationships between William, Hester, and Oliver will develop. She is anxious that the Monk books don't take on too many aspects of the Pitt series, and therefore she doubts that Latterly will ever marry either man. "I have brought Oliver to the brink of asking Hester to marry him," she says, "but when she realizes what he is going to say, she steers the conversation in a different direction. The shadow of Monk is too heavy between them." Monk, in turn, could never marry anyone but Latterly, and though it may not happen, nothing will ever break up their friendship. Perry has played with the idea of William asking Hester to marry him, only to break off the engagement because he discovers something appalling in his past. "He would decide she shouldn't be saddled with him, and Hester would be absolutely livid. 'How dare you decide for me!' Hester would say," she concludes, laughing.

One of the other common elements of the two series are strong female characters, and Perry disagrees that her women and their relationships with men are ahead of their time. "I write about strong women because it would be anachronistic not to," she says. According to the author, the cause of women's rights saw significant activism and progress during the nineteenth century. Perry uses her grandmother as an example that progressive attitudes existed in Charlotte's era. "My father was born in 1908, and his mother worked like the blazes and put both him and his sisters through university," Perry states. Her father studied mathematics, physics, and astronomy; her aunts studied politics, philosophy, and law rather than humanities, the usual subject for those few women who attended university at that time. "This for a family from an ordinary, working-class background in Salford," Perry continues, adding, "and my paternal grandmother would not have been much younger than Charlotte."

The decision to make Hester Latterly one of Florence Nightingale's Crimean War nurses was again very specific. "I wanted Hester to be a woman with courage," she says, "and she needed a reason to have the courage, experience, and independence that she has. She'd be completely out of her time if there was no explanation for it, if she were this extraordinary woman having grown up in ordinary circumstances. Being a nurse in the Crimea, she would have gained this independence and experience of exercising judgment, authority, and decision. She would have been through more than enough to prompt her to act contrary to her earlier upbringing. Yet, without that background, she would be quite unbelievable."

Anne Perry had always intended to have male and female protagonists in both of her series, but the inclusion of both sexes also had specific purposes, practicality not being the least of them. "The reason was to get more than one point of view," she explains. "If I limited myself to the female role, there would have been so many places I couldn't have gone. It would be very restricting, especially in Victorian times when male and female roles are so different. Also, because I am a woman, I wanted a woman's point of view. I think women observe things differently from men. They particularly notice body language more than men do. We can hold a trivial conversation about the weather, but what we are really communicating can be a lot more important. Men are a lot more literal, I think, and in the past, they didn't have to pay as much attention to body language because they had all the power, be it physical or financial," she ends.

Anne Perry relies on two kinds of research. The historical research mostly comes from reference books. "However," the author says, "they aren't a great deal of use when it comes to what a person was thinking or feeling, and that is far more important." When it comes to human behavior, Perry counts on her experience of relating to people. "If you know only people who are roughly similar to yourself, with the same sort of interests, that narrows your world a great deal. So, being interested in and knowing as wide a variety of people as possible is one of the best ways of research I know," she says, "and I would say the key thing is to like them."

Perry is less certain how her culpability in the death of Mrs. Parker has influenced her writing. "I don't know," she says. "Everything in life influences who you are, and probably I'm a much more thoughtful person because of it. I probably leap to judgment on others a great deal less because of it, but it's not something I think about very often. I have come to terms with it, but obviously, you can't have something like that happen in your life without it affecting you unless you're totally mentally out of it." She pauses momentarily to consider her words. "It informs who I am, and who I am informs my writing."

While she was living in the United States in the late 1960s, Anne Perry came across what has been a major influence on her life and work ever since. "I didn't encounter the Church until I was about twenty-seven, some twelve years after I'd come to terms with what had happened in New Zealand," Perry says. "I'd gone to a lot of the different Christian churches that had crossed my path, and each one had offered a lot, but there was always something I couldn't agree with. So therefore I decided I was going to walk my own path, be a religious person but not attached to any church." This changed when she learned about the Church of Jesus Christ of Latter-day Saints, also known as the Mormon Church. Recalling her feelings at the time, Perry says, "I thought, *Just a minute, this is what I believe!* It was what I had worked out myself, plus a whole lot more I hadn't even thought of."

While she is observant of her religion, Perry is not fanatical about her faith. However, it is significant to know why the Mormon religion appealed to Perry because its teachings find their way into the author's books not as dogma but as a strong guiding philosophy.

Unlike most Christian religions, the Mormon faith does not see the human banishment from Eden as a punishment. For them, it is the first step in a process of progressing and growing into becoming a full individual. Being able to make the right choices and distinctions and making the necessary mistakes along the way is part of this process. Ultimately, people will progress to knowledge where they can choose good because they understand what it is, and they realize it is what they want. "It is the idea that you continue to learn and to grow until you become braver, wiser, more generous, more compassionate," Perry explains. "A purity of heart is not being unblemished, it's learning to understand your faults so that you can erase them yourself. It's purity of intent."

Perry feels forgiveness is an important part of erasing one's faults. "If God will forgive after a certain period of appropriate understanding and repentance, then you can not be self-indulgent, and you've got to forgive yourself as well. Self-castigation really is pretty selfish. You have the responsibility to say, 'I did something I shouldn't have done. I understand that it was wrong and why it was wrong, and if I can put it right, I will. If I can't, then I will absorb myself in becoming as good a person as I can. I will forgive myself, and I will jolly well forgive others as well, because another part of Christianity is that you will be forgiven as you forgive. If you cannot forgive others, you can not expect to be forgiven, and if you truly wish to be forgiven, you will want to forgive others because you will know what it is like to need to be forgiven. That again is very basic Christianity; it's love of other people."

A further important point of distinction is that while Anne Perry's work is morally grounded, it is also infused with humor and is never moralistic. "I don't go to the scriptures with the idea of finding a theme," she says. "If you are true to your religion, it's got to be a way of life that informs everything you do; otherwise, it's simply a Sunday observance." Having said this, Perry also stresses, "It is never 'What does the Church teach?' that I want to write about, it's 'What do I believe? What do I care about?' " She presumes that all writers feel the same way and base their work on their own ethical beliefs, whether they are religious or not. "If you're not writing what you care about or what you believe in, then I suggest you do something else."

For some years now, Anne Perry has been living in Ross-shire,

Scotland. Her beautiful home has a stunning view over the Dornoch Firth, and the house is situated on what can only be described as a miniature estate. Most days there are at least two people working on the property, and the author also has two part-time secretaries to assist with her writing one Pitt and one Monk novel a year. In addition, there are various manuscripts in the offing: two French Revolution novels—one of which is the start of another historical crime series—and also a fantasy trilogy.

Perry explains that she is able to keep up a consistent output because she enjoys what she does, and she usually works six days a week. "I normally start about nine in the morning, pause for a little while at five, before going back at maybe ten, often working till after midnight."

Invaluable to Anne Perry's work is friend and next-door neighbor Meg MacDonald. "Not only is she a good, constructive critic," the author says, "she is very good for brainstorming and helps with the creative side of things. We work two mornings a week together."

It was MacDonald who saved one of the supporting cast members from a very nasty death. "The character is gang-raped," the author explains, "and he was going to be so badly wounded, psychologically as well as physically, that he was going to die. Meg said, 'Do we have to kill him off?' I thought, *Well, no, it really isn't necessary.* So I changed my mind on that. I, and I hope the readers, too, have got fonder and fonder of him as time has gone by, and it would just make the book too dark if I had let him go. The whole story's pretty tragic in a lot of other respects, so I hope I've balanced it out."

It would not have been the first time that Perry had disposed of one of the figures who previously had played a prominent supporting part in her books. Yet, as long as the reaction of both the surviving characters and her readers is strong enough, she has no great difficulty in killing them off. When writing about death in her books, it is not the corpses that concern her so much, "It's the pain and the fear involved that bothers me," she says, adding, "The deaths in my books are intended to leave you shaken." Such traumas also have a lasting influence on the remaining characters in her books. "Some authors do not change their principal character. I don't mean make them a different person," Perry explains, "I mean the protagonist is not altered by what happens. Do you think that anybody could experience those things and be worth a damn and not be altered?"

Before she begins to write, Anne Perry has plotted and planned her novel thoroughly. She has summarized each chapter, scene by scene, on a foolscap page, explaining, "I need a pretty good structure, or it's going to be a lousy book." Earlier on, she has already established the nature and the reason for the crime. More importantly, Perry will have asked herself why the perpetrators would have felt that committing it was the only course open to them. "If there's another, easier way, they're going to take it," she says. "I don't want to write about somebody who kills because it amuses them, and I also don't find financial gain is a very interesting motive."

What is a frequent motive in Perry's books, however, is the human desire for power, and this desire is most strongly represented by the Inner Circle in the Pitt novels. Thomas Pitt, who is identified by Perry as most often voicing her own convictions, has frequently been offered membership in this organization, which very much resembles the secret Freemason institutions of the time. He has always refused to join what he sees as a faceless entity on the grounds that he would be relinquishing his right to heed his own conscience.

The latter is again inspired by Perry's personal convictions. "I believe the one thing you must hang on to for eternity is your free agency; it's basic Mormon philosophy. Free agency means your right to follow your own conscience, and you never, ever give up your individual freedom of conscience. Obviously, if you are going to do something that is outside the law of the land, you are going to have to pay the consequences for it, but our articles of faith state that you must obey the law of the land in which you live." Realizing that there are situations where this might contravene basic human rights, Perry admits that in those instances, fighting for change is permissible, "but," she stresses again, "you would accept the consequences."

These thought processes go a long way to explaining the depth of the author's characters, including her villains. On numerous occasions, even the latter earn the reader's sympathy, perhaps due to the fact that they are often victims themselves of the oppressive Victorian society in which they live. Perry will only partially accept this reasoning. "I don't think society can be blamed for everything," she says. "I like to think we are responsible for our own actions to a considerable degree, varying with the person and the circumstances. In one of my books, two girls, who were sold into prostitution at the ages of eight and ten, go on to kill men making profit from child prostitution. In that book especially, I would say society was to blame and, while I don't advocate murder, those men certainly had it coming. I can understand people having compulsions, but to use other people's compulsions and to feed it for profit . . ."

Yet despite her understanding of people with addictions of various natures, she dislikes the victim mentality. "It means you are helpless," she says. "I would far rather think that most of my problems are my own fault, because then that means I can fix them. I can stop being that way and do something about it."

Anne Perry has numerous projects in the pipeline. Among them are television adaptations of both her book series. The BBC had the initial option to the rights of the Charlotte and Thomas Pitt books, but let their contract lapse after numerous script writers were unable to produce satisfactory adaptations. Other production companies were interested in optioning the Pitt novels, but Perry chose to sell the rights to Ardent, a company owned by Prince Edward, Queen Elizabeth's youngest son. "Ardent already had the option on the Monks through an actress-turned-producer called Jane Merrow," the author explains. "So I chose Ardent partly because I wanted to keep the books with the same people rather than have them conflicting with each other. I also went with Ardent because I already knew the people there. I trusted that they would do adaptations in line with what I would feel happy with."

Despite alterations to the structure of *The Cater Street Hangman*, Perry is happy with the direction of the adaptation. "I think they are improving it in every sense. *The Cater Street Hangman* was my first book, and it was a bit raw. Obviously, for a two-hour drama, the plot has to be condensed quite a lot. The intention is to play up the love story and leave the mystery a little bit in the background. I think that they are correct in that and, if I were to write it again now, I would have the nerve to make the love story stronger as well. At the time I thought, *No, you're writing a mystery, don't dare do this. It isn't done.*

The two French Revolution novels and the fantasy trilogy will debut some time in the future. Perry thinks it will be "a wee while" before her publishers feel ready for these books. "The more you get known for one genre, the harder it is to break out," she says. "I will keep on polishing these manuscripts, tightening them up, and getting them better until they're good enough, until they reach the point where an editor says, 'This we've got to have.'"

Perry worked out the characters and plot for her French Revolution mystery while she was developing them for Otto Penzler who, as editor, was overseeing a series of novellas by different writers for Orion, a publishing company. "I liked the protagonists," she says, "so I want to carry on with them. The novella finishes with the September massacres in 1792, and I'm going to pick up the story in October, taking it through to the execution of King Louis XVI in January 1793." The author concludes, "Maybe, if somebody believes I can do a French Revolution crime novel, they might take my straight novel of the same period as well."

Tathea, Anne Perry's fantasy, is the book closest to her heart. When she talks about fantasy novels, she does not mean "dungeons and dragons" as she puts it, but stories that have a profound moral suggestion. "The best fantasies are explorations of perhaps not so much good and evil, but right and wrong," she says. "I don't think there's anything in the world that interests me quite as much as what we should do and what we sometimes do that's not right." Surprising herself, Perry suddenly formulates a definition for the genre. "I have never said this before, but this is what I think a fantasy should be: a spiritual truth or reality, illustrated in some dramatic yet concrete form."

As Perry talks about *Tathea*, it certainly seems that her fantasy novel will live up to her definition. The title of the book is the name of the protagonist, a woman who asks the universal questions: Who am I, and why do I exist? Tathea finds her answers in spiritual truth, which she brings back to Earth, but truth has many consequences. "Truth forces people to grow," Perry says. "The experiences that are most profound, offering growth, are also those that are most painful, and therefore, we often decline them. They force people out of what the Americans call 'the comfort zone,' but when you are in the comfort zone, you are not growing, and growing hurts! What we're scared of is that we'll be alone, that we'll be hurt, and that we'll fail and make fools of ourselves, but if you don't go out there and try, you'll certainly fail."

BIBLIOGRAPHY

The Cater Street Hangman (Pitt). New York, St. Martin's Press, and London, Hale, 1979.

Callander Square (Pitt). New York, St. Martin's Press, and London, Hale, 1980.

Paragon Walk (Pitt). New York, St. Martin's Press, 1981.

Resurrection Row (Pitt). New York, St. Martin's Press, 1981.

Rutland Place (Pitt). New York, St. Martin's Press, 1983.

Bluegate Fields (Pitt). New York, St. Martin's Press, 1984; London, Souvenir Press, 1992.

Death in the Devil's Acre (Pitt). New York, St. Martin's Press, 1985; London, Souvenir Press, 1991.

Cardington Crescent (Pitt). New York, St. Martin's Press, 1987;
London, Souvenir Press, 1990.

Silence in Hanover Close (Pitt). New York, St. Martin's Press, 1988;
London, Souvenir Press, 1989.

Bethlehem Road (Pitt). New York, St. Martin's Press, 1990;
London, Souvenir Press, 1991.

The Face of a Stranger (Monk). New York, Fawcett, 1990; London,
Headline, 1993.

Highgate Rise (Pitt). New York, Fawcett, 1991; London, Souvenir
Press, 1992.

A Dangerous Mourning (Monk). New York, Fawcett, 1992;
London, Headline, 1994.

Defend and Betray (Monk). New York, Fawcett, and London,
Headline, 1992.

Farrier's Lane (Pitt). New York, Fawcett, 1993; London,
HarperCollins, 1994.

A Sudden, Fearful Death (Monk). New York, Fawcett; and London,
Headline, 1993.

The Hyde Park Headsman (Pitt). New York, Fawcett, 1994;
London, HarperCollins, 1995.

The Sins of the Wolf (Monk). New York, Fawcett, and London,
Headline, 1994.

Traitor's Gate (Pitt). New York, Fawcett, 1995; London,
HarperCollins, 1996.

Cain His Brother (Monk). New York, Fawcett, and London,
Headline, 1995.

Pentecost Alley (Pitt). New York, Fawcett, 1996; London,
HarperCollins, 1997.

Weighed in the Balance (Monk). New York, Fawcett, and London,
Headline, 1996.

Ashworth Hall (Pitt). New York, Fawcett, 1997; London,
HarperCollins, 1998.

The Silent Cry (Monk). New York, Fawcett, and London,
Headline, 1997.

Patricia Cornwell

INTERVIEW BY PAUL DUNCAN

W hen she was five, Patricia Cornwell's parents broke up. Two years later, she moved with her mother and two brothers to Montreat, a small town in North Carolina, just two miles from the home of evangelist Billy Graham. Growing up, she heard many stories about the kind things Billy's wife, Ruth, did. One Christmas, Patricia's mother had a nervous breakdown and tried to give her children to Ruth. Ruth got the children accommodation with local missionaries for three months until Patricia's mother was well again. Later, Patricia became friends with Ruth, who became a sort of surrogate mother and a great influence on a troubled teenager with low self-esteem. Patricia was encouraged by Ruth to write short stories and poems. In 1981, after winning an award for her crime reporting at the Charlotte Observer, Patricia had to leave to move with her husband to Richmond, Virginia, where he studied for the ministry. It was here that she wrote a biography of Ruth Bell Graham called A Time for Remembering (1983).

While at the chief medical examiner's office, Patricia Cornwell wrote three unpublished crime fiction books—full of poisonings, buried treasure, and wills—in which Dr. Kay Scarpetta was a minor character. One of the editors who rejected her advised her to write about what she knows, and to let Scarpetta take center stage. Patricia was looking for a story for Scarpetta. Around that time, a serial killer was raping and strangling professional *women in Richmond. Patricia was separated from her husband, living alone, frightened, and bought her first gun for her own protection. This became the kernel for* Postmortem *(1990). The book became an immediate worldwide success, winning all five major mystery awards.*

Paul Duncan met Patricia at the Waldorf Hotel. Patricia's words were accompanied by the theme to Gone with the Wind *endlessly repeating in the background.*

PD: Where does the character of Kay Scarpetta come from?

PC: I have a suspicion that—and this may sound bizarre—one of her genetic coils is from my own relationship with Ruth Graham when I was growing up. She is a very powerful woman, very beautiful, and very, very kind. She has a heart of gold and is a compassionate person but, in her own way, is reserved. She was certainly a heroic character to me at a period of time in my life when I had no power, when I was very young. That's the sort of person you want to come save you when something bad happens.

PD: Is Kay similar to anyone?

PC: No. It probably has something to do with the fact that I didn't have anyone in mind when I came up with her. Also, because I'm so rooted in reality—to the real professionals and the real cases—I tend to get somewhat removed from literary, TV, or film characters. They, to me, are not reality, so they have no bearing on my work. This means I have a difficult time trying to explain my characters because people like to categorize them by comparing them to other characters.

PD: However, having created this popular character—a female medical examiner who works for the FBI at Quantico—all sorts of variations of her have started to appear in the past eight years. The most notable is probably Dana Scully in *The X-Files*, who has expressed some of the same ideas and thoughts as Kay Scarpetta.

PC: This is one of the reasons why Peter Guber and I are not wasting any time in producing the first Scarpetta film. Unfortunately, my books are the inspiration for other people to come up with other strong female protagonists, particularly in the FBI or medical fields.

I won't even watch or read these other things that people tell me about because they'll probably just aggravate me.

One of the reasons I've been fortunate enough to have access to a lot of places and information is because I have a platform of legitimacy from my profession and background. You also earn your credibility through word of mouth and by meeting people. I can't continue to enjoy the world these people live in unless they know they can trust me. They read the books, think I'm okay, and the doors open.

PD: You work to get the facts right.

PC: It's an unforgiving world. If you get something wrong, people turn off you just like that. Besides that, I want to get it right for myself, keep it honest. It's very important to me, personally, to get it right, to know what it feels like, and to experience it as much as I can.

PD: With access to all this information, and with two years experience as an award-winning crime reporter for the *Charlotte Observer*, I would have thought that you would be writing fact, not fiction.

PC: Sometimes fiction is truer than fact. Actually, I do both, because the scaffolding of all my stories is fact, whether it is a procedure, or the type of case, or the kinds of individuals. It is all rooted in experience and research. That's the fact. The fiction of it is the way that I want the characters to work the cases.

People have asked me over the years why I don't write true crime, and I tell them that I could not bring myself to victimize people all over again. If you have a son or daughter murdered in what turns out to be a sensational crime about which books are written, and you have been on the side of the fence where I have been—seeing relatives sitting in the waiting rooms and the looks on their faces as they come to find out what's happened to their child—I don't want to write about things in gory detail that could upset those relatives all over again. There are cases where people find it cathartic to write about their experiences, and I don't bump the people who do it, it's just that I couldn't, and I don't want to.

PD: The books have very little violence in them. All we see are the effects, both physical and emotional, of violence committed off screen.

PC: That's because that's all that Scarpetta sees. It's very rare that Scarpetta will witness a violent act unless she herself commits it, as she's had to do in several books when she's had to defend herself. I only show violence when the bad guys are getting it, not when the victim is getting it.

PD: Is that planned, or is it just the way it's worked out?

PC: That's the way I feel. Violence is a reality to me. I mean, I've had my hands on these dead bodies, I've been to the murder trials, I've been to the crime scenes. I've seen people roll through doors who've had their lives viciously ripped from them. I have no use for the people who commit those kinds of acts. My sympathy is for the victims. That's why I'm very comfortable with Scarpetta, because she is their defender. That's the way I feel. I couldn't do it any other way.

PD: Scarpetta is very single-minded. She's on a crusade.

PC: I'd say she and I both have lives consumed by what we do and what we believe. It's that I express mine in a different way than she does. She actually works the cases, and I tell the story of the cases. I have said many times that what I really consider myself to be is a scribe to the people out there doing the real work, whether it is the forensic pathologists, the FBI agents, the police, the scientists, the prosecutors . . . Someone needs to tell their stories, go in their labs and find out exactly what they're doing today. "Well, I'm using a gas chromatograph to do this . . ." or ". . . the scanning electron microscope to determine which element this is . . ." They need someone like me to do that, and that's really what I consider my job.

PD: She is so driven or obsessive about her job that it seems, perhaps, sad that she has so little life outside her job.

PC: It's not so much obsessive or driven as it is being devoted. For one to say that Scarpetta is obsessive or driven is like saying that a priest is. It's like a calling. She has taken on a mantle to help people who have no power. She's like a missionary, or a minister, or priest to the people who can no longer speak in a language that other people can understand. That's the way I regard what I do, too.

People can also say the same thing about me. I'm divorced, I haven't remarried, I have no kids, you never read in the papers about me dating someone, and so on. It's not that I don't have a private life or friends and attachments—I think I have a very rich life in that way—but I deal with people in snatches. I can't have weeks on end with people I like unless I happen to be working with them. It's for the same reason. I'm not driven to be the number-one crime writer in the world—it's not an ambition of mine—it's just that I'm devoted to what I'm doing as she is to what she's doing.

In the same way, I have to be as devoted to her so that I can tell her story and always learn the latest advances in technology or medicine that would be applicable to what she does so that I'm knowledgeable enough to deal with it in a book. And that takes a lot of time.

PD: Certainly, the temptation is to compare Patricia and Kay.

PC: We're the same, but we're different. Certainly, some things are the same. How could they not be, because they're coming out of me? So we probably share the same genetic code, by and large, but we're not exactly the same people. Maybe she's another manifestation of what I would be like if I did what she did for a living. Certainly, there are parallels.

I think it would be difficult to write about somebody like her if you didn't share some of the same qualities. Like, for example, a devotion to justice, integrity, and decency, fighting for people who can't fight for themselves, trying to make the world a little better.

You can't fake that. You either feel it or you don't. I couldn't make you feel what she feels if I didn't feel it.

For each book, I come up with a case I want her to work and then I go through the pilgrimage with her, and I simply put things down pretty much the way I see them and the way I know them from reality. In reality, of course, nobody is pure good and nobody is pure bad, but there are certainly good and evil people. Without a doubt, Temple Brooks Gault is evil. That doesn't mean that he doesn't have good qualities. I don't know what they are, and I don't care what they are, and I'm sure Kay doesn't care what they are either.

If you work in these professions, when people do things which are this heinous, you're not interested in their good qualities. You just want to figure out enough about them so that you can catch them, or at least give them a name so you can find them.

As far as Kay is concerned, she is not perfect, but she is purely good in terms of her integrity and morality where justice is concerned. She is having an affair with a married man, Benton Wesley. That's not moral. That's not even smart. She knows it, too, and she has trouble with it. She's not always done the right thing with Lucy, and she knows it. And Lucy knows it, too. But Kay tries.

I think it's on the personal front that it's more difficult, which, I think, is true for most of us. You will never catch me being dishonest in the business world or even in my profession, but sometimes I might be dishonest in my personal life because I don't say something I should say because it's too hard for me to say it. That's where Kay's weaker.

PD: Reading *Cruel and Unusual, The Body Farm*, and *From Potter's Field*, these books read as a trilogy.

PC: In those three books, as a matter of fact, I was trying very hard to get Kay to loosen up a little bit. I think you see that because she has more emotional situations on her hands.

PD: So there was no design for the three books?

PC: No. I start each one with a case, and I never know where each will go. For instance, *The Body Farm* was a really hard book for me to write because I set it in my own childhood, in the foothills of western North Carolina. In a way, it was almost like killing off myself as a little girl, by putting myself imaginatively in that environment.

If you're a little girl with no power, like Emily Steiner was, buried beneath the cold earth, and people don't know the truth about your death, who would you want to find out who did it? You'd want Scarpetta.

She can't make the child alive again, but she can make her talk. Kay can do something for the living, to make it easy for them to cope with this evil that has occurred. That's really what she does in each of her books.

Maybe we see it more and more in subsequent ones because it becomes more defined to me what her mission is. After all, just like you, I get to know her better each time. I know her a whole lot better now than I did in *Postmortem* and, I suspect, three years from now, I will know her even better than I do now.

PD: I wouldn't be able to attend an autopsy. I would see the bodies as people and think of their past lives and emotions. I would find that too upsetting.

PC: That is why you would probably be a good forensic pathologist. That's exactly what the good ones do. They don't look on the body they're cutting as a thing. The bad ones do because it's easier to divorce themselves from their humanity. The dead won't talk to you if you don't know them as a person.

If you really want to hear what they have to say, you have to believe in their humanity. Yes, it is a sacrifice because it takes a lot out of you, but I think it takes more out of you not to do that, because I think a part of you dies by degrees if you refuse to give a person their humanity. Even if they are dead.

I think one of the reasons that people stay with Scarpetta for four hundred pages is because she does give people their humanity—she gives them names. She went through the whole of *From Potter's Field* determined to give the dead woman her name. When the man was beating his horse, she went up to him and asked him the horse's name and then asked him, "Do you beat Snow White every day, or just on Christmas Day?" She always gives a name to the victim, whether it's a horse or a bald lady found in Central Park. That's what a good forensic pathologist will do. So you might be surprised at yourself. You might do better with it than you think.

I mean, it's not fun, but quite honestly, the only way to endure some of the most difficult cases is if you give them their humanity. For example, one day I was with my friend Dr. Marcella Fierro, who's now the chief medical examiner. She's one of the best forensic pathologists in the world, and I've been very lucky to have her as a mentor. We were going down to the morgue in the elevator, and there was this horrible smell from a body we had found in the river. It had been there for several weeks in the middle of summer. I had smelled bodies before, but this was the worst. It was really, really wretched. I was going down to help, to scribe the labels. I looked at Marcella and said that sometimes I really didn't know how she could stand this. She looked at me and said that she just tried to remember who he was.

And when you think of that, suddenly you no longer see this

bloated, hideous corpse but a man wearing a hat, T-shirt, shorts, and tennis shoes, and he's out on the river fishing with his son. I saw him for the rest of the morning, and I was a good trouper and I did my job. If you cannot give that much humanity back to that person, why in the world would you want to spend that much time with what's left of him?

Contributor Notes

Crow Dillon-Parkin was born in Yorkshire and holds degrees in English and American literature and art and design. She has worked as an artist, office clerk, office cleaner, charity worker, retail manager, and dressmaker, and has stood in local elections for the Green Party (not all at the same time). Currently, she edits *Crime Time* magazine, fitting it in between making art, freelance proofreading and copy editing, and working at Birmingham (U.K.) City Archives. She is married and has two children.

Paul Duncan was born at a young age, grew up, and now has the body, if not the mind, of an adult. He lives two-thirds of his life in a house. He co-founded *Crime Time* magazine and is presently writing a biography of Gerald Kersh, a survey of Alfred Hitchcock's murder movies, and researching Brit Noir.

Jan Grape, along with **Dean James**, is a coeditor of the Edgar-nominated *Deadly Women: The Female Mystery Writer*, published by Carroll & Graf. She also has sixteen short stories in anthologies ranging from *Deadly Allies I* and *II*, *Lethal Ladies I* and *II*, *Feline & Famous*, *Cat Crimes Takes a Vacation*, to the recently released *Ven-*

geance Is Hers. Her nonfiction articles are in *The Mystery Writers Sourcebook, The Fine Art of Murder*, and *How to Write a Private Eye Novel*. A regular columnist for *Mystery Scene* magazine, she also writes for the British publication *A Shot in the Dark*. She edits the Private Eye Writers of America newsletter, as well as being the vice president of that organization. She has also been a past president of the Southwest Chapter of Mystery Writers of America and holds memberships in Sisters in Crime and the American Crime Writers League. Along with her husband, she owns the Mysteries & More bookstore in Austin, Texas.

Dean James is the manager of Murder by the Book, Houston's nationally known mystery specialty bookstore. He earned a Ph.D. in medieval history from Rice University in 1986, then spent the next ten years as a librarian in the Texas Medical Center before joining Murder by the Book full time. He is the coauthor, with Jean Swanson, of *By a Woman's Hand: A Guide to Mystery Fiction by Women*, the second edition of which was released in 1996. The first edition of this popular reference book on contemporary women mystery writers was nominated by the Mystery Writers of America for the Edgar Award for Best Critical-Biographical Work, and it won the Agatha and Macavity Awards for Best Nonfiction. With **Jan Grape**, he is the coeditor of another volume on women mystery writers *Deadly Women*, published in 1997 by Carroll & Graf. For the past three years, Dean has taught courses on mystery fiction for Rice University's School of Continuing Studies: recent topics include historical mysteries, women detectives in mystery fiction, and a history of England via murder mysteries.

In less than two years, **Adrian Muller** has become a notable international figure on the mystery scene, selling articles, interviews, and opinion pieces to a variety of mystery publications around the world.

Robert J. Randisi is the author of more than three hundred books, the founder of the Private Eye Writers of America, the creator of the Shamus Award, and the cofounder of *Mystery Scene* magazine. His new novel, *In the Shadow of the Arch*, will be published by St. Martin's Press in 1998. Dominick Abel has been his agent since 1981.

Lee Server is best known for his extraordinary books examining the paperbacks of the fifties in *Over My Dead Body*, the pulp magazines in *Danger Is My Business*, and his prizewinning interviews with early Hollywood screenwriters in *Screenwriters: Words Become Pictures*.

Charles L. P. Silet widely reviews crime fiction and interviews crime writers for such journals as *The Armchair Detective*, *Mystery Scene*, *Clues*, *Mostly Murder*, *The Drood Review*, and the Australian mystery magazine *Mean Streets*. He teaches film and contemporary literature and culture at Iowa State University. He is currently editing a collection of critical articles on Chester Himes.

Jerry Sykes is a Britisher who has just started selling short stories and is working on his first novel. He contributes regularly to *A Shot in the Dark*, *Crime Time*, and *Mystery Scene*.